Cover Copy

There can be only one…for both of them.

Fae-blooded Julia holds the ability to read another's aura and determine their true intent. Her skill has only ever aided her in life, until the day when their neighboring enemy clan arrive to discuss a marriage of alliance between her and their chief's son. She misjudges their enemy's intent and all goes horribly wrong. Her parents are captured and imprisoned and now she must find a way to free them. Only now standing in her path is a fiercely protective warrior who has traveled from the future into the past, a man who insists they are soul bound, and a man whose aura shows no sign of such a bond. She is wary, yet still, she can't deny how much he stirs her deep within.

Highland warrior shifter Tavish Matheson has traveled through time to find the woman his soul demands is his, yet convincing her will be a mission all unto itself. When Julia is kidnapped by the enemy while on a mission to save her parents, he sets out in fierce pursuit. All he desires is to keep her close, rescue her parents, and most of all, to offer her his love.

He's a warrior who will not be denied. She's a lass devoted to her kin.

Books by Joanne Wadsworth

The Matheson Brothers Series
Highlander's Desire, Book One
Highlander's Passion, Book Two
Highlander's Seduction, Book Three
Highlander's Kiss, Book Four
Highlander's Heart, Book Five
Highlander's Sword, Book Six
Highlander's Bride, Book Seven
Highlander's Caress, Book Eight
Highlander's Touch, Book Nine
Highlander's Shifter, Book Ten
Highlander's Claim, Book Eleven
Highlander's Courage, Book Twelve
Highlander's Mermaid, Book Thirteen

Highlander Heat Series
Highlander's Castle, Book One
Highlander's Magic, Book Two
Highlander's Charm, Book Three
Highlander's Guardian, Book Four
Highlander's Faerie, Book Five
Highlander's Champion, Book Six
Highlander's Captive (Short Story)

Billionaire Bodyguards Series
Billionaire Bodyguard Attraction, Book One
Billionaire Bodyguard Boss, Book Two
Billionaire Bodyguard Fling, Book Three

Books by Joanne Wadsworth

Regency Brides Series
The Duke's Bride, Book One
The Earl's Bride, Book Two
The Wartime Bride, Book Three
The Earl's Secret Bride, Book Four
The Prince's Bride, Book Five
Her Pirate Prince, Book Six

Princesses of Myth Series
Protector, Book One
Warrior, Book Two
Hunter (Short Story - Included in Warrior, Book Two)
Enchanter, Book Three
Healer, Book Four
Chaser, Book Five

Highlander's Kiss

The Matheson Brothers, Book Four

Joanne Wadsworth

Highlander's Kiss
ISBN-13: 978-1-99-003434-3
Copyright © 2015, Joanne Wadsworth
Cover Art by Joanne Wadsworth
First electronic publication: September 2015

Joanne Wadsworth
http://www.joannewadsworth.com

All Rights Are Reserved. No part of this book may be used or reproduced in any manner whatsoever without written permission, except in the case of brief quotations embodied in critical articles and reviews. The unauthorized reproduction or distribution of this copyrighted work is illegal. No part of this book may be scanned, uploaded or distributed via the Internet or any other means, electronic or print, without the author's permission.

AUTHOR'S NOTE:
This book is a work of fiction. The names, characters, places, and incidents are products of the writer's imagination or have been used fictitiously and are not to be construed as real. Any resemblance to persons, living or dead, actual events, locale or organizations is entirely coincidental. The author does not have any control over and does not assume any responsibility for third-party websites or their content.

Published in the United States of America

First digital publication: September 2015
First print publication: September 2015

Acknowledgements

I have an incredibly supportive family who allow me so much time to write. Huge thanks go to my hubby, Jason, and kiddies, Marisa, Caleb, Cruise and Rocco. Hugs.

For my readers, I can't thank you enough for joining me, and taking this journey to where imagination and magic soar.

Gilleoin – The Legend

In the twelfth century, a man named Gilleoin became the first and only known man to hold bear shifter blood, an ability gifted to him by The Most High One. His clan was called Matheson, and when he mated with a woman carrying faerie blood, they created a line shrouded in secrecy, a line that far into the future, now neared extinction…

Cherub – The Fae Angel of Love

The ancient House of Clan Matheson, led by Gilleoin, the Chief of Matheson, Scotland, 1210.

Cherub dashed out from under the high arch over the front door of the castle and into the inner courtyard. She twirled around, her gown of white silk billowing in the wind whipping around her, the golden ribbons at her waist rippling and tangling around her hands. Arms raised, she reached out with her fae senses and allowed the very wind itself to bring to her the secrets it held, as she'd done for over a thousand years.

As an immortal time-walker and the faerie king's daughter, her duty was to aid those of fae blood who walked this Earth and she did so by ensuring the newly soul bound were brought together across the centuries and no longer separated by time.

Kirk, her warrior soul bound mate, swept in behind her, his chest a delicious wall of heat at her back. Gently, he caught her hands, whirled her around to face him then dipped his head to hers. His beautiful golden shifter gaze devoured her. "My elusive imp, it appears you sense lost souls this night."

"I do, far into the future, within your own shifter clan."

"Who exactly?" His excitement thrummed along their

merged mind link to her.

"Tavish and Tor, your second cousins, although 'tis Tavish's need that strikes me the strongest." Tavish and Tor, brothers and identical twins, had recently sensed their mates on the last full moon, and now, once she brought them here into the same time as their chosen ones, their senses would rear even stronger. Their desire to find the other half of their soul would consume them.

"Tavish is committed to his kin and being on call as our clan doctor. His patients come first, Cherub."

"Aye, but he will stop at nothing to find his mate, to ensure he makes her his." She closed her eyes and searched for the lass Tavish's soul was bound to. There, the intricate golden thread that belonged to Tavish swirled toward Julia's soul, her dear friend and one of her fae kind right here in this time. Bringing Tavish and his chosen one together across this wide chasm that separated them would require a little of her mischievous fae intervention, but 'twas naught she wasn't up for. Aye, a mated male longed for the chase and part of his journey in finding his chosen one was in the hunt, one she'd ensure Tavish was given.

On her toes, she reached up and kissed her mate's stubbly chin. She and Kirk had completed the bond such a short time ago, but she couldn't imagine her life without him. The moment they'd joined together as one, she'd taken a piece of his soul into her keeping and from that moment on, he too had become an immortal as she was. Her mate would stand by her side, for now and for all time. The exquisiteness of all she'd been gifted made her giddy with need.

Cloaking them both and ensuring none could see them, she rubbed the entire length of her body against his, her heart and soul singing at the luscious contact. "What did I do to deserve you?"

"I could ask the same question. What did I do to deserve you? I was certainly granted my ultimate wish the day I found you." He seized her mouth with his, his desire hot and hard and so very needy, the very same as hers pulsed. "To the skies, my elusive imp. I wish to show you just how very much I love you."

With a swish of her fingers, she swept them upward toward the heavens and gave herself over to the depth of the bond they shared and the fierce love they held for each other.

Tomorrow, she'd ensure Tavish and Julia met. Tavish's coming hunt would be one of the most intriguing she ever set in motion and she grinned wickedly at the thought. What a journey they would have ahead of them. Of that she had no doubt.

Chapter 1

Near the ancient House of Clan Matheson, Scotland, 1210, the following day.

Julia bowed her head as she stood before her parents' memorial stone wedged high on the cliff top ocean trail between the castle and her people's fae village. A good hundred feet behind her, the sea crashed hard and sprayed high, while before her, the forest rose sure and strong, the tall pines swaying in the fierce wind that rushed across the choppy waves of Loch Alsh and swept up the sheer rock wall and over them. High above, gray clouds bubbled ominously and she shivered and drew her white shawl tighter around her shoulders. "I'm so sorry, Arabel." She clasped her sister's hand and faced her. "I didnae mean to drag you all the way out here on this miserable day, but I just couldnae come alone."

"Dinnae be sorry. I needed to come as much as you did." Her twin squeezed her fingers then rested her other hand on top of the craggy stone holding their parents' names chiseled into the front.

Aleck and Adair.
Beloved parents of Arabel and Julia.
Taken from us far too soon.
Our hearts are broken.

"Sometimes, I can sense they're close even though that cannae be." Julia's heart heaved. Her fae skill of aura reading rose and her senses cried out for the gentle hum she'd always heard when her parents were near. The silence of their lost auras tore at her, as did the weight of her guilt. "'Tis my fault they're no longer with us."

"Nay, you must cease saying such a thing." Arabel gripped her shoulders and frowned. "'Tis Colin MacKenzie's fault that they are dead, as well as his snake of a son. I wish we'd never set eyes on Colin or Jeremiah."

"As do I, yet 'tis I who misread Colin and Jeremiah's auras. Mother and Father would never have traveled without a guard to our enemy's lair if I'd seen and heard correctly." Unlike any other fae aura reader in her clan, she was the only one who could sense both one's true intentions by the color of their aura and also the supporting sound their aura made. Even her aunt who held the same skill couldn't pick up the clear and concise sound that fully confirmed what the one they focused on truly intended. Her stronger skill had never set her wrong before, until the day she'd met the MacKenzies.

"Father and Gilleoin both believed Colin MacKenzie wished for a marriage of alliance, that his word was the truth. We were allies at the time, no' at war as we currently are." The war between their clans this past year had grown bitterer and bloodier than ever since the kidnapping and slaughter of their parents. Arabel squeezed her shoulders. "The Chief of

MacKenzie is the one who killed them, and with his own hand no less."

"But—"

"No buts are permitted. You arena to blame." Determination flared in Arabel's blue eyes and lit the golden sparks glittering around the edge. Her sister was her closest confidant, identical to her in every way except for their fae skills. Arabel was a fire-wielder and held one of the greatest of the battle skills.

Breathing out, Julia tried to shake off her current frustration, but no matter how many times her sister told her that their parents' death wasn't her fault, she still struggled to fully believe it. She too was at fault.

"Come, let's discuss this no more and instead leave Mother and Father an orchid." Arabel lowered to her knees before the stone and tugged her down beside her.

Tears burned behind Julia's eyes as she carefully removed the marsh orchid from her gown's pocket and placed the brilliant burst of fuchsia-pink against the rough gray stone. Father had always picked Mother one of these orchids every time he'd crossed the wetland farther along the loch, and Mother had always tucked the precious bud behind her ear or within her long braid. At least her parents had left this world together, a blessing since Mother would never have survived without Father for long. Theirs had been a soul bound match, the same as what Arabel now shared with Finlay. Her sister was most fortunate to have been gifted with such a bond.

Arabel touched the orchid's velvety soft petals, her bright aura clouding over and emitting a soulfully sad tune that tugged at Julia's heart. "We'll never forget them, Julia, and one day we'll make certain Colin MacKenzie pays for our parents' unjust death. He cannae be allowed to slaughter innocent people and get away with it."

She would ensure he paid for it too. Her own aura, usually a melding of rainbow colors, now held a mournful black haze. She ran her fingers over the colors flickering on her arms and upper body and settled it back down. She'd never allow the MacKenzie to take another of her kin's lives, would seek retribution, for both her and Arabel, somehow and some way. She rose to her feet and drew Arabel up along with her. Across the other side of the loch, several miles away and not visible from here, lay the MacKenzie's lair. White caps rode the heavy swell of the sea, the rising storm gaining in momentum, just as the storm of despair did which raged right in her heart.

"Oh." Arabel touched her head. "Finlay calls to me along our merged link." Finlay had recently arrived here from the future with his brothers, Iain and Kirk, the three identical warrior brothers known as the 'power of three.' Their arrival had fulfilled a prophecy Nessa had spoken over twenty years ago, and along with their fae skilled mates, they were a force to be reckoned with. Finlay had discovered Arabel was his chosen one, a match their mischievous Fae Angel of Love had instigated when she'd first opened a portal and brought the 'power of three' into their time.

Julia adored Finlay, considered him a wonderful new brother. From the moment her sister had joined with him, she'd witnessed the telltale sign of their auras tugging toward each other's, just as those who were soul bound did.

"You're not returning to the future already are you?" She'd miss her sister and Finlay terribly when it was time for them to return to Finlay's time. Aye, she'd struggle to survive the separation. Goodness. Just the thought of her sister soon leaving sent her dismal mood spiraling downhill even further.

"Nay, we'll be here for some time. Finlay gave Uncle Gilleoin his word he'd remain at the keep with Kirk to care for our clan while he traveled to Stirling." Gilleoin had been summoned to Stirling Castle by William, the King of Scots, and he'd left with his son and the seer of their clan, hers and Arabel's grandmother, Nessa. So too Iain and his mate, Isla, had traveled with them, the two so eager to see all that they could of this time while they were here.

"What does Finlay need?"

"He said Cherub would like to see you, that she's waiting at the sea-gate landing and would like us to return."

"I wonder what Cherub would like to see me about?" It must be important. Cherub wouldn't have asked her to come otherwise. The wind whipped Julia's long golden hair about her waist as she turned toward home and followed the curve of the bay to where the House of Clan Matheson rose like a sentinel, its massive gray stone turrets and towering walls topped with battlements and double the guardsmen roaming the ramparts. 'Twas her sanctuary, and that of her clan's as well. Never would she allow the MacKenzie to take their home from them.

Along the sea-gate landing next to two moored birlinns, Cherub stood with her hands raised to the sky, her cherry colored gown with its cinched bodice making her a bright beacon of color. The Fae Angel of Love controlled the *air* element, could halt the wind or send it churning if she so desired. She could also cloak her form and become unseen to another, or if she wished, so too she could become as one with the very air itself and take on a mist form.

"I'm no' sure, but we'd best be away since Cherub awaits." Arabel brushed her hands against her forest-green skirts then crossed to her horse and untethered it from a low tree branch.

Julia collected her own mare, mounted and with the reins in hand, slapped her knees into her animal's sides and rode back toward home. Bent low over her mount, she rode beside her sister along the high trail veering steeply downward toward the bay.

Arabel arched a challenging brow at her. "Do you care for a race? It might help clear our minds."

"Always. Catch me if you can," she challenged right back.

Never one to allow her sister to win a race, Julia tucked herself tighter against her horse, her gown's cream skirts beating against her legs as she urged her mare faster and whizzed along the trail. Stones scattered along the gravelly track, flew over the cliff's verge and rapped down the rock face before disappearing into the churning, watery depths below.

"Cheat!" Arabel yelled and laughed and pushed her horse harder.

"How does one cheat when riding a horse?" She galloped down the trail and along the grassy verge of the loch and as she arrived at the sea-gate, a mere horse-head in front of Arabel, she slowed her mount and brought it to a halt. With her mare snorting frosty air, she rubbed its neck, tossed one leg over the saddle and—

"Julia, wait." Arabel shot a look at her foot. "Your shawl is—"

She couldn't halt her momentum, or free her slippered foot caught in the trailing ends of her shawl. She toppled over and went down, hard. She hit her head on the edge of the stone landing and black spots danced before her eyes. All went dark.

* * * *

"Julia, please, wake up." Arabel's voice floated over her. "Now."

"I'm—" Oh dear, her head thumped as if horses stampeded within.

"Do as your sister says." Soft hands fluttered over her temple. Cherub's.

She forced the darkness away and blinked her eyes open. Arabel and Cherub wavered into view, their faces awash with worry. "I'm all right, just a bit—Oooh, everything is swaying."

"Which means you arena all right at all. You're also bleeding, and rather profusely." Arabel gripped the hem of her forest-green skirts, exposed her shift underneath and tore a strip from the bottom of the ivory cotton. Carefully, Arabel wrapped the strip around her head and tied it off in a knot at the back. "This should help stem the blood flow until I can get you inside. You're going to need stitches, several of them."

"Nay, please, no stitches." She touched the bound cloth at the back, her fingers coming away wet with blood. "I hate stitches, and I hate even more how rough you are when you administer them."

"I'm no' rough. But stitches are stitches. One cannae halt the pain when taking needle and thread to one's self." Arabel patted her hand. "Although I promise to be as gentle as I possibly can."

"Ladies, wait a moment, there's another option." Cherub slid one arm under Julia's back and helped her sit up. "I know of a healer within my mate's clan. Tavish is known as a doctor in the twenty-first century and I've been to see him a time or two when I've had an injured kinsman who required far more aid than what a healer in this time can offer." Cherub looked into her eyes. "Julia, in the future there are great advancements in healing and Tavish can ensure your wound is stitched without you experiencing any pain whatsoever. If you wish, I can take you to him."

"You're going to take me to the future?" She would gladly take Cherub up on her offer for that reason alone. Seeing the time and place where Arabel would soon live with Finlay enticed her to no end. "I would love to go to Ivanson Castle."

"Then we shall." Cherub glanced at Arabel with a slightly impish tilt to her lips. "'Twill be best if I take just Julia since Finlay willnae appreciate it if I take you so far from his side, even if only for a little while."

"I'll remain but only if you promise to bring Julia back here as soon as you can." Arabel crawled to Julia's feet and unhooked her shawl still snagged around her slippered foot.

"I give you my word I will." With one arm wrapped around Julia's waist in support, Cherub aided her to her feet. "Julia, you're to hold on to me while we're traveling through the vortex I open. No letting go, otherwise you'll experience a far rougher journey than what is necessary."

"I understand. I'll hold tight." She'd never traveled through one of Cherub's portals. Eager, she gripped Cherub's arm.

"Be careful as you travel." Arabel stepped back, blew each of them a kiss.

"We will." Cherub swirled her fingers through the air and the wind rose and whipped all about. A portal opened and she and Cherub fell away into the churning abyss.

Stars whirled through the dark and lightning flashed. Excitement buzzed through Julia and she gasped at the sheer beauty of moving through both time and space. What an adventure. She'd gladly fall from her horse again just to experience this.

* * * *

Far in the future and on guard in the misty moonlight, Tavish Matheson patrolled the battlements of Ivanson Castle. All remained quiet beyond the curtain wall, the surveillance cameras mounted on the topmost corners of the ramparts capturing the stillness of the night and nothing more. Beyond their keep, the forest stretched for miles upon miles within the mountainous ranges of the Highlands, providing their shifter clan with the perfect level of isolation they needed from the rest of the world.

Deep within the woods, an owl hooted then a second joined the first's nightly call. He scanned the woods, his shifter sight alone allowing him to see so very well in the gloomy dark. Unease rolled through him and his bear pricked under his skin. Something was off, although he had no idea what.

"Anything interesting going on tonight, brother?" Tor strode toward him in his belted plaid and shirt, his golden shifter eyes bright in the near dark.

"Not a thing, although that alone is making me even more restless." The wind rose and fog swirled over the treetops. The brisk breeze lifted his black hair and plastered his white shirt against his chest. He palmed his belted sword resting snug at his side. "Are you here to take over?"

"Aye, I'm on watch until dawn."

"Good, then I might just go for a quick walk, let my bear have a wee stretch before I head to bed." He clapped Tor's shoulder as he walked past him then bounded down the stone stairs and jogged out the gate under the raised portcullis. Allowing his bear his release, might just help to settle him down.

More fog swirled, the wind rushing around him. Within the churning haze, two women suddenly appeared, one of them Cherub. He'd never mistake the Fae Angel of Love, not when she'd visited him a time or two along with the odd patient from far in the past. The lass she held onto with one arm around her waist staggered on her feet and clutched her head. Blood oozed through the ivory strip of cloth bound around her head. She must be another patient, and with her velvet gown of cream sweeping to the ground, its sleeves draping over the backs of her hands, quite clearly a lass from another time. Aye, her clothing was from centuries past.

"Tavish, there you are." Cherub waved out to him. Her creamy skin sparkled, the glimmer a physical attribute held only by the eldest child born within the ancient royal line of the fae. "My apologies, I lost my focus as I opened a portal and missed arriving in your medical rooms, although no' by far. I need your aid."

"What can I do to help you?"

"This is Julia. She's close kin, and took a nasty fall from her horse and wounded herself. Could you take a look at her injury?"

"Of course I can."

"You all right down there, Tavish?" Tor gripped the crenellation as he leaned over it, his black hair falling forward over his brow. His gaze darted to Cherub and he grinned.

"Welcome back, Cherub. So you're the one causing the air to stir."

"Evening, Tor. I brought Dr. Tavish a patient, a very important patient from Gilleoin's time." Cherub smiled at his brother. For so long Cherub had hidden her true self from their clan, preferring to remain cloaked on her visits due to her sparkly skin, but no more, not since she'd become mated to Kirk, one of their chief's three sons.

"Let's get the two of you inside and I'll see to this very important patient." Tavish went to scoop Julia up so she needn't walk but then stopped. She wasn't from his time, might find his actions far too forward. Instead, he offered her his arm.

"Thank you." Julia slid her trembling hand through the crook in his elbow and curled her fingers around his wrist, her touch so sweetly warm and making his bear stretch deep inside him, as if itching to get closer to her. That had never happened to him with a woman before.

He shook the thought off as Julia glanced all about, taking in the high curtain wall, the forest then the gravel driveway which led around to the back of the keep to a large parking area in the rear. "I take it this is your first time here?"

"It is, although I expected to see something...different. Particularly since I've traveled over eight-hundred years through time." She watched her feet with each unsteady step she made.

"Just wait until you get inside." He guided her across the stony ground. "You'll see 'different' then. That I promise you."

"Julia, you'll love seeing all that this time offers." Cherub led the way under the arch and into the bailey. "Like electricity and running water. I have a home in this time which is located not far from here at Angel Bay. I dearly miss being there when I flitter all about."

The brisk breeze rose, swirled Julia's scent around him, a sweet white rose fragrance that tickled his nose. She smelled so soft and feminine and he dragged in an even deeper breath to capture more of her elusive aroma. His bear fairly purred his pleasure from deep within.

Julia's gaze lifted to his, her blue eyes as stunning as a clear summer sky and holding glittering sparks of gold around the edges. "Did you say something? I heard a purr."

"That was my bear." Although how she'd heard his beast deep inside him was intriguing. He hadn't emitted any sound. Only he could hear his bear. "My other half likes how you smell, and so do I."

"You do?" Her cheeks flushed an adorable pink. "I sprinkle rose oil in my bath, ah, water." The pink bloomed even brighter as she lowered her gaze. "Goodness, I cannae believe I just said that."

"I'm rather glad you did." He halted in the middle of the bailey next to Cherub, right beside the center well with its swinging wooden pail and sweeping ivy.

"Oh dear, Kirk calls." Cherub touched her head. "There's another emergency. Our connection can cut in and out sometimes when we're separated by time so 'tis fortunate he could reach me as he has." She gripped Julia's hands. "I must go, but just know I'm leaving you in the best of hands. I trust Tavish. He's a wonderful doctor, so kind and caring."

"If you need to go, I understand."

"I'll return as soon as I can." Cherub patted his shoulder. "I expect you to take good care of my kin."

"I'll take the utmost care. You do what you need to. I'll keep Julia with me until you return."

"Of course you will. I would expect naught less." With a mischievous smile, Cherub backed away then twirled the air. She opened a vortex and as the wind rushed all about, she disappeared within the swirling dark.

"Cherub said you're close kin. How close?" He steered Julia toward the front door of the keep.

"My sister, Arabel, is Cherub's sister by marriage, so very

close."

"I've heard of a lass named Arabel. She's mated to Finlay, right?" Which meant her sister held the fire-wielder skill. Even though Finlay hadn't yet returned to this time, he'd heard all about what Arabel could do from Finlay's brother, Kirk, during his flying visits in and out with Cherub. "Iain, Finlay, and Kirk are my second cousins."

"Then 'tis a very small world indeed…or mayhap time." She smiled and swayed, grasped his arm firmer.

"Here, let me carry you. You're not stable on your feet yet."

"I'm truly—"

He scooped her up and she gasped and clutched his shirtfront.

"—fine."

"No, it's best I carry you. I wouldn't want you falling and hurting yourself again." Too bad about the protocols between times. He wanted to hold her. Up the front step, he bounded then upstairs and along the passageway of the second floor toward his well-lit medical rooms at the end. Once inside, he set Julia down on the white-sheeted medical bed positioned in the center of the room, washed up at the sink and pulled on a pair of surgical gloves. With a tray of utensils in hand, he walked in behind her and set the tray on the side table. "Head wounds can be dangerous, but I promise to take good care of you."

"Cherub trusts you, which means I trust you too." Her words warmed his heart and he smiled.

"Thank you. I don't intend to lose that trust." He picked up his scissors, carefully sliced the bloodied cloth away then gently separated her hair. The wound was long but thankfully not too deep. "Tell me all about yourself, Julia." He yearned to know more. "Everything about the past intrigues me, particularly your time when Gilleoin reigned as chief of our clan."

"I'm an aura reader and can sense another's true intentions by the color and the sound of their aura, and Gilleoin is my uncle, wed to my Aunt Sorcha."

"I've never met an aura reader before." But that went someway to explaining her earlier comment. She'd heard the sound of his bear's contentment. "What does my aura tell you?"

She glanced over her shoulder at him, her smile making his heart lose a beat. Those sweetly pink lips of hers with their perfect pout, enticed him, made him want a taste. "Your aura is a pure white with a tinge of sizzling red at the edge, just as Gilleoin's is. 'Tis a shifter's aura you have, but there is more. When I focus on you, I can hear a gentle purr and that tells me you and your bear are as one, that your other half is rather content right now."

His bear was certainly content, any and all restlessness he'd felt earlier having disappeared the moment she'd arrived. "Your assessment is absolutely correct. Where do you live when not buzzing through time with Cherub?"

"At the House of Clan Matheson on the shores of Loch Alsh." She rubbed her forehead and grimaced. "There is an ache and it worsens."

"Did you lose any awareness when you fell from your horse?" He'd give her medication for the headache, the moment he'd stitched her wound.

"How did you know I fell from my horse?"

"Cherub said so when you first arrived. Do you recall her saying so?" Her clear confusion likely came from her losing consciousness.

"I do now you've jogged my memory, and aye, I lost awareness, Dr. Tavish. My sister woke me from the dark."

"Call me Tavish. There's no need to stand on formality while you're here." He reached up and tugged the overhead light on its metal arm closer. Light blazed and Julia's eyes went wide as she ogled it.

"Oh my, you have light without fire."

"This light comes from a light bulb, and definitely no fire is needed. This is a form of the electricity Cherub mentioned before. Lower your chin if you can. I'd like to flush this wound and clean it well. I'm also going to numb the area too. The most you should feel is a slight pinch when the injection goes in then maybe the odd little tug as I stitch the edges together."

"What is an in-jec-tion?" She twisted her tongue around the foreign word as she touched her chin to her chest for him.

"Doctors in this time use different tools to aid us in healing our patients, and since I've no intention of allowing you to feel any pain, I'm going to use an injection with a numbing agent inside." He cleaned the wound then smeared each side with numbing gel to ensure she didn't even feel the needle going in. No pain at all was his ultimate goal.

"Tavish," she whispered his name, her voice so soft as she leaned back a little against him. "Did you know your name means twin?"

"Which I happen to be." Injection in. "Did you not see Tor on the battlements outside? He's the one who called out. We're identical." He threaded the needle and set to work stitching the wound. "He was pretty hard to miss."

"I'm afraid I only saw a dark shadow. My vision was still a little spotty at that time. Arabel isnae just my sister but also my twin. She's a whole five minutes older than me, and always reminding me of it."

"Tor's a whole five minutes younger than I am. I have no trouble reminding him of that either." He ran another quick check over her head for any sign of swelling but there was none. Keeping a close eye on her throughout the night though would be a necessity, and he wouldn't allow Cherub to take Julia away until at least the morning, that's if Cherub returned before then. Another stitch. "Twins actually run strongly in my shifter clan. More often than not two cubs are born at once, although Iain, Finlay, and Kirk are the first triplets we've had."

"Twins run strongly through my fae line as well." She

gripped the edge of the thin mattress either side of her, her knuckles going white. "I'm nervous. I've never been all that good at getting stitches and I fear the first one. 'Tis an awful kind of pain."

"There's no need to be nervous." He covered one of her hands with his and her grip relaxed under his touch. "I've already made the first stitch, as well as the second." He began the third stitch.

"You have?" She jerked her head upright and stared at the long length of thread that led from the back of her head to his hand. A smile lifted her lips. "Well, would you look at that. You are a very clever doctor indeed, with a most magical touch. Should I ever need stitches again, I am coming right back here to see you."

"Thank you, but I hope you'll never require stitches again. Look front and center for me."

"Of course. My apologies." She resumed the right position and he returned to his work, bringing each side of her wound nicely and neatly together. "Are you mated, Tavish?"

"As yet I'm not, although on the last full moon my senses arose just as the other unmated males in my clan's did since the 'power of three' was unveiled and the fae village saved." He inspected his stitches, five altogether, which would dissolve on their own in another six or seven days' time. "All done, Julia."

"Already?" She glanced at him with the sweetest smile. "I shall never forget your kindness. You have my most grateful thanks for your aid."

"And I shall never forget the aura reader who paid me a visit from the past." He dropped his utensils into the automated cleaning machine on the bench, collected a bottle of water from the small corner fridge then with two painkillers in hand, returned to her and held them out. "I want you to swallow these pills. They'll chase away any lingering pain and allow you to sleep with ease throughout the night. I'll also need you to sleep over so I can ensure all is well."

"I would like to stay longer, to see what else this time offers. What herb are these made of?" She accepted the pills and humming under her breath, rubbed them between her fingers.

"Those pills aren't actually made of herbs but a proven medication." He uncapped the bottle lid.

"Would you look at that." She nabbed the bottle from him, swirled the water within then fingered the notches on the rim. "How clever to put a top like this on the bottle. I see the cap can wind itself over the head of the spout through these ridges. What is this bottle made of?"

"Plastic, a manmade substance. Pop one of those pills on your tongue then scrape it to the back with your teeth. As soon as you've done that, take a sip of water and gulp the pill down, then repeat again with the second pill." Her questions and delight at seeing so many new things touched his heart. He'd love to show her around his home, take her to some of his favorite places and watch her excitement continue to grow and bloom.

She swallowed the pills.

"Would you like to bathe and wash the blood from your hair before I organize a place for you to sleep?"

"Am I allowed to bathe? Whenever I've had stitches in the past, my sister hasn't allowed me to get them wet."

"Just this once you may bathe, then you're to ensure your stitches remain dry for the next few days. I've actually used dissolving stitches, so there's no need for me to even physically remove them once your wound has healed."

"Then a chance to bathe would be most appreciated."

"Good. Come with me. I'll show you to my bathroom and get you sorted." He set his hands on her waist and lifted her off the bed then slowly set her down in front of him.

Wobbling, she grasped his shirtfront and leaned her forehead against his chest. "I still feel so woozy."

"Lean on me as often as you need to." He tucked a lock of

her wind tangled blond hair behind her ear then once she appeared steady on her feet, offered her his arm once more and guided her out the door and into his bedroom down the hallway. His four-poster bed took up half the large space, the remainder holding a blue suede settee and an armchair angled in front of a wide screen TV. His bathroom sat off to one side and he steered her across his room and through the door. Sandy colored tiles led to an open shower in the tiled corner, one without any glass sides. The shower curtain though could be pulled across if needed, although he rarely used it. The bathroom flooring was designed to funnel the water away into the sink hole.

Julia ogled the room and gasped as she sighted the massive mirror over top of the white marble vanity. "I can almost see my entire self in that looking glass. That is the largest one I've ever beheld."

"We call them mirrors in this time, and it is a beauty." He picked up the metal shower chair, set it in the center of the showering area then flicked the overhead fan on. It whirred and fluttered the white towels on the side rail. "Come here, Julia. Take a seat." She did and he lowered to a crouch, bringing them eye to eye. "I don't actually have a bath as such for you to bathe in, but instead I've got a shower in which you'll sit underneath. That is how you'll be able to bathe and wash up."

"I see." With one finger, she touched the button on his shirt then glanced at the ceiling above and each wall surrounding her. An intriguing look crossed her face. "And how does one shower inside a bathroom when there is no way for a shower of water to reach me?"

"Showers are a modern invention and it's best if I show you, rather than try to explain how they work." He removed her slippers and lobbed them toward the heated towel rail. There, they'd remain dry and out of the spray's reach. From the shower caddy, he handed her shampoo and a bar of soap. "Feel free to use anything in this room you might need. What's mine is now yours."

"Are you certain I need to be sitting right here to have this…ah…shower?"

"Very sure." He chuckled and popped a kiss on her forehead. "I've never met such a woman as you, and it feels like forever since I've had such an enjoyable conversation. Seeing your delight in all these new things reminds me of how lucky we are to live in this time with all our modern conveniences."

"I've never had such an interesting and enjoyable conversation either." She touched her forehead where he'd kissed her. "What do I do next?"

"You'll need to take your gown off to shower." She had a full-length shift on underneath, the top lacy edge of it showing along her neckline. "Will your shift cover you adequately? You can borrow a towel if not, but it's best I remain with you while you shower since you're not yet steady enough on your feet. The last thing I want you to do is fall and hit your head on these hard tiles."

"Aye, I usually swim in my shift when needed so it will cover me adequately, although I cannae reach the stays in the back of my gown. Could you aid me?" She set the shampoo and soap on the floor next to her chair, rose to her feet and gave him her back.

"Absolutely." He swept her long blond hair to one side and exposed the creamy length of her neck then with her gown's cream and gold ribbons in hand, he unlaced her stays. "There, all done."

"Thank you." She wriggled the loose fabric down over her hips and the cream velvet swished to the floor. She scooped it up and hung it on the wall hook then wavered in her step, pressed her hands to her knees and drew in a long breath. "Everything spins when I move too fast."

"Then take a seat. I set it there for you for that very reason." He led her back to the chair and she plopped onto it and eyes closed, slowly breathed in and out. He hunkered down, rested his hands on her knees and gently rubbed. "I promised Cherub I'd remain with you and I will. Also, with dizziness usually comes nausea. Let me know if you feel sick so I can give you some meds to ease your symptoms."

"There is no nausea, just dizziness." She opened her beautiful blue eyes with their glimmer of gold at the edge and covered his hands with hers. "'Tis so comforting to be near you. You make me feel quite at ease."

"It's comforting for me to be near you too." More so with each minute that passed. Gently, he turned one of her hands over, picked up the shampoo bottle and squeezed a dollop of apple scented shampoo into her palm. "This is shampoo, what we use to clean our hair."

"It smells delicious." With one finger, she swirled through the creamy colored mix then cupped the back of his head, drew him closer and buried her nose in his black locks. "Mmm, whenever I eat an apple, I shall now think about you and this very moment." She rubbed the shampoo in her hands and grinned as the mix bubbled up. "Show me how to shower."

This he couldn't wait for, to see her surprise at the sight of running water streaming from the shower head. With the nozzle unhooked from the slide rail, he flicked the lever on then with his hand under the spray, waited for it to hit just the right heat— nice and warm and not too hot.

"That is so fascinating." Julia scraped her chair closer and grasped his hand being hit by the spray. "'Tis like a waterfall of water, a heated waterfall."

"There are metal pipes that bring this water right through these walls into this very bathroom. When one turns the lever on, water flows, or when the lever is turned off, the water halts." He passed her the shower head. "You're to control where the water goes."

She turned the nozzle on herself and the spray hit her front and flattened the thin cloth to her body. Lifting it over her head, she laughed as water sluiced through her locks and down to her feet tucked under the chair. Her big blue eyes met his, the twinkle within making him catch his breath. Comforting didn't even begin to describe how he currently felt around her. Inspired, thrilled, at peace and bursting with happiness, did.

"Here, let me help you." He picked up the shampoo and squirted more into his palm since she'd washed what he'd given her away. From behind her, he gently worked the bubbles through her wet hair, the silky strands sliding so sensuously through his fingers.

"I feel like I'm in heaven. Thank you for taking such wonderful care of me." She tipped her head back farther and sighed with delight.

Transfixed, he couldn't take his gaze from her. Tiny dimples either side of her lush lips begged for his touch and her sheer exuberance warmed the inside of his heart.

She waved the shower head up and down her body until the wet cloth was plastered against each and every inch of her. Slim legs and shapely calves, soft hips and the roundness of her full breasts. Hell, even a heavenly tease of her pink nipples showed. His mouth watered and his bear fairly purred for more. Never had the sight of a woman ever caused such a staggering need to rear to glaring life within him, not once, not ever.

He took the shower head from her and rinsed the bubbles away.

Was it possible the Fae Angel of Love had brought his chosen one right to his doorstep? Never had he imagined meeting his mate like this. He mulled the thought over, although not for long. Everything about Julia captured and enticed him. There was only one woman for him, his soul bound mate and it was her. Of that he was certain.

His chosen one sat right before him, and his soul lifted and rejoiced.

* * * *

Warm water streamed through Julia's hair and with it eased the thumping in her head, or mayhap that was from the pills Tavish had given her. No matter which it had been, she'd never felt so relaxed and alive as she had in this moment. For so long she'd grieved for her parents, but this trip here into the future had relieved a little of the terrible burden she always carried.

Tavish leaned in behind her, touched his cheek to her cheek and whispered, "You're all done."

"Thank you." She reached back with one hand and cupped his stubbly jaw. Being near him soothed her, in a way she'd never experienced around a man before, and the red edging his pure white aura shimmered even brighter. So too the gentle purr emanating from him rose to a wickedly low rumble. She swiveled around on her chair, rested one hand on the metal back and used it to keep her balance as she stood. Goodness. Her shift was plastered to her. She plucked it away from her chest, swiped a drying cloth from the rail and wrapped it around her. Such fluffy white cotton. Never had she wrapped herself in such a decadent cloth before. She rubbed her cheek against it. Tiny loops had been woven into the weave that thickened the cloth and made it lusher. "What is this called?"

"A towel." His shifter eyes blazed with smoldering heat as he gazed at her. "Feeling warmer?"

"Very." Heat flushed through her and she swayed.

"Hold onto me if you feel faint."

"I cannae halt this dizziness." Leaning against him, she nestled her cheek against his chest, his white shirt damp and clinging to his skin from the shower water she must have accidentally sprayed him with. "I wouldnae mind that bed to rest in now."

"I'll grab you something to sleep in first. I don't have any women's clothing in my wardrobe and I'd rather not wake one of the ladies in the keep to procure what you'll need, but I could offer you a shirt, some sweatpants as well."

The thought of wearing his clothing sent tantalizing thoughts swirling through her mind. She probably should say no and don her gown again, but any form of refusal wouldn't leave her mouth. "I'd like that."

"My clothing it is then." He disappeared out the door into his bedchamber, those dark trews he wore hugging his tight backside, a backside she truly shouldn't be admiring quite the way she was. Knocking her head had certainly scattered her usually good thoughts.

She shuffled about within the thick cloth, shoved her arms out of her soggy shift and tugged it down. The ivory linen fell in a wet plop to the floor and she stepped out of it, the towel still well secured around her.

"Here you go." Tavish returned with a bundle of clothing in hand, a royal blue shirt and men's trews, or what he'd called sweatpants. He scooped up her shift from the floor, wrung the water from it then laid it over top of the rail before he slipped back out the door and closed it after himself.

Against the wall, she leaned, dropped the towel completely and pulled his shirt over her head. The soft linen flapped down to her knees. She rolled the sleeves up to her elbows then tugged her wet hair out from underneath the collar and used the towel to dry it.

"Are you almost done?" His voice floated to her through the thick paneling of wood.

"One moment." She flapped out his gray sweatpants and stepped into them although they slithered right back down her legs and fell in a soft puddle. She stepped out of them and picked them up. "The sweatpants are too big."

"Let me see." He stepped inside and eyed them in her hands. "I might have a smaller pair, one that shrunk in the wash not long ago."

"Nay, this shirt will do." 'Twas decent enough with only

her calves and feet showing. She handed the pants to him, lifted the shirt collar over her nose and breathed in his warm and fresh scent trapped within the cloth. "I like your shirt."

"I like seeing it on you as well." He foraged in one of the drawers under the counter with its wide basin, nabbed a brush and gently detangled her locks before dropping the brush back in the drawer. With one hand at her back, he guided her into his chamber where the covers had been pulled back on one side of the bed. "Hop in. I want you to get as much rest as possible for what remains of the night."

"I'm to sleep in your bed?"

"I've used the settee before as a bed, and I'd rather you sleep right here where I know you'll be comfortable and where I can keep a close eye on you. You took a nasty fall and I intend to wake you every hour or two to ensure all is well."

"Our clan healer does that too with warriors who've lost awareness during a battle. She fears they may no' wake in the morning, so to set her mind at ease, she stirs them often during the night." She eased under the covers and jiggled about on the thick mattress. "This bed is so soft and so big. There's no need for you to sleep on the settee if you wish, provided you can keep to the other side of this bed."

"Are you sure?" He toed off his boots, removed his sword belt and propped his weapon against the wall.

"I dinnae mind at all." She pulled the covers back on the other side and wriggled back to make more room for him. He slid into the bed fully clothed then reached up behind him on the wall and flicked a switch which turned the overhead light off and plunged the chamber into near darkness. Only a shimmer of the moon's glow trickled in through a gap in his navy curtains. The gentle moonbeams played over his high cheeks and firm jaw. "I hope Cherub takes her time in returning. I would dearly love to see more of your keep and these fascinating things of your time."

On his side, he faced her. "When Cherub returns, I don't

intend to let you go, to just simply disappear back through time and never see you again." His aura flared and the gentle purr emanating from him rose to a low growl.

"I'm sorry." She rubbed his arm to soothe him and the growl tapered away. "I didnae mean to say something that would upset you."

"I'm not upset."

"Aye, you were. Your aura told me so." One's aura never lied, other than for Colin and Jeremiah MacKenzie's auras. Theirs lied with a lethalness that could kill.

"I just don't care for the thought of you leaving. That's all."

"I can ask Cherub if she will bring me back to visit. Since Arabel will be living here and our parents—" Her gaze misted and she blinked the hot rush of tears away. "Never mind."

"No, tell me what you were just thinking that upset you."

"My thoughts have dwelled on my parents a great deal this day. They passed away and now my sister is all I have."

"I'm so sorry for your loss." He curled his hand over her hip, his fingers warm and soothing. He tugged her closer, his gaze intent. "Do you want to talk about them?"

"I miss them, terribly."

"What are their names?"

"Aleck and Adair." Talking might help. "My father was a great warrior who held fae blood and my mother had the most caring heart. She studied herbs and aided our healer when needed. Both came from the fae village."

"How did they pass? If you don't mind me asking." He stroked her hip and she wriggled closer at his gentle touch.

"No' long after Arabel and I came of age, the Chief of MacKenzie requested a meeting with Gilleoin and my father. He wished to enter into negotiations for the marriage of his son, Jeremiah, to one of Gilleoin's nieces since Gilleoin had no daughters. That marriage was to be between Jeremiah and me. At the time our two clans were no' yet at war as we currently are."

She covered his hand with hers. She couldn't halt her need to share even more. "Unfortunately that meeting was just a ruse. I sat in on it at my father's request in order to keep an eye on Colin and Jeremiah MacKenzie's auras. They lied, which I didnae pick up on, and in doing so I misread their true intentions."

"What happened next?"

"Later that week, as soon as my parents arrived at Colin MacKenzie's keep to complete the negotiations, he had them tossed into the dungeon and then a demand sent to Gilleoin. My uncle was told to hand over his lands on the tip of Loch Alsh and in return the MacKenzie would release my parents. Of course many demands volleyed back and forth between them, and for several months until it became clear to Gilleoin that the MacKenzie was unable to listen to reason. That's when my uncle set out for their stronghold with an elite contingency of his warriors. Gilleoin's intention was to sneak in under the cover of darkness, rescue my parents and then return with them, but instead he discovered they'd been slain at the MacKenzie's own hand, several months prior and afore the first demand had even been sent. Gilleoin was furious and attacked. When he left, 'twas with a bloody trail in his wake."

"No one should have to lose their parents, and certainly not the way you and Arabel did."

"I would never wish what my sister and I have gone through on anyone." She plumped her pillow under her cheek. Her eyelids fluttered down and she pushed her eyes back open. All that had happened this day had tired her. "It has helped to speak to you of this." It truly had.

"I'm glad you've shared this with me." He tucked her closer, slid his hand right around her waist and palmed the lower curve of her back. "Go to sleep. I'll watch over you as you rest."

"Do you always watch over your patients with such dedicated care?"

"Always, but I shall be watching over you as if my very life depended on it."

"You are so very kind and caring, exactly as Cherub said." She focused on his aura then hers. No tugging.

'Twas a shame their auras didn't move toward each other's, as those who were soul bound did. He would make a wonderful mate. Certainly, the woman he was soul bound to would be one lucky lass.

She closed her eyes and drifted.

The dark rose and took her swiftly away.

Chapter 2

The ancient House of Clan Matheson, 1210.

As dawn broke the following morning, Cherub paced the chief's solar, the missive she, Kirk, and Finlay had received from the Chief of MacKenzie scrunched in her hand. Their enemy had sent them yet another demand, one that had her frustration and fury rising. She clasped her hips. "The nerve of the man."

"Calm down, my love." Kirk stepped in her path and gripped her shoulders. Sheathed wrist daggers glinted from under his rolled cuffs, his tan leather vest stretching tight across his broad shoulders. "We'll sort everything out."

"Aye, we will." She unraveled the scrunched missive and traced her finger along the top line.

A marriage of alliance is what I seek. Bring Gilleoin's niece to me, the aura reader Julia, and following her marriage to my son Jeremiah, I shall forthwith return Aleck and Adair Matheson into your hands.

You have a fortnight to answer this summons. Expect their death if you dinnae.

"Kirk, in this missive MacKenzie states that Arabel and Julia's parents live, which is a complete and utter lie. Gilleoin himself snuck into MacKenzie's lair with an elite team of his own men and searched the dungeons for Aleck and Adair. When he didn't find any sign of them, he seized one of the guardsmen and learnt exactly what had happened. The MacKenzie slaughtered them, with his own hands no less. They've been gone for so long, well over a year. Why is MacKenzie now attempting to revive them from the dead?"

"What if they never truly perished?"

"That's exactly the question we need to consider." Finlay tossed another log on the roaring fire. "Aleck and Adair's bodies weren't returned for burial, and other than Gilleoin being unable to find them, we have only one lone MacKenzie guardsman's word that they perished at MacKenzie's hand."

"There is also the fact that the MacKenzie's demands ceased once Gilleoin had discovered the truth. Nay, I believe MacKenzie is playing some sort of game with us." She tucked her cheek against Kirk's chest. Heartache at the loss of her kin still consumed her. "I'm certain of it. This missive is naught but a lie." Except what if it wasn't? She couldn't deny that thought nagged at her.

"Yet if there's even an inkling of truth to it, and Aleck and Adair do in fact live, have survived this entire time, then we have to do all we can to find them and free them." Determination flashed in Finlay's eyes. He nodded at Kirk. "You know what needs to happen."

"Cherub and I will breeze on into Colin MacKenzie's lair and investigate further." Kirk slid one finger under her chin and tipped her gaze up to meet his. "Do you agree?"

"I do, although if they do live, MacKenzie would never keep them in his dungeons, no' when he's well aware of all I can do. They could also be imprisoned anywhere by now. His lands spread from Loch Alsh all the way to Loch Broom, far across the mountainous plateau to the north. There's so much land to search. MacKenzie also has strong ties with his surrounding allied clans. He could call upon any one of them to hold his captives for him." Her heart ached for Arabel and Julia and what they'd soon be going through once they learnt of the MacKenzie's latest demand. Fury would take hold and then no doubt hope would blossom. That was what Colin MacKenzie wanted, to ensure they all held that hope.

"Yet we still need to start our search somewhere." Kirk stroked her back. "Perhaps he's even counting on us eliminating the most obvious place to check first."

"I agree with Kirk." Finlay planted his feet wide and crossed his arms. "We need to search MacKenzie's keep, then we'll devise a plan if you come up with nothing. We'll spread our search area out from that point. Certainly once Arabel learns of this missive, she'll be forever haunted by the possibility of 'what if.' We have to take action. Doing nothing isn't acceptable, which I'm sure Gilleoin would agree with."

"We won't rest until we discover exactly what happened." Kirk crossed to Finlay and clasped his forearm in a firm warrior's hold. "Gilleoin left this castle, his people, and his lands in our keeping until he returns from Stirling with Kenneth and Iain. He'd want us to search for his kin, until we'd scoured every inch of MacKenzie land."

"He'd also never allow us to give into the MacKenzie's new demand. If Arabel and Julia's parents live, then we'll bring them safely back home and not fall prey to the rest of what he's demanded." Finlay returned Kirk's strong forearm hold. "We stand together as one, just as we've always done."

"Aye, as one."

Cherub nodded her agreement. The MacKenzie was clearly after control, and taking Julia from them would only end in more demands if they allowed such a marriage to occur. MacKenzie had lost the recent battle at the fae village, then failed at gaining the eternal life he'd been after by taking her and forcing her hand to spell his soul to hers and now he wished to raise the dead and gain a hold over Gilleoin's clan through marriage to one of her closest. She'd never allow it. Julia was bound for another, the man who held the other half of her soul.

"What are you thinking that has that fierce frown on your face?" Kirk asked, his mind moving swiftly through hers as he sought the information he desired.

"We've spoken of this afore." She sent all thought of Julia and Tavish's mated bond from her mind. "A mated male longs for the chase, and part of his journey is in what he must overcome in order to be with his chosen one. That journey builds the foundation for their bond and all that 'twill be."

"Are you speaking of Tavish and Tor and the other unmated males within our shifter clan?"

"I am."

"What have any of them got to do with this missive from Colin MacKenzie?"

"For now, that I cannae say, but in time all will be made clear."

"Is this one of those instances where you prefer I don't deprive my clansmen of the chase that awaits them?"

"Exactly." She tucked the missive into her plum gown's pocket and glanced at Finlay. "You speak to Arabel and we'll update Julia once we've completed our search." She caught Kirk's hand. "Are you ready to leave?"

"Always." He wrapped his arms around her. "My place is at your side, just as yours is at mine. You can take me to wherever you please, whenever you please."

Love overflowed her heart. She'd been gifted with such a wonderful and loyal mate and every day she thanked the fates that had brought them together. On her toes, she reached up and kissed his chin. "Hold tight, my tempting bear. We have a new mission to undertake.

"Be careful, both of you." Finlay lifted a hand. "I'll see you on your return."

"That you will." She smiled at Finlay, cloaked herself and extended her veil over Kirk then whisked them out the open window and soared toward the MacKenzie's lair. If Aleck and Adair lived, she would see them freed. She wouldn't rest until she had.

Chapter 3

The dawn's rising sunshine streamed through the gap in Tavish's navy curtains and fluttered over Julia's closed eyelids. Birds twittered outside and she wriggled, her legs trapped under one of Tavish's muscled legs. On his belly, he lay half over top of her, his arm a warm and solid weight around her waist.

Soundly, he slept, her movement not even making him stir. He must be exhausted. He'd woken her throughout the night, each time for only a moment or two but his worry for her had been clear to see each time he had. She smoothed one thumb under the dark shadows lining his eyes then slid her fingers through his silky black shoulder-length hair. Tingles raced across her fingertips.

Sometime during the night, he'd taken his shirt off and tossed it onto the end of his bed and now his shoulders, so wide and heavy with muscle, lay temptingly before her. They rippled with strength and she pushed the covers back a little more and exposed his broad back and tapered waist. Black trews clung to his hips and his golden skin gleamed. Oh my, she truly shouldn't be looking her full quite like this.

She pulled the covers back up and continued to mentally berate herself as she snuck out of bed. She tiptoed across the cold polished floorboards toward the corner oak chest. In the topmost drawer, a pair of white socks poked out and she tugged them free and pulled them onto her chilled feet. She trailed her fingers down the front of the shirt Tavish had loaned her. The buttons were quite shiny and made of a similar substance to that of the water bottle she'd sipped from last eve. They must be plastic too. Never had she seen buttons made of anything other than bone, wood, or sea shells. There was so much in this time she wished to see.

Propped on top of the chest, a colorful image was wedged inside a dark wooden frame. She picked the frame up and stroked the glass covering the image within, one incredibly lifelike and completely captivating. Tavish stood impeccably attired in pleated tan trews and a pale blue collared shirt and leather belt, his arm slung over another man's shoulders, a man identical to him in every way. His twin. Tor wore a similar pair of trews to Tavish but in a forest-green and a pressed tan shirt. The two stood underneath a large elm tree with a thick matting of amber colored leaves at their feet, the stone walls of Ivanson Castle rising high behind them. Such a precious image. She would adore having one like this of her and Arabel.

Gently, she set the picture back in its rightful place then hopped across to the window. She slid one finger between the navy curtains and opened them an inch. Below in the stony inner courtyard, muscled men in billowy shirts and belted Matheson plaids strode toward the training area near the far curtain wall. They stretched then partnered up and tapped their swords together. With a heave, they struck and fought, each strike of their blade against the other's ricocheting toward her. She jumped at the fierce clanging and checked on Tavish over her shoulder.

Eyes closed, he stretched then patted the space where she'd been. "Julia?" He jerked upright, flung his eyes open then as he spied her at the window, sighed raggedly. "You gave me a fright.

I didn't hear you wake up. What are you doing over there?"

"I wanted to see more of your time."

"It's cold out of bed." He shoved the covers back and marched toward her. Those broad shoulders she'd not long admired led to a glorious chest holding a smattering of hair as dark as his head, and defined abs that had her fingers itching to touch him once more. Goodness. He must train daily with the sword to have built such strength within his body. He wrapped his arms around her and swamped her in his heat. "Let me warm you up. My shifter blood runs hotter than mere human blood alone."

Her hands were squished between them, right against his chest. She spread her fingers wide, closed her eyes and breathed in his warm and fresh scent. "Mmm, now I'm much warmer."

"I see my clansmen are already at training." Over her head, he pushed the curtains right back and flooded the chamber with sunshine. "Sorry for sleeping in. I didn't mean to. Let's turn you around so I can check your wound, then I can show you around so you can see more of my time."

"There is no pain."

"I still need to ensure everything looks well." He perched his backside on the stone windowsill, turned her around and tugged her in between the V of his spread legs. With her hair separated at the back, he began his examination.

She gripped his muscled thighs either side of her hips. Never had she been in such close proximity to a man before, and neither did she want to be anywhere else. What was wrong with her? Never had she acted so wantonly before. Perhaps the bump to her head had caused her to lose all good sense?

"There's no sign of any infection, although there is a bruise. If you feel sore, or if your head aches, just ask me for some more painkillers and I'll ensure you get them."

"I'm sure I shall be fine." She stepped out of his hold and walked around the bed toward his private bathroom. If he intended to show her around, she needed to dress, and in far more than just his shirt.

"Wait up a moment." Stealthily, he followed her then swept in front and blocked her path. He slid one hand over her hip and the other around to the small of her back. "Would you like me to rustle us up a breakfast tray and bring it up here for us both, or for me to take you downstairs to the great hall so we can eat with my clansmen?"

"I would love to meet your clansmen." She pressed her hand against his chest, right over his heavily beating heart. Its beat, so sure and strong, pounded underneath her palm and the red tingeing the white of his aura blazed brighter and surged with more heat. Even the gentle purr he emitted rumbled louder, his bear incredibly close to the surface. "What's your bear like?"

"He's been antsy of late, particularly since the last full moon should have led me to my mate but instead led me nowhere." He covered her hand with his and trapped her fingers against his warm skin. "Julia, we need to talk. I actually wanted to speak to you about something very important last night, right after you showered, but with your injury I thought it best I keep this coming discussion until this morning."

"What did you wish to discuss?"

"As your doctor, I'm not permitted a relationship with you, therefore I'm giving you notice I'm no longer your physician."

"Oh, ah, all right."

"Instead, I would like to ask for your permission to court you."

"Pardon?"

"I would also like to ask your permission for a kiss." He ran one finger along her lower lip. "Every time I woke you, all I wanted to do was kiss you. I still do, and it's becoming a craving I can't ignore."

"But what of your mate?" She couldn't allow him a kiss, not when he was soul bound to another.

"You are my mate."

"Nay." She stepped back from him. "I can see when two are soul bound, and your aura does no' tug toward mine or mine toward yours." Only those who were soul bound did. "I'm sorry, but we arena mated."

"I say we are." He drew her back against him, until the entire length of her body touched his. "You also have the lushest lips and I need to know what you taste like."

"We truly arena mated." She shoved one hand up between them. Desire had never risen in her before, but it had with him. 'Twas a shame they weren't soul bound, that he was meant for another. "No kissing is permitted."

"Your scent is driving my bear crazy right now." Leaning in, he breathed deep. "So too you're wearing my shirt and I love it." He nuzzled her neck, right over her pounding pulse. "The need to bite you, to mark you as mine is strong. Forget about the aura-tugging. Every sign I can see leads me to only one conclusion. You are my chosen one."

"Aura-tugging is the only sign that matters to me." She ducked under his arm and whipped into the bathroom and shut the door. She couldn't be his chosen one, even if she wished it. She pulled his shirt over her head then folded it carefully on top of the counter. From the heated rail, she nabbed her shift and slipped the dry linen over her head. Thank goodness for the wonderful inventions of this time. Heated rails. Truly impressive. She lifted her gown from the hook on the back of the door and brushed the odd bit of dry dirt away. In the basin, she rinsed a spot of blood from one shoulder then donned the cream gown as best as she could with the stays that laced at the back. With her slippers on, she searched the drawer for the brush Tavish had tidied her locks with the night before and ran it through her hair.

"I have some clothes for you, Julia." Tavish knocked.

"Come in."

He opened the door wearing faded blue trews and a billowy black tunic with ties that swayed free at the neckline. Belted at his waist, his mighty sword gleamed while in his hands, he carried a bundle of clothing which he set on the counter. "Megan heard you were here from Cherub and just dropped these off. She's the chief's wife. I also informed her that I've found my mate."

"I've met Megan. She and Michael are Iain, Finlay, and Kirk's parents. Cherub brought them to my time to attend their sons' wedding. That was a wonderful day."

"She said Cherub and Kirk are waiting for you downstairs in the great hall." His aura became flushed with a haze of blue, the color always signifying frustration and turmoil, not that she couldn't tell by his clenched fists and rigid stance of his current emotions.

"Then Cherub's here to collect me and I must go." She wrapped one hand around his forearm and the blue haze of frustration in his aura receded. "You must believe me when I say we're no' mated."

"A mated male knows when he meets his chosen one." A look of longing flashed across his face as he lifted a lock of her hair and curled it around his finger. "Your hair is so soft and silky, and you look beautiful in your gown."

"And you are a charmer with your touching words." She let go of him and walked from the bathroom, through his chamber and out his open bedroom door. The passageway, lit with bright overhead lighting led toward a stairwell at the far end. She strode along the burgundy and blue runner as Tavish jogged in beside her.

"Julia, I don't need the full moon to guide me to my chosen one, not when being near you tells me all I need to know. I've also no idea why our auras aren't tugging toward each other's as you've said, but that matters little to me." He lifted a challenging brow. "Do you not feel anything toward me?"

"I dinnae have the right to speak of it if I do." He was taken, and she would never come between a soul bound pair.

"That's not what I asked." He caught her hand, slowed her step then pressed her back against the wall. Head dipped, he touched his nose to hers, and murmured, "My desire for you is growing, in leaps and bounds. All I want to do is hold you, kiss you, to discover everything there is to learn about you."

"The only thing you need to learn is that I'm not yours." She fluttered a hand over her racing heartbeat. Those words sounded wrong even as she uttered them and they clashed inside her, made her cringe. "Let me go, Tavish."

"That is still the wrong answer." Smoothly, he slid his hand under her hair and palmed the bare skin of her nape, his gaze moving over the sensitive area where her shoulder and neck met. He rubbed one thumb over the spot. "I want to bite you, to mark you as mine, just as those mated pairs in my clan do."

"'Tis an anomaly for sure." She touched his neck in return, right over his thumping pulse point.

"It's no anomaly, but the early stages of the bond taking form." He eased closer, brushed his nose through her hair and nuzzled her neck. "Since the moment we met, I've struggled to let you out of my sight. When you walked into the bathroom and away from me, all I wanted to do was tear that door down so we were no longer separated. Now I'm about to take you downstairs to Cherub and Kirk when it's the last thing I want to do. You are mine."

"Tavish!" A man bounded up the stairs, a man identical to Tavish in every way, even down to the blue trews and the billowy black tunic he wore. "I got your message from Megan, that you've found your mate."

"Allow me to introduce Julia to you." Tavish lifted his head, wrapped one arm around her waist and drew her forward. "Julia, this is Tor, my brother. Tor, Julia."

"It's wonderful to meet you." Tor hugged her then stepped

back with a grin. "I'll enjoy finally having a sister."

"'Tis wonderful to meet you too, although mayhap you could speak to your brother for me. He believes we're mated and I cannae seem to convince him otherwise."

Tor cast a worried look at his brother. "She doesn't believe you?"

"It appears my mate holds the fae skill of aura reading and as yet hasn't seen the signal that proves we're mated. Our auras should tug toward each other's. For now, I'll have to convince her in other ways."

"Word has already spread of her arrival, and our clansmen are eager to meet her. Cherub and Kirk also asked you to hurry. They need to speak to Julia about an issue of great importance."

"Which means I must go." She snuck out of Tavish's hold and descended the stairs. At his rumbling growl from behind, she picked up her pace. "Dinnae let you bear control you, Tavish."

"My bear is about to burst from me and snatch you away."

"I'm sure your bear would never do any such thing." Not when she truly wasn't his. She reached the bottom of the stairs and stepped through the front foyer. The main doors leading into the great hall were embossed with the chief's arms that held two bears as supporters either side, those bears signifying all that they fought for—the survival of a loyal race of shifters— Gilleoin's line. A line which must continue to grow from strength to strength and not be permitted to falter.

"If you remained at my side, neither my bear or I would have an issue." Tavish swept in beside her, pushed open the door and motioned for her to move ahead of him into the great hall.

A good hundred of his clansmen sat eating at trestle tables, their boisterous chatter lightening her heart. "Now, this is wonderful to see. There are so many shifters. In my time, there is only Gilleoin and his two sons, my cousins, Kenneth and Ivan."

"Ivan's line alone lives here at Ivanson, while in this time Kenneth's firstborn line continues to hold Matheson Castle, your home." He captured her hand and slipped it through his crooked arm. "We have around two-hundred clansmen in all, although not all are present here today."

"Where are the others?"

"Many are out and about seeing to their duties. We have specialist teams who work high level government cases. Even though we keep our shifter status to ourselves, there are a few trusted people outside of our clan who are aware of what we can do and keep our secret." He leaned closer. "Our numbers are slowly dwindling though. Unfortunately it's been over five years since our last clan birth."

"Isla is expecting twins with Iain, so your clan shall have two new births in a few short months." She slid her fingers down to his wrist and tangled them with his. She shouldn't touch him so, except she just couldn't help herself and his aura calmed when she did. Easing his frustration seemed to ease hers. "Iain and Isla are currently in Stirling with Gilleoin and Kenneth, as well as with Nessa. Iain and Isla were so eager to see all that they could while the chance presented itself."

"What took them all to Stirling?"

"Gilleoin was summoned by William, the King of Scots, and had no choice but to go and attend him. He left Finlay and Kirk in charge of his castle and lands until he returns. They are doing a most admirable job. One can tell they are your chief's sons."

"All three of Michael's sons are born leaders." He lifted her hand to his lips and kissed her fingertips. "I still want to kiss you."

"I'm sure the urge will abate." It had better, otherwise she might very well begin giving into him since she liked his touch so much. She turned her attention back on those within the great hall. Ahead at the dais, Michael Matheson, the Chief of Clan Matheson, sat dressed in a tan leather vest over a collared shirt, his sword gleaming at his side. Megan sat next to him in a cherry-colored ankle-length skirt and blouse. Kirk sat near his father, his plate brimming with slices of cooked meat and bread and he cut a sliver of meat and fed it to Cherub.

"Come and choose what you'd like to eat then we'll sit with Kirk and Cherub." Tavish steered her toward a side table filled with an array of steaming foods. He picked up two plates and passed her one then loaded his plate with crispy bacon, hot scrambled eggs and cooked tomato slices. She selected the same, although a much smaller portion. With her plate filled, Tavish set a hand at her back and guided her across the room to the dais and pulled out a chair for her next to Cherub. She set her plate down while Tavish sat next to her and Tor sat on his other side.

Cherub smiled and squeezed her hand, the sleeves of her regal plum gown accented with gold satin fluttering over her wrists. "How do you fare this morn?"

"I'm very well. Tavish stitched my wound and I felt not a pinch of pain as he did." She leaned closer, lowered her tone. "Although I'm afraid Tavish seems to be under the impression that we're mated, even though his aura tells me otherwise."

"His aura does no' tug toward yours or vice versa?" she whispered back.

"Aye, that is exactly what I'm saying."

"How strange." Cherub appeared confused. "Do you feel aught toward him? I ask that because the air itself brings me the secrets it holds, including the call of those who are soul bound. A few days past I actually caught Tavish's soul's need for yours, and I've yet to be led astray."

"You did?" She snuck a look at Tavish. He and Tor spoke to each other and she breathed out then leaned back toward Cherub. "Well, I must admit I do feel desire for him, but I cannae tell him that. 'Twould only raise his hopes. One's aura does no' lie, or at least not an honorable man's aura. Tavish is clearly honorable."

"Hmm." Cherub patted her hand. "Let me think on this new

development a little and I'll see what I can uncover." She straightened then motioned toward Kirk's parents. "You've met Michael and Megan afore."

"Of course." She smiled at them. "Thank you for the clothes, Megan, but with Cherub's return for me, I shall no' be needing them. Michael, I would love to see your home but I fear I willnae be here long enough to do so."

"Since you're mated to Tavish, I'm sure there will be here plenty of time over the coming days and weeks ahead for you to see everything." Michael cut into his sausage and took a bite. "You're always welcome at Ivanson Castle. I hope you'll now consider it your home."

"I heartily agree with that welcome." Smiling, Megan picked up the tea pot in the center of the table and filled a cup and passed it to her. "I can't wait to show you and Arabel around, that's when Cherub finally brings my new daughter-in-law here for a visit. There's honey in the bowl before you if you wish your tea sweetened, my dear. Milk is in the jug."

"Thank you." It seemed everyone believed she and Tavish were soul bound, his word alone ensuring it was so. And Cherub too had sensed the bond. She added a spoonful of honey to her tea and sipped the sweet brew as she mulled it all over.

Cherub nudged her knife and fork toward her. "You need to eat, then we need to talk further about why Kirk and I are actually here. There's been a development since you last left, one regarding Colin and Jeremiah MacKenzie."

"I can eat while we talk." She picked up her fork, speared a bacon slice, chewed and motioned for Cherub to continue. If there'd been a development with their enemy, she wished to hear about it.

"I'm afraid I bring some quite startling news. We received a missive from Colin MacKenzie and in it he states"—she cleared her throat—"that your parents are alive."

"Surely you jest?" She dropped her fork and it clattered

against her plate. "What kind of game does Colin MacKenzie think to play?"

"Those were my thoughts exactly when I first read the missive."

"What's going on?" Tavish slid an arm around her shoulders, his full attention on her. "You're very tense."

"Cherub has received a missive from Colin MacKenzie and in it he states my parents are alive. A lie for certain."

"There's no chance his words could be true?" He glanced at Cherub for confirmation.

"'Tis unlikely, Tavish, although we cannae discount MacKenzie's new demand. Earlier this morn, Kirk and I actually visited the MacKenzie's lair and ran another full and complete sweep of his dungeons and keep. There was no sign of Aleck or Adair." Cherub set her elbows on the table and pressed her hands together. "The only thing we know for certain is that the MacKenzie wishes to hold supremacy over us, in whatever way he can. He also wants to ensure fae blood runs in his direct line, which is why his demand included a request that Julia be wed to Jeremiah in a marriage of alliance afore her parents are released."

"I wish to see this missive." She needed to read Colin MacKenzie's demand for herself.

"Of course. I brought it with me." Cherub pulled a folded piece of parchment from her pocket, one wrinkled from being scrunched up and handed it to her. "Finlay has spoken to Arabel and she is both furious and distressed. She worries for you and what you might do."

"My sister knows my feelings well. If our parents live then I will do whatever it takes to free them." She unfolded the parchment and read,

"A marriage of alliance is what I seek. Bring Gilleoin's niece to me, the aura reader Julia, and following her marriage

to my son Jeremiah, I shall forthwith return Aleck and Adair Matheson into your hands.

You have a fortnight to answer this summons. Expect their death if you dinnae."

Julia tapped the paper. "'Tis all as you've said, Cherub, although any possible marriage of alliance will never bring a halt to the war between our clans. MacKenzie must certainly know that."

"There also isn't a chance I'll allow you to marry another man." Tavish plucked her from her chair and dragged her onto his lap. "That I can promise you." His aura spiked with black, his anger rising hard and fast. "Do we understand each other?"

"I miss my parents, Tavish." Hot tears burned behind her eyes. "Even though I've no desire for a marriage of alliance, if there's the slightest chance the MacKenzie has spoken the truth and they're actually alive, then I would do whatever it took to see them freed. There is less pain in accepting an unwanted marriage than in losing my parents all over again."

"I feared this would be what you'd say." Cherub sniffed as tears pooled in her own eyes. "Even though we found no sign of your parents at the MacKenzie's keep, we still need to search our enemy's lands. They spread from Loch Alsh all the way across the mountainous plateau to Loch Broom in the north. Colin MacKenzie has holdings elsewhere too, as well as alliances with other clans with whom he might have asked to hold his captives for him. So too all we have is a fortnight in which to find them."

"A fortnight will have to be enough." She rolled her shoulders and firmed her resolve. She'd do whatever it took to discover the truth. "Cherub, you're aware I can hear the gentle hum of my parents' auras when they're close. I'd never mistake the sound for another's. I need to be present when the search begins."

"How close do you need to be to hear the hum?" Cherub

squeezed her hand.

"Quite close, within a hundred yards." She snuck off Tavish's lap and pulled Cherub to her feet. "We must go. There is little time to waste."

* * * *

"Wait." Tavish shoved to his feet. There wasn't a chance he'd let Julia go anywhere without him, not now he'd finally found her. "I'm coming."

"I willnae pull you away from your kin. Your clansmen need you. You're their doctor."

"Don't you feel the strength of the mated bond already taking a firm hold between us?" He cupped her cheeks in his hands and looked deep into her eyes. "Where you are, is where I need to be."

"I—I—" Such pain and anguish swirled within her gaze. "I'm sorry." She snuck in behind Cherub. "We must leave, with all haste."

"I agree." Cherub winked at him, and far too impishly for his liking. "Tavish, 'tis time to see if you two are truly soul bound. I highly recommend you dinnae fight the pull. We will need your aid in this search if you're willing to offer it."

"Of course I'll offer my aid, and what pull?"

"Cherub, this isn't a good idea." Kirk stood, his sword gleaming in a baldric across his back as he snagged one arm around Cherub's waist. "We need to take Tavish with us. A mated male knows when he's found his chosen one, and by the way, you really should have told me these two were mated."

"I'm thinking only of Tavish right now, my tempting bear. 'Tis all about the chase, remember?" Cherub disappeared, right along with Kirk and Julia. They vanished, right into thin air.

He was up for any chase.

The wind swirled and the front doors flew open and banged shut.

Now he knew exactly what pull Cherub referred to, the pull

of the vortex which would take him through time. He raced outside in full pursuit, Tor one step behind him. In the center of the inner courtyard, dust churned into a swirling mass. Sprinting, he yelled into the rush of wind, "Tor, I have to follow where she leads."

"Then I'm coming along for the trip."

He dove into the dark abyss, Tor right at his side, just as he'd always been in life. The churning darkness swept him and his brother away. He'd never allow Julia to escape him, not even through time itself. His hunt for his mated one had begun and it was a chase he'd never relinquish. Finding Julia and completing the bond with her would drive him. She was his chosen one and he intended to prove it to her, however he must.

Chapter 4

Lightning slashed and thunder boomed within the pitch black. The wind heaved and twirled Tavish about. Traveling over eight-hundred years into the past would be a trip unlike any he'd ever experienced before. Searching within the misty gloom, he saw not a soul, not even his brother who'd been right beside him as he'd jumped. "Julia! Tor!"

"Here." Tor flew toward him and clasped his forearm. "It seems we've lost the others."

"I also don't know exactly how long we'll be in this vortex, or where we'll come out. I'll need your aid in finding my woman."

"You'll always have it." Determination slashed Tor's face, likely the same fierce expression that lined his own. "Maybe we should pick up our speed."

"Let's do that, together." He clasped Tor's forearm in return and with unwavering intensity, dove deeper into the churning, murky dark with his brother.

"Tavish!" Ahead, Julia tumbled and turned in the fierce wind, her cream gown lit with gold flashes as lightning sizzled all around.

"I'm coming." Like an arrow zooming toward its target, he

zeroed in on her and nabbed her around the waist. Tor, still gripping his forearm, swung around her other side and grasped his other forearm. Together, they kept Julia safely pinned between them. "Are you all right?" he bellowed over the rushing wind, his heart a wildly beating mess.

"I am now you're here." She wound her arms around his neck and clung to him, her long golden locks whipping around them both. "If one holds onto Cherub when traveling then one never experiences this kind of mad free-fall."

"You let go?"

"Aye." She burrowed her head into his neck and nipped his ear. "For some reason, I knew you'd dive in after me. I had to find you."

"You knew because like me, you too feel our bond taking form. You're my mate, mine to protect and care for." Something he intended for her to learn, and fast. "We'll search for your parents together. I'll never leave your side. That I promise you."

"It appears we're slowing down." Tor stared ahead through the dense fog that loomed.

A cloying mist rose up and swirled all around them. Lights flickered, as if the stars themselves had escaped the sky then an unearthly force sucked them all apart and they plummeted into the frosty depths of a loch.

Chilly water closed in over Tavish's head and he kicked through the murkiness in search of Julia. Her cream gown glowed under the water and he grabbed her around the waist and powered upward. They broke the water's surface right alongside Tor. White-capped waves crashed over them and he gulped in air and held Julia tighter to him in order to protect her from the rougher waters as best as he could.

"Look, land," Tor yelled as a seagull squawked overhead then flew down and skimmed the choppy waves toward shore.

"Welcome to my home, and to the year twelve-hundred and ten." Julia motioned toward a four-story castle a hundred feet or so inland. Its massive gray tower house overlooked the loch and the castle's fortified walls were topped with battlements and guardsmen roaming the ramparts. A forest rose tall and strong behind it, the wooded land sweeping around toward the entrance of the loch where it jutted to a point. Smoke curled into the air from thatch-roofed houses cloistered tightly together and surrounded by a high stone wall. "That's the fae village, Tavish."

"I almost can't believe I'm here." He shook his head as he tried to take it all in. This was where their shifter clan had first begun, so far across the Highlands from his own home at Ivanson. At the sea-gate landing, four moored birlinns bobbed with the incoming tide, and on the tip of the landing Cherub and Kirk stood, both waving out. "I see we have a welcoming party."

"Oh no." Gasping, Julia clutched the back of her head.

"Is something wrong? Are you hurt?"

"Nay, but I got my head wet and you said I wasnae supposed to."

"It could hardly be helped." He pressed a kiss to her forehead. "Do you care to show me your home?"

"Since you've arrived for a visit, it would be rude of me no' to. Let's swim in." She slipped out of his arms, caught a cresting wave and rode it in toward land.

"Wait up, woman." Hell, she was a slippery lass to hold on to. He took off after her and he and Tor caught the next wave and cruised with it into land. Once his feet hit the sandy sea floor, he slogged through the water and scooped Julia off her feet before she made the beach. "No more disappearing with Cherub, or swimming away from me. For a mate, you're certainly a handful to keep in my sight."

"Julia." Cherub rushed from the landing onto the pebbly shore and hugged Julia as he held her in his arms. "You should never have let go of me. Are you all right?"

"I'm absolutely fine. Dinnae worry over me." Julia snuggled into him and his chest pumped out. As much of a handful as she was, he wouldn't want her any other way. Her feistiness drew him toward her, her devotion and love for her clan as well. Lucky didn't even begin to describe how fortunate he was to have been gifted with a mate such as the woman he held in his arms.

"At least you've all arrived safe and well." Cherub glanced at Kirk. "Since everyone has arrived without any issue, you and I should continue on. We need to update Gilleoin and Nessa about the MacKenzie's decree, then get started on a search plan. There's little time to waste."

"I agree. We'll go now, head to Stirling then return." Kirk eyed him and Tor. "It's great to have you both here. I'll catch up with you as soon as we're both back."

"You do what you need to." Tavish nodded, his grip on Julia firm. "Travel safely."

"We will." Kirk wrapped his arms around Cherub and the two of them disappeared in a rush of wind.

Julia tapped his chest. "You can put me down now. I need to find my sister and assure her all is well."

"I prefer to carry you." His bear growled at the thought of releasing her. "That way I'll know exactly where you are. We'll find her together."

"Julia!" A woman hurried down the winding castle trail toward them, her golden locks streaming behind her in the fresh breeze, a lass who looked identical to his mate in every way.

"I take it that's Arabel?"

"Aye, please, set me down, Tavish. She'll believe I'm injured if you're carrying me about."

"I'll set you down on one condition, that you promise not to disappear on me again." He'd keep her within arm's reach, no matter what she promised.

"I'll do my very best." She kissed his cheek and smiled. "I can see you're going to be a very demanding mate."

"You better believe it." Warmth rushed through him. Had

she actually acknowledged their mated bond? Carefully, he set her on her feet, knelt and wrung her soggy skirts out.

"Look at you," Arabel tsked as she arrived and hauled Julia into her arms. "You're soaking wet. How's your head?"

"All stitched, although I'm no' supposed to get the stitches wet." She motioned toward him and his brother. "Meet Tavish, my doctor, or he was my doctor afore he gave me notice he would no longer tend to me. Next to him is Tor, his brother."

"'Tis lovely to meet you both." Arabel smiled wide. "Welcome to the House of Clan Matheson."

"Thank you." Tavish wound one arm around Julia's shoulders and in her ear, murmured, "By the way, I will be tending to you, although not as your doctor but as your mate, which you can be assured will be with the greatest attention to detail."

"Your mate?" Arabel's eyes widened and her mouth popped open. She darted a look between him and Julia. "Tavish said you're his mate. Do you care to explain?"

"Tavish believes I'm his chosen one, although his aura does no' tug toward mine, nor mine toward his. I should have seen it do so by now." She tipped her head toward him, a curious look on her face. "Although you're not the only one to believe we're mated. Cherub too said she'd sensed your soul's call toward mine. I also cannae deny that I find it very difficult to be parted from you."

"It's extremely difficult for me to be parted from you too." He tucked her closer under his shoulder, even though all he truly wanted to do was kiss her, then lay claim to her in every possible way. The mated bond had formed between them and of that he had no doubt.

"Well, this is an interesting turn of events." Arabel grasped Julia's hands and squeezed. "Speaking from experience, as one half of a mated pair, these shifter men know when they've found their chosen one, no matter what your auras say. Now"—Arabel took one step back and rubbed her hands together—"allow me to dry all three of you."

"That I would love." Julia clasped her skirts and stepped away from him. "Arabel is a fire-wielder and holds one of the deadliest of the fae battle skills. You'll both need to hold perfectly still while she moves around us and dries us all."

"You make me sound far more dangerous than what I am." Arabel smiled as she smoothed her palms over Julia's shoulders and along her front then circling her, swished across her waist and down her skirted legs until her gown flapped dry in the breeze. Arabel circled him and Tor next, sending a delicious wave of heat over them both.

"That's incredible." He plucked at his now dry shirt. "Even my feet are all cozy and warm within my boots. That's a spectacular skill."

"Well, it does come in handy from time to time." Arabel linked arms with Julia and motioned for him and Tor to follow her as she walked up the grassy trail winding upward toward the castle. To Julia, she said, "Finlay will be thrilled to see his kin, as well as rather surprised. Did Cherub and Kirk drop you all off then leave for Stirling?"

"Aye, they've gone to update Gilleoin and Nessa, then they'll return as soon as they can."

They all passed through the arched gates with its raised portcullis and armed guardsmen in their Matheson belted plaids. The bailey's stone walls rose tall around them while up ahead, the front doors held the carved image of their clan crest emblazoned on the front, just as the front doors of Ivanson Castle did. Tavish stepped inside and entered the great hall with its sweeping ceiling rising to a high crown. Iron chandeliers hung from the wooden beamed rafters, while large tapestries of hunting and landscape scenes graced the walls.

"This way to the chief's solar." Arabel led the way around the edge of the great hall.

He passed two maids clearing trenches and tankards from the trestle tables while a lad swept the area around the wide arched stone fireplace. Logs crackled in the hearth and sent the fire's heat wafting toward him.

"Finlay, I've brought you some guests." Arabel stepped inside a side room and held the door open for them as they entered.

"Well, well, it's Tavish and Tor." Before a chunky wooden desk, Finlay grinned as he eased out of his chair and stood in tan pants and a brown leather vest studded with steel, his sword sheathed at his side glinting from the light beaming in through the narrow window behind him. "What a surprise to see you two here."

"Cherub brought us, which was a bit of a bumpy trip, but we got here all the same." Tavish caught Julia's hand and lifted it to his lips. "I've found my chosen one."

Finlay's grin widened. "That's the best news. You have my congratulations." He set the quill he held in hand down, strode around the desk and clasped his and Tor's shoulders. "I take it then you've both heard about the MacKenzie's missive?"

"We have, and we're here to aid in the search for Aleck and Adair." He stroked Julia's arm. "I'll never allow my chosen one to wed another man."

"Neither will we ever allow it." Finlay nodded. "And on the search front, this morning I sent an additional twenty men to our warrior encampment on our eastern border with Colin MacKenzie, while another twenty will head out tomorrow. I've been considering the encampment as the base point from where we could begin our search. Not only do we have a strong presence there but the camp sits in just the right position to allow for multiple search routes to be taken, across land and sea, and also with Cherub on board, through the skies as well."

"That's a wonderful idea." Arabel sat next to the fireplace and raised her hands to the sizzling flames.

"I agree. The encampment offers us a prime position." Julia leaned her cheek against his shoulder. "So too I would like to be included in the search team. I can hear the gentle hum of my parents' auras when I'm close to them."

"Exactly how close do you need to be?" Finlay asked her, his gaze flaring with interest.

"Within a hundred yards."

"Well, that's a hundred yards more than what we currently have in pinpointing their location." Finlay perched on the arm of Arabel's chair, rested a hand on her knee as he said to her, "I can't be a part of the search team since I need to remain here. I'd also rather you stay with me. I'm not sure I could handle having you too far from my side. Your help too in ensuring the keep runs smoothly, is invaluable. Do you mind staying?"

"Aye, I've no wish to be parted from you either, and I cannae aid in the search quite like Julia can." She squeezed his fingers. "We'll remain together."

"Then Cherub and Kirk, Tavish and Julia and Tor will make up the first search team," he instructed as he glanced at each of them in turn. "You'll make the camp your base and join with Cherub as she takes you through the skies. Another team can head across MacKenzie's land via horseback, and yet another via the loch. We can sort out the finer details once Cherub and Kirk return. I take it they've continued on to see Gilleoin and Nessa?"

Julia answered him, "They have. When do we leave for the camp?"

"Tomorrow, with the team of warriors I have leaving at that time. That'll give Tavish and Tor some time to become familiar with this keep."

"I'll show them around." Julia slipped away from his side and opened the door.

"I'll join the tour later, brother." Tor patted his back.

"Thank you." Tor understood him as no other could. Right now he needed time alone with Julia and their coming discussion really couldn't wait. He followed her as she led the way out of the chief's solar and around the perimeter of the great hall toward the stairwell at the far side. As they climbed the winding stairs, he set a hand at the small of her back. Touch was vitally important to shifters, and even more so between mates. His need for her roared even stronger since they'd yet to complete the bond. "Where are we headed to first on this tour?"

"My chamber. I can see you have a need to talk, and so do I." She strolled along a darkened corridor that remained bare of any other, each of the doors leading from it firmly shut. Before the fourth door on the left, she gripped the knob and glanced over her shoulder at him. "This feels like a monumental moment."

"It is, and it'll be one we'll forever remember." He covered her hand with his, turned the knob and steered her inside then closed the door after him.

She crossed the room and opened the shutters over her window. Sunlight beamed in and played over her four-poster bed with its sweeping golden bed curtains and plush white pillows stacked against the carved headboard. A three pronged candelabra stood on the bedside table next to a red-leather bound book. He wandered toward the side table where an oval mirror was propped behind a dish overflowing with silk hair ribbons in an array of vibrant colors.

Julia swished in behind him and his bear rose and prowled under his skin. "Your bear is growling. I can hear him."

"He wants to meet you, to ensure you know that you're ours." His claws sliced out and back in as he faced her.

"Even your eyes are aglow with shifter gold." She touched his chest and leaned in. "He calms right down when I touch you."

"We both like it when you touch me." Fur rippled across his arm then retracted, there one moment and gone the next. "We need to speak of our bond. Until we complete it and create the merged link of the mind, one that's inherent in my shifter blood, then both my other half and I will never truly be at peace. I need to join with you, Julia, in all ways, for us to be able to speak to each other at will along a merged pathway known only to us. I want you to accept me and all that I am. My word is the truth. We are mated." Hair rippled across his other arm. His bear needed to be set free, couldn't be contained anymore. He gripped his shirt hem, hauled it over his head and tossed it onto the end of her bed. "I need to shift, and since I detest shredding my clothing, it has to go."

"Then allow me to give you some privacy while you make the Change." She walked to the door.

"No." He nabbed her hand and tugged her back to his side. "Don't leave me. It'll make my bear antsier if you're not here. We both want you, him and I."

"You wish for me to stay?"

"I'll use the dressing screen to shift behind if you wish, but I have no problem changing before you. You are my mate and I will hide nothing from you." He motioned toward the hand-painted silk screen propped in the corner. "Although I'll give you the choice."

"Aye, use the screen, please." Her cheeks flushed.

"Of course. Thank you for staying." He toed off his boots, unstrapped his sword belt and set it on the side table then strode in behind the screen. Faded blue jeans unzipped, he shoved them down his legs then tossed them onto the table with his weapons. It was time to shift, to show her his other half. No more could he delay. "Are you ready?"

* * * *

"As ready as I'll ever be." Julia clasped a hand to her chest as she waited for Tavish to shift. Suddenly, a sizzling display of bright lights flared behind the screen then a large bear plodded out, reared up onto his hind legs and roared. Goodness. Tavish's bear was huge, with black fur the same beautiful shade as his head and his golden eyes alight. He dropped down onto all fours and prowled toward her, his pure white aura with its sizzling red tinge at the edge glowing even brighter.

Overwhelmed, and with a fierce need to touch him rolling through her, she dropped to her knees and held out one hand. "Come closer, Tavish. Let me pet you."

Slowly, he padded around her, rubbed against her sides then came back in front and nudged her hand with his head.

"Thank you." She sank her fingers into his silky pelt and scratched between his ears. One deeply satisfied purr rumbled from him, the heavenly sound of his content bringing tears to her eyes. "Your bear is beautiful, Tavish, as beautiful as you are."

He bumped his muzzle into her belly.

"You wish another pat?" Heart lifting, she wrapped her arms around his neck and rubbed her cheek against his furry one. She couldn't deny her need to be close to him in his bear form, just as she'd needed to be close to him in his human form. She truly hadn't wished to leave him so he could shift, had been secretly thrilled when he'd asked her to stay.

She sank down, tucked her legs underneath her and smiled as he too lowered then rolled onto his back and exposed his belly. With his paws up, he offered her a hopeful look. He definitely wished for a tummy rub.

"I like touching you, almost too much." She smoothed her hands over his belly, her fingers sliding through his decadently soft fur. With one slow stretch, his purr deepened. "There's been the odd time I've actually stumbled upon Gilleoin out in the woods with Aunt Sorcha. Gilleoin adores lying on the grass in a pool of sunshine while Sorcha sits beside him and rubs his belly." She spread her hand over his heart, its steady and powerful beat soothing her further. "I need to ask you something, and dinnae get mad when I do."

He remained still, so she continued, "If you're wrong and we arena mated, then I shall never keep you from your true mate.”

Lights shimmered, in a blaze so bright she toppled back and Tavish loomed over her, all man and hard and hot flesh. "I've waited a lifetime for you and would wait forever until you accepted your destiny, but my bear won't. He wants you and I'm not sure how much longer I can continue to hold him back. There will be no more talk of 'what if I'm wrong.' You are my true mate, and I'll do whatever it takes to prove that to you. Allow me to court you."

"I—I—" She palmed his wide chest, shocked he'd changed so swiftly in front of her. The smattering of dark hair on his chest thinned as it traversed between his defined abs and led downward in a teasing trail. Gulping, she couldn't keep her gaze from moving lower. Dark curls covered the apex of his groin and his manhood rose from it, his shaft firm and long and lengthening even more as her gaze roamed over him. His shaft brushed against her belly and her fingers itched to touch him there.

"Want me, the way I want you. Touch me, Julia."

"I…" She shouldn't, yet she stroked down his sides and over his trim hips. She lifted up, pressed her nose into his neck and drew in more of his intoxicating scent. There was no halting what was between them, this all-consuming need or desire. "I wish for more."

"Tell me exactly what you want and I'll give it to you. I don't want to push you for more than what you're willing to give, so you need to speak your mind and be utterly clear with me. This bond is about the two of us, although your needs will always come first."

"I'm no' sure what I need." She wrapped her arms around his neck and rocked her hips against his, until his hard body carved its powerful heat right into hers. "These feelings are all so new and unexpected."

"Then let me show you what you might need. Do you trust

me?"

"Aye." Her agreement came swift and fast, her trust in him absolute.

"That's my mate." He rubbed the tip of his nose to hers then cupping the back of her head, he covered her mouth with his. Moaning, he licked across her tongue then growled and dove deeper. He kissed her, so sweetly and so seductively, his warm and fresh scent swirling all around and embedding itself deep within her.

Kisses. She definitely wanted his kisses. A surge of heat flared in her core and pooled between her thighs. She wriggled against him, needing even more although she knew not what.

"Let me kiss more of you." He ran his hands down her back and over her hips as he moved from her lips and nibbled along her jawline. Laving a path down her neck, he nipped and licked her skin until he reached the sensitive hollow where her neck and shoulder met, where her pulse pounded. Sucking her flesh into his mouth, he released a low rumble. "The urge to bite you is strong. Say aye. I willnae do so until you give me your agreement."

Everything pointed toward a soul bound match between them. Threading her hands deep in his shoulder-length black hair, she stroked his scalp, her nails lightly raking over him. "Bite me. Show me that we're soul bound. Prove to me that I dinnae need to see the aura-tugging as my skill usually shows."

"I'll make sure I prove it, and that you don't regret giving me your trust. Give me a few moments though before I do. I need to taste more of your skin first, to calm and settle my bear." He buried his head at her neck and licked her skin. He swiped his tongue over her, back and forth until he dipped a little lower and laved the upper swells of her breasts where the low-cut neckline of her gown grazed her flesh. As he licked into the gap between her breasts the rough rasp of his tongue made her nipples bead and poke the thin cloth.

Another hot flare of desire burst to life within her and she stroked one thumb over his neck. Her mouth watered to take a bite out of him too. Wanting more, she nuzzled his neck, his pulse a heavily pounding beat under her tongue. She licked the spot, scraped her teeth back and forth and almost cried out at the intense wave of need that washed through her. Sweet heaven. She had to bite him, now

"Do it," he whispered, so tantalizingly. "Then I'll bite you."

"I—" He seemed to know her every thought.

He slid his hand underneath the shoulder of her gown, eased the fabric down her arm and exposed her breasts. "I want your mark, Julia. You are my true mate. Bite me. I'll never deny you what you need."

She closed her eyes and unable to turn away, sank her teeth into his flesh.

"Harder," he growled as he arched into her, his tone fierce and demanding. "Mark me so well that each time you see the evidence of what you've done, you'll know deep in your heart the truth, that I'm yours, just as you are mine."

"Being this close to you scatters all my thoughts." With her heartbeat a pounding roar in her ears, she licked the other side of his neck then bit down a second time, stamping him with her mark.

"Aye, you're mine, now and forever." He buried his head at her neck and razzed his teeth over her skin. She moaned and rocked underneath him as she waited, as she held her breath in anticipation. He bit down and she clutched his shoulders, her nails digging into his flesh.

"More," she whispered. "Give me more."

* * * *

Julia's demand made Tavish's pulse race with fierce satisfaction. His mate wanted more and he intended to give it. He swept lower, nipping around her breasts, each of his bites a mark of claim she'd asked for and which he desperately needed to give her. He flicked her nipple with his thumb then sucked the pebbled treasure deep inside his mouth. As he did, she pressed her breasts deeper into his touch, her nails digging into his shoulders, her claim a physical one that both he and his bear reveled in. His beast purred a mile a minute inside him. Aye, he'd known from the moment he'd met her that she was his and now he intended to ensure she fully embraced their bond as he did.

He licked his lips. Her breasts were full and lush and he ached for another taste of them. Heat surged in his loins and he bent his head and laved first one nipple and then the other. Nice and slow. She tasted heavenly. He razzed his teeth over one rosy tip, taking a second before drawing the aureole deep inside his mouth to treasure each and every inch of her. Sheer pleasure radiated through him and hardened his cock further. He rocked his hips against hers to alleviate some of the pressure, only he hardened even more. Never had he ever known such pleasure as this. He tweaked her other nipple and she arched her back, curving fully into him.

Easing both her breasts together, he gorged, kissing and licking, taking her nipples between his lips and rolling his tongue around them before nipping each one. The bites intensified his feelings for her, pulled his heart and soul ever closer toward hers.

"Tavish." She moaned and rubbed against him. "That feels so good, too good."

"For me too." He lapped the tight buds until she clasped his face between her hands and dragged his mouth back to hers. He kissed her again, plunging his tongue inside her mouth and drinking in her sweet innocence. She met him kiss for kiss, entwining her tongue with his and driving him near mad in a delicious dance that had both him and his bear clawing for her.

His claws sliced out and he dug them into the floorboards to help curb some of his lust.

"Julia?" A knock sounded at the door. "'Tis Cherub."

He shook his head, tried to penetrate the heavy fog of desire taking him. Had someone knocked on the door? Pulling back, he fought for a breath. His mate's lips were plump and pink and wet and the last thing he wanted to do was to cease kissing her.

"Julia?" Another knock.

"Dinnae stop, Tavish." Julia clutched his head, her eyes dazed with passion. "I need another kiss."

"Cherub's at the door."

"What door?" Gasping, she jerked upright and stared at the door. "Oh, that door. I didnae hear her."

"I barely did either." He shoved to his feet, helped her to hers then dropped a quick kiss on her very full and tantalizing breasts before lifting her gown back up and covering her. "I hate losing this delicious sight."

"You need to cover yourself as well." She reached up on her toes, nipped his lower lip then whisked to her golden curtained ambry. She nabbed a fresh gown hanging from within and dashed behind the dressing screen. "Hurry," she whispered in a rush.

While she changed, he grabbed his clothing from where he'd scattered it. He hauled on his shirt and tried to adjust his uncomfortably tight jeans. He left his black shirt flapping free and opened the door, and likely with a scowl on his face.

Cherub arched a far too innocent brow as she stood in the passageway with two bags in hand, one his medical case which he always kept fully stocked next to his chamber door, the other a case from his closet, one now stuffed with his clothing that poked out from under the top flap. "I hope I didnae interrupt anything important, but I come bearing gifts."

Chapter 5

Breathing slowly and surely, Julia tried to clear the sensual haze in her head that kissing Tavish had caused. Her man had sent every rational thought from her mind the moment he'd touched his lips to hers, thoughts she wouldn't mind him scattering all over again. Mmm, and when he'd bitten her and nipped and devoured her breasts, such heat had shimmered through her and intensified all her emotions. 'Twas as if he'd pulled her heart and soul closer toward his, and all with his delicious touch alone. Aye, he'd shown her they were soul bound, a bond she fully intended to accept, tugging auras or not.

After shedding her clothes, she eased a clean shift over her head and donned a rich burgundy velvet gown that shimmered over her hips and swished to her ankles. The low neckline, embellished with white crocheted detailing, was mirrored with the same adornment along the ends of the sleeves that draped over the backs of her hands. She added a matching white crocheted girdle, belted it at her waist and adjusted the tasseled ends sweeping down to her knees. Her hair was likely a mess, so she quickly ran her fingers through it and tried to tame her long locks as best as she could.

Slippers on, she gripped the edge of the screen and peeked

around it toward the door. Tavish's broad back blocked all sight of Cherub in the passageway, so she stepped out and swished in behind him. Her mate, her fierce protector. She leaned against his back, rubbed her cheek against the soft cotton of his black tunic and tried heartily hard not to slip her hands underneath the flapping hem and stroke over his warm skin.

Over his shoulder, he glanced at her, such hunger in his gaze and his smile wide. He set two bags down just inside the door and tucked her underneath his shoulder. "Cherub brought me my medical bag and some clothes. I hope you don't mind if I leave them here in your chamber?"

"Not at all. Come inside, Cherub." She motioned her in. "I want to thank you for all you've done for me, particularly for taking me to Tavish's time and introducing us. 'Twas wonderful that you did."

"You're most welcome, and does this mean you've actually accepted that the two of you are soul bound?" Cherub's plum skirts brushed the floorboards as she stepped inside.

"It means…" She looked into Tavish's eyes, and likely with the silliest smile on her face. "I have. I trust my mate and his word. He has fully convinced me I am his."

His golden gaze flared brighter and almost scorched her with its heat. "I want to kiss you again." Sensuously hot words that nearly melted her on the spot. "And you'll need to cease looking at me like that or else I'll completely forget Cherub's standing in this room with us and do exactly as I please."

"If that was a warning, 'twas a very bad one." She twirled a lock of her hair around her finger. She wanted his kisses, however she could get them.

"Oh, this is good news." Cherub beamed then grasped her hands and pulled her attention back to her. "I also come bearing more gifts than just Tavish's bags. I've had the chance to speak to Nessa and she asked me to impart a vision she saw regarding you. Are you ready?"

"Aye." Her grandmother's words always rang true, her visions a gift each and every one of her clansmen embraced. "Tell me what she said, word for word."

"I shall." Cherub squeezed her fingers and began, *"Live as you've never lived afore, my dear. There is warmth and an all-encompassing heat at the end of the tunnel. That is the place you seek. All your heart longs for will soon come to light and from that sacred place, your journey shall begin."*

She mulled over Nessa's words, considered them from every angle.

"That's interesting." Tavish turned her by the shoulders to face him. "What do you think Nessa means by it?"

"The first part must refer to my parents. Since the day I lost them, I ceased living, and no matter how many times Arabel and my grandmother tell me their death wasnae my fault, I still cannae release the burden that it was. It didnae help too that I saw such hope shimmering within Father and Uncle's auras the day they met with Colin MacKenzie. They both hoped to strengthen the ties between our two clans and ensure we were allies. I've always sensed that I let them down."

"You didn't let anyone down." He lifted her hands to his lips and kissed her fingertips. "So too your parents' death isn't your fault, but that of the man who took their lives. You were only trying to do what was best for your clan."

"Yet what if they're truly alive and we cannae find them in the fortnight of time given to us? What if I'm left with no other choice but to wed Jeremiah in order to save them?" 'Twas a very real possibility and one that frightened her greatly. "My head and my heart are often at war, and in truth, I fear giving into their demands."

"I'll never allow you to walk away from me, or wed the enemy. Trust me to take care of you, to ensure that it so."

She nodded. She would trust him, and fight for what was growing between them. "I wish to see our bond deepen."

"We'll deepen it." He kissed her forehead. "That I can assure you."

Cherub cleared her throat. "What of the last part of Nessa's vision? *There is warmth and an all-encompassing heat at the end of the tunnel. That is the place you seek. All your heart longs for will soon come to light and from that sacred place, your journey shall begin.*"

"I'm not sure what she refers to with that." But she'd keep Grandmother's words close. "Was there anything else she said about the vision?"

"Nay, that is all." Cherub tapped her hands against her sides. "Kirk and I also spoke to Gilleoin and he's urged us to begin the search."

"Finlay has already devised a plan. We are to head out with the warriors leaving tomorrow for the encampment, all except for Finlay and Arabel since they're needed here. We'll make the camp our base and from there head out in teams, the first being led by you as you take us through the skies, another team heading across MacKenzie's land via horseback and another via the loch."

"That is a sound plan, and one I'm in full agreement with. Let me tell Kirk what's happening." Cherub went quite as she spoke to her mate across their mated link. "Kirk too is in agreement. He's outside tending to an issue but will join Finlay and Tor in the chief's solar as soon as he's done." Cherub eyed Tavish. "He would like to talk to you further as well."

"Then I'll go downstairs." Tavish scooped his weapons from the side table and stopped at the door, cast her one last smile. "Wait here with Cherub. I won't be gone long."

"Take as long as you need. I would like to hear more of Cherub's trip."

He blew her a kiss as he walked out the door and disappeared down the hallway. His leaving hurt, squeezed at her heart and she grasped her skirts and stepped into the hallway.

"Wait." Cherub nabbed her hand, pulled her back into her chamber. "Give Tavish some time to do what he needs to. Our mated men cannae stand to see us worry or be in pain, and you are clearly consumed by both."

"I miss him." Her very soul ached at his leaving.

"I understand the feeling well." Cherub closed the door and leaned against it. "There is something else Nessa spoke to me about which I've yet to mention. You and I are about to embark on a little trip."

"To where?"

"To the MacKenzie's lair. Nessa insisted I take you, for you to have the chance to listen and see if you can hear the gentle hum of your parents' auras. Even though Kirk and I have searched his keep from top to bottom, Nessa said you too will need to see and hear with your own eyes and ears as well. Only the truth will set you free."

Cherub tugged her toward the window and opened it wide. "I'll cloak us both then take us to the skies. We're traveling across the loch, although without the use of a portal since we've no need to travel a great distance. Are you ready?"

"Aye, as I'll ever be." To visit the MacKenzie's keep for herself was what she desired. Her grandmother knew her well. She needed to know for certain if her parents were there, but even more than that, she truly wished to allow the truth to set her free, to ensure her head and heart no longer raged with confliction.

"Then let's be away." Cherub cloaked them both, whisked them through the open window then out and over the treetops. Cherub soared high and Julia's heartbeat raced. Never had she traveled like this with her people's princess before—cloaked and through the air. They soared, like birds in the sky. Far below, the castle became a mere dot of gray amongst the sparkling blues of the loch and the rich greens of the forest.

"This is incredible." Excitement shimmered through her,

worry too, as well as an abundance of hope. Her parents might truly be alive, and that was the one thought she'd now hold onto. For today and throughout each day of the coming fortnight as they searched.

Swiftly, Cherub took them even higher, through a layer of puffy white cloud, the air swirling mistily all about. Cherub sped across the loch and along the land toward the east then as they closed in on their destination, she slowly descended. She skimmed a cloying gray fog sitting low over the water then arched up and over the fortified walls of the MacKenzie's lair and settled on top of the foggy battlements.

Below their high perch, men trained in battle leathers, dust rising at their feet and mingling with the hazy air. Their claymores crashed, steel ringing loud against steel.

"Do you hear aught?" Cherub murmured, her hand wrapped tightly around hers as the two of them remained unseen, even to each other.

"I'll need a moment to focus. There's so much noise." Eyes closed, she deadened the clanging of swords and the screeching of a seagull somewhere out on the water as it sought its catch. Those sounds fell away and with her mind narrowed in on her parents, she held her breath and waited for the gentle hum.

* * * *

Palming the hilt of his belted sword, Tavish sat in the chief's solar with Tor and Finlay as they awaited Kirk's arrival for their meeting. His heart grew heavier. Leaving Julia behind had been the hardest thing he'd ever done, each step he'd taken from her making his breath come harder. She was his chosen one and of that he had no doubt.

"You look distressed, brother, and for a man who's just found his chosen one, you shouldn't." Tor closed the front of the armoire that held the chief's armor and set a battle axe down on the table. He rubbed it clean with a soft cloth then slid the axe into the belt hoop on the opposite side of his hip to his sheathed sword.

"This mated bond is strong and I've a deep need to complete it and ensure I tie Julia to me in every way."

"I remember the feeling well, that desperate need to cement the bond." Finlay motioned toward the armoire. "Help yourself to whatever weapons you too might need, Tavish. Gilleoin would want you to be well armed while here in this time. The enemy lurks everywhere."

"I'd appreciate the additional weaponry." He accepted Finlay's offer, selected an axe similar to Tor's and sheathed it at his side.

"Excuse me." A knock sounded. "'Tis Layla. I bring refreshments."

"Come in, Layla," Finlay called out. "Refreshments would be most welcome."

With a tray of tankards in hand, a young woman with golden spiral tresses and her hair pinned with a crown of pretty red flowers and red and white ribbons fluttering down her back, swished in. "The cook bid me to bring you all some ale and oatcakes."

"Give her my thanks." Finlay shuffled some of the seneschal's accounts littered across the chief's large desk to the side. "Leave the tray right there, Layla. Meet my second cousins, Tavish and Tor, both recently arrived from the future."

"Aye, word has already spread around the keep that we have newcomers." She set the tray down then carried a tankard to Tavish, excitement flushing her cheeks. "Is it true? You're mated to Julia?"

"It's very true." He accepted the earthenware mug and gestured to Tor. "My brother though has yet to meet his chosen one."

"Oh, 'tis so wonderful you're both here to find your mates, although 'tis unfortunate you've arrived at this most difficult time." Layla whooshed across to Tor with a tankard, her deep red skirts billowing around her. "Since the 'power of three' arrived, I've been so curious about the future. All the lasses would love to travel to your time. We hear there is far more freedom for women in the twenty-first century. Julia is certainly quite lucky to have already witnessed your world."

Tor smiled at her as he accepted the ale. "It's been foretold our mated ones will hold a touch of fae blood. Do you hold fae blood, Layla?"

"Aye. My father comes from the village, is one of the leaders, although we've lived here at the castle since I was born. Father is also one of Gilleoin's captains. You will likely meet him afore too long. Father holds the same skill as I do, that of the 'power of thought.'"

"You mean telekinesis?" Tor's brows rose in interest.

"I've heard Finlay call it that as well. 'Tis the same thing."

"What of your mother?"

"My mother passed away at my birth." She ducked her head. "Nessa is my godmother, and alongside my father, has raised me."

"I'm so sorry for your loss."

"It has been some time, although Father misses her greatly. They were mated." Her gaze moved over the loose laces on Tor's billowy black shirt and they slowly tightened. She touched the swaying ends of his ties with her fingers then smiled and tucked her hands away behind her. "I can levitate or move objects, can manipulate whatever I wish. If you find I do things you dinnae like, please tell me. I can be too forward at times, so Father always says."

"Be as forward as you like. You've a most interesting skill and I'd love to learn more about it."

"I've a very distracting skill too." Her cheeks flushed a rosy pink and she dipped her head. "Oh, but I am rattling on when I've clearly interrupted a meeting of great import. I must cease doing that. Please excuse me."

"There's no need to go."

"I must." She dashed out the door and waved over her shoulder. "Enjoy your ale."

Tor stood at the door watching the lass as she disappeared into the kitchens beyond the great hall. Once she'd disappeared, his brother frowned as he faced Finlay. "What's her father's name?"

"Gregor, and Layla is also betrothed to Donnan MacDonald, the Chief of MacDonald's son. They're to be wed soon, once Gilleoin and Nessa have returned." Finlay grumbled as ink blobbed from his quill onto the parchment. "I sure miss my computer with its spreadsheets, not to mention a regular old pen. I keep asking Cherub and Kirk to bring me a ballpoint. You'd think they'd remember one tiny little pen, but no, it always slips their minds."

"I wish I had one on me to loan you." Tavish selected a whetstone from the armoire, withdrew his sword and sharpened his blade.

"Sorry I'm late. I had to see to an issue." Kirk strode in, his white tunic tucked into his belted plaid and his ever-present sword sheathed.

"We've sorted out the details regarding the search. You'll all be leaving with the warriors who'll be riding out to the encampment tomorrow, around midmorning." Finlay lobbed his quill to him. "I need a pen, a real pen, with the ink contained within. Tell me you remembered to get me one on your trip home this morning."

"Ugh, so sorry." Kirk tossed the quill back to him. "I'll get it the next time I'm home."

"That's what you always say."

"I do get a little distracted by Cherub at times, and honestly, those are very interesting distractions." Kirk dropped onto the seat next to the fire. "Before we leave on the search, Cherub and I also need to see to one more issue. Nessa requested my mate and I take Julia to the MacKenzie's keep, for her to have the chance to listen and see if she can hear the gentle hum of her parents' auras."

"I'm coming on that trip." Tavish halted mid-stroke with the whetstone. "Where Julia goes, I go."

"Understood." Kirk nodded. "Let me just reach Cherub and find out where she's at so we can get that trip underway." He tapped his head then frowned. "That's strange. I can't reach her along our merged link. Sometimes it cuts out when she flitters about, but she never said she was going anywhere."

"Is it possible she'd take Julia to the MacKenzie's keep on her own?" Cold fear chased down Tavish's spine. He set the whetstone back and sheathed his sword. "I left the two of them upstairs together."

"There's every chance." Kirk shoved to his feet with a low growl. "Unfortunately my mate has been on her own for over a thousand years and is still getting used to having me around and not acting on her own. If she's gone to the MacKenzie's lair though, then she's going to be in a world of trouble with me."

"We need to check." Tavish raced out the door and bounded upstairs with Kirk at his side. He flung Julia's chamber door open and stepped inside. Neither women were there, not even a trace of their scent.

Kirk gritted his teeth as he eyed the open window. "That is not a good sign. Change into your battle attire now and arm yourself well. We're about to sail across the loch."

* * * *

On top of the enemy's battlements with Cherub, Julia focused on her parents. If they were anywhere in this keep then she'd hear them, only not one soft hum echoed back toward her. Hot tears burned behind her eyes and she squeezed Cherub's hand. "I hear naught."

"Then we continue to search farther afield, but 'tis good you came." Cherub hugged her. "Keep the faith that if they live, we'll find them."

"I shall." She wouldn't fail her parents a second time, not as she'd done in misreading Colin and Jeremiah MacKenzie's auras. "Thank you for bringing me, even though 'twas a—"

"Who goes there?"

"Shh." Cherub dragged her into the closest recessed archer's resting spot. Even though they couldn't be seen, the battlements weren't all that wide.

"I said who goes there?" A warrior strode through the swirling fog in dark battle leathers, one gauntleted hand firm on his sword hilt and his fiery red hair brushing his wide shoulders. His aura, a dirty blood-red, saturated him and the thunderous rumble that accompanied his aura surrounded and smothered her. 'Twas Jeremiah, his aura so very different to what she'd first seen during their meeting. This was his true aura, and one that would have warned her to steer well clear of him had she been aware of it.

Jeremiah marched past their hidden spot then stopped, sniffed the air and backed up with a thumping step. He gripped the stone ledge above them, bent and peered into their darkened nook. "I smell vanilla and white roses, a woman's scent, and there is only one woman who can remain unseen to a man's eye. It appears we have a visitor. Come out and stand afore me, Cherub."

Cherub squeezed Julia's hand in a silent entreaty that she remain quiet, then she pushed her farther back into the nook and rose and uncloaked before their enemy. With her hands planted on her hips, she arched a brow. "You called, Jeremiah?"

"You're on MacKenzie land, have trespassed and will pay dearly for doing so."

"I also received your father's missive and you've no doubt been expecting me. Where is he keeping Aleck and Adair, that's if they're truly alive?"

"They're alive and far from here. When they first arrived, I was the one to personally escort them to their new accommodations, and they've remained there the length of their imprisonment. You can be certain though that when the deadline expires and Julia hasn't been brought to me, then their death will be assured. I'll see to it myself." He spat on the ground.

Julia searched his aura but the inherent deceit that already swarmed through the dirty blood-red was so thick she couldn't tell if his words were the truth and her parents truly lived.

"I'll never allow one of my kin to wed you." Cherub shoved him back then dissolved into a mist and reappeared in full form on his other side. She walked backward, drawing Jeremiah farther away from her hidden position in the nook.

"An alliance by marriage is what my father and I seek between our clans." Jeremiah stalked Cherub. "There will never be peace unless Julia and I speak vows and wed. Does she no' care for her parents? Does she wish them dead?"

Never would she wish her parents dead. She shoved out of the recess, rushed along the walkway and pounded her fists into Jeremiah's back. "Tell me where they are! Tell me where they are!"

"Wed me and I shall." He snagged her hands and rammed her into the wall behind her. "Guards," he shouted, "come."

Her head hit the stone and her breath whooshed out. Everything swayed then the wind rushed and Jeremiah was thrust from her. Cherub gripped her hand, cloaked them both and swept them high into the skies.

"Fire your arrows," Jeremiah bellowed to his men.

Arrows flew, arched high and sailed right past them as they sped back toward the House of Clan Matheson.

"Are you all right, Julia?" Cherub's hold on her tightened.

"I shall be. I'm sorry. I shouldnae have attacked him but I couldnae help it." She rubbed her achy head. "This time I saw his true aura and heard the venomous strength of it as well."

"Could you tell if he told the truth about your parents being alive?"

"All I could sense was his evilness." The pain of her loss welled up again and suffocated her.

"Just breathe." Cherub rubbed her back. "Put all thought of what's happened from your mind. We'll find your parents, and then we'll free them. This I promise you."

"Thank you." Touching her heart, she strengthened her resolve. She had an entire clan who would aid her in her search, as well as a soul bound mate who would stand by her side no matter what the future held. Grandmother had been right when she'd said she needed to see and hear with her own eyes and ears as well. Her parents would never have wished for her to wed their enemy, not now she'd seen exactly who Jeremiah was.

Find her parents, she would. There was no other choice.

Chapter 6

Across the inner channel of Loch Alsh, Cherub whisked Julia back toward the House of Clan Matheson while overhead, the afternoon skies darkened with the promise of rain. Foamy white waves crashed onto the pebbly shore.

"Oh dear, it looks like we've arrived just in time." Cherub settled them gently down on the slick stone landing as Tavish and Kirk, wearing full battle attire, raced down the winding castle trail toward them. Cherub uncloaked them both and gently squeezed her hand. "Might I recommend you give Tavish a kiss. I've found distracting one's mate in such a way works rather well, particularly when I've inadvertently gotten myself into trouble. Kiss your mate, and dinnae stop until you've completely muddled his mind. That is what I shall be doing."

"Cherub!" Kirk stormed toward her, the claymore holstered in a baldric across his back bobbing with each step he took. Hands firm on his sides, he halted before her. "You, my elusive imp, have some serious explaining to do. I couldn't reach you along our link. Where have you been?"

"To the MacKenzie's lair." She sidled up against him, lifted up on her toes and wrapped her arms around his neck. "I should have taken you, but sometimes I cannae help but act alone, particularly when I've done so for over a thousand years. Allow me to apologize the right way."

"Don't go thinking you can get out of this argument by—"

Cherub kissed him and he moaned, gripped her tight and kissed her back. The wind swirled and the two of them disappeared on the breeze as Cherub took them away.

Right. Kissing seemed to work a real treat.

Glowering, Tavish stomped along the landing in black leather trews and sturdy boots, his war coat flapping open over a white tunic. His weapons gleamed at his side, a great two-handed claymore on one hip and a battle axe on the other. "We too will be having words. You're never to leave me in such a manner again, or set one foot on MacKenzie land without me by your side. Are. We. Clear?"

"I couldnae hear my parents' auras." She rested her forehead on his chest, her burgundy skirts fluttering in the wind against her legs. "Nessa said I'd need to see what was there with my own eyes afore the truth could ever set me free."

"Did going there do so?" His voice gentled as he gripped her upper arms, skimmed downward and threaded their fingers together. "Tell me what happened."

"Jeremiah spoke to Cherub and I listened in on their conversation. He said my parents are alive and far from here, that when they first arrived at their keep, he was the one to personally escort them to their new accommodations and that they've remained there the length of their imprisonment. When the fortnight expires and I've not been brought to him, then their death will be assured. He'll see to it himself." She lifted her chin, looked deep into his golden eyes. "The truth is, my parents would be furious if I ever agreed to marry Jeremiah MacKenzie in order to see them freed. My resolve is now firm. We shall search for them, find them, and bring them home. There can be no other way."

"I'll never allow you to wed Jeremiah MacKenzie. You're

my mate. I'll never lose you to the enemy."

She untangled one of their hands and cupped his cheek. "My heart tells me we're mated, even though my skill does no'. I've no wish to wed any man, other than you."

"Then you and I need some privacy to talk, just the two of us, without any possible interruption. I certainly intend on showing you exactly how very completely mated we are." He led her farther along the landing, bounded into a skiff, reached back and swung her on board beside him. "Take a seat."

"Where are you taking me?" She plopped down on the bench at the stern, as eager and needy as he was for this stolen moment in time. Just the two of them. She longed for that.

"Where there isn't another soul except you and me." He released the mooring rope, coiled and stored it then with the oars in hand, sat on the center seat and rowed out of the bay. Once he'd cleared the rougher waters, he tucked the oars away, removed his war coat studded with bits of steel and tucked it under the seat then grasped the ropes.

The wind filled the sail with a hearty slap, and with his feet braced wide along the side, the skiff shot off like an arrow. "The wind is strong. Come here, Julia."

She climbed over the center seat and seized his waist. The crosswinds at the tip of the loch slapped into the sail and pulled it taut. The skiff rose farther out of the water on the other side and as Tavish leaned back to counter the balance, so did she.

Flattened against his chest, his arms either side of her as he harnessed the wind power in the tight sail, he sent them flying across the water. Goodness, if she reached out, she might very well be able to touch the white-capped waves. "Do you sail like this often?"

"Tor and I often race together along Loch Bear near Ivanson Castle. There's nothing quite like sailing the seas or enjoying Scotland's freshest air. It clears the mind as nothing else can."

The wind whipped her golden locks into a frenzy and she giggled at the sheer freedom that rolled through her. The sea swelled and crashed into the shore they sailed alongside and the forested hills of her homeland rose high and far into the distance. "This is wonderful, and just what I needed."

"Me too. Don't let go of me," he yelled over the heavy thrashing of the waves.

"I shall never let go of you." With her arms tight around his waist, she held onto him and smiled as his beautiful aura shimmered with sparks of silver, his enjoyment in their trip clear to see. She kissed his chin and nuzzled his neck.

"Do that again." He dropped a kiss on the top of her head. "Keep touching me."

"You are one very demanding mate." But she obeyed his request. Such peace invaded her soul as she held onto the man who'd taken over her world. With the ropes in hand, his biceps bulged and his billowy white tunic flapped free, his hair now a wind-tossed mess which she completely adored. She stroked over his broad shoulders and arms, along his trim sides. Muscles bunched and rippled under her palms. Her mate was a man who held great strength, would fight to protect her and his clansmen, but also a man who held the gentlest touch when healing another. The fates had certainly shined on her. She'd been gifted with such a wonderful man, one her parents would have loved.

"What are you thinking?" His warmth enveloped her.

"Of how you make me feel, safe, protected, cherished."

"Aye, you're mine to protect, my mate, the only woman I will ever hold in my heart."

"And you're the only man I will ever hold in my heart." She slid her fingers under the flapping hem of his tunic and smoothed over his muscled back.

They rounded the tip and as the wind eased and the skiff settled back down, Tavish jumped from the edge into the hull and took her with him as he did. "You can take a seat again if you wish."

She plopped back onto the bench at the stern and rubbed her achy head. Jeremiah MacKenzie's attack had caught her unawares and hitting her head a second time hadn't been all that helpful. 'Twas just as well she hadn't reopened her wound.

"Does your head hurt?" Tavish tied the ropes off to hold the sail in place then dropped in beside her. With the rudder in hand, he guided them alongside the rugged coastline toward one of her favorite places. "I noticed you're rubbing it."

"Nay, my head is fine." She shoved her hands in her lap. She didn't wish to speak of Jeremiah's attack, not when she'd rather embrace this moment and the precious time she'd been afforded with him. "Will your kin be missing you and Tor back home?"

"They'll know where we've gone since we ran straight out into the courtyard chasing you, Cherub and Kirk."

"What of your parents? I didnae get to meet them while I was in your time."

"You wouldn't have anyway. Mum and Dad are away on holiday, touring a place far from these shores, two countries yet to be discovered in this time." He spread his hand over hers in her lap. "Mathesons have traveled the whole world over and continue to do so."

"Which countries are they visiting?"

"Australia and New Zealand. They'll be back in another month, or maybe two. They're enjoying their travels too much to return, although that might change when they hear I've found my mate, and that Tor will soon be searching for his chosen one. They'll want to be close, offer their aid if we need it. For certain they'll want to meet you."

"I would love to meet them too. Tell be about the countries they're visiting."

"Australia and New Zealand are right around the other side of the world. Australia is around a hundred times the size of

Scotland, while New Zealand would be three times the size of our fair land. There are so many countries and large continents that have yet to be explored, places I would love to explore with you when we return to my time. One can almost travel around the entire world in twenty-four hours should they wish to."

Surely he jested. "One cannae even travel the length of Matheson land in one day, let alone the entire world."

"We fly by airplane, a large contraption that can seat hundreds of people and fly thousands of feet high above in the sky." His aura remained pure, ringing with complete honesty.

"And you'd truly take me in such an…airplane?" She'd always been such a curious child, yet her parents had never taken her or Arabel far from their Matheson lands due to the skills they held. Holding a touch of fae blood was both a privilege and a burden and they took extreme care as to who might see all that they could do.

"Of course." He pointed ahead. "That looks like an interesting place to stop."

A white sand beach curved around a glorious bay scattered with the odd boulder while a jagged rock wall rose high behind it and a river gushed into the swirling incoming tide to one side.

"That cove is one of my favorite places. Deep underground there is a large array of caverns just beyond the rock wall, caves that hold both hot and cold pools. I've explored this place often with my parents. Arabel too."

"I'd love to see the caverns, although no swimming just yet for you. That wound isn't to get wet. It needs time to heal."

Thunder rumbled along the horizon and the clouds above swirled into a muddier gray. A drop of water splashed her nose and another hit her cheek. "We need to hurry and make landfall, otherwise I'll get wet regardless."

"We're almost there."

"I cannae wait to show you the caves. I'm so glad we've come."

"As am I." Tavish adjusted the rudder and sent them cruising toward land then lowered the sail and steered them into shore. Once the hull scraped the sand, he bounded out and hauled the boat half up onto the beach. The waves rolled in and splashed his leather trews as he held out his arms for her. "Come here, my true mate. I'll carry you."

She scampered to the bow, climbed onto the seat then jumped into his arms.

He caught her with a chuckle. "You're clearly eager to be back on dry land."

"Nay, I'm eager to be here and alone with you." She kissed his cheek. "Thank you for bringing me. I needed this, to get away for a little while."

"Let's seek shelter." He set her feet down on the soft sand then leaned into the skiff and collected his war coat and a Matheson plaid, which he slung over his shoulder. After tying the mooring rope to a boulder and fully securing their skiff, he guided her across the beach to the cavern's entrance carved into the solid rock cliff face.

She skipped across the white sand and ducked inside just as the clouds opened up and the rain slashed down. "We made it, just in time."

"How deep does this tunnel run?" He caught her hand and twined their fingers together as he walked with her along the darkened, slickly wet tunnel carved of stone. Water trickled through cracks above and splashed into puddles at their feet.

"For some distance, but we are no' going very far." She pulled Tavish to a halt. "The cold and hot pools are straight ahead, but since I'm no' allowed to swim we should instead take this side vent. There's a steamy cavern which is glorious to see."

"What side vent?"

"'Tis right here." She patted the wall and found the slim opening. Through the craggy gap, she squirmed then as the fissure opened up, she stopped and waited for Tavish on the other side.

He wriggled through and smiled. "Well, that was a tight fit. I never would have found that side vent if you hadn't of shown me."

"The first time Father found it, 'twas quite by chance. Come. We're almost there." She strolled to the end of the passageway and leapt onto the white sand a few feet below. Heat shimmered all around, the steamy air thick and humid. "You'll need to breathe slowly until you get used to the heat."

Within the round earthen cave with its high craggy ceiling, a thin shaft vented skyward and allowed a shimmer of light to beam through the tiny cavity above. Light rippled over the slick black boulders in one corner where cold water trickled over hot rocks. Steam plumed and filled the cavern. "Dinnae touch those rocks," she warned him. "They're very hot. The cold water flows in from the fresh water stream close by."

"This place reminds me of a sauna."

"What is a sauna?"

"A manmade room designed to replicate exactly this." He turned her by the shoulders and parted her hair at the back to run another inspection of her wound. "Everything's still looking good. This steam will be fine for you, even if your skin gets damp. It's just soaking wet I don't want."

"Come, I'd like to show you something special." With her hand in his, she tugged him past the boulders toward a chiseled rock basin carved into the ground across the other side of the cavern, one that held a bath-like pool of cool water. "The carved bath is rather shallow, knee deep at most, but if you get too hot, a quick sit down here is wonderful. Mother never used to be able to get Arabel and I out of this pool."

"I'm so glad you've enjoyed so many wonderful times here. So too we shall share an equal number to come." He knelt at the basin's edge and swirled a hand through the water. "This is incredible."

"I wish to dip my feet." She unbelted her white crocheted girdle and dropped it on the dry sand at the rear then tipped off her slippers.

"If you're hoping in then so am I." With a wicked grin, he flapped his plaid out and settled it on the sand. He kicked off his boots, unstrapped his sword belt and laid his weapons next to her belongings then stripped off his tunic, rolled the hems of his trews to his knees and sat on the edge of the tartan. Feet dunked in the water, he patted the space beside him. "Come here."

"One moment." In no time at all she'd be far too hot with all these clothes on. She eased her burgundy gown over her head, dropped it on top of his shirt and sat next to him in her linen shift. With her long hem bunched over her knees, she dunked her feet next to his and swished them back and forth though the deliciously cool water, her toes just touching the smooth, stony base. "Since we're all alone, I would like to speak to you about our bond."

"Go right ahead. I'm listening." He settled one hand on her leg, curled his fingers around her thigh and gently caressed. His white aura with its tinge of shifter red glimmered with sparks of gold and the gentle purr emanating from him vibrated stronger, deeper, his and his bear's need for her shimmering through.

"What if I'm ready now?"

"Ready for what?"

"To complete the bond and create the merged link of the mind."

"Are you certain?" Such hungry hope swirled within his gaze.

"I wouldnae want to push you, if you were no' ready, but aye, I am." She leaned closer, touched her lips to his. "Are you?" she whispered, sharing her breath with him.

"I've been ready since the moment I met you, but since you're not from my time, I need to first ask you a very important question." He lifted the edge of the tartan they sat on, tore a thin strip from it then moved onto one knee before her, clasped his right hand with her right and wrapped the thin tartan strip around both their wrists.

"What are you—" Her heartbeat raced at the symbolic gesture she understood well. "This isnae necessary."

"You are my mate, the only woman I'll ever desire. If we're to complete the bond, then I'll only do so once I've made you my wife in truth. I wish for a handfast marriage, Julia. Bind yourself to me as my wife for a year and a day, and the moment we can, we'll speak vows before a clergyman."

"Oh my." Her hands shook. "You truly wish to handfast with me?"

"I want you as my wife, and that is my one and only stipulation before we complete the bond and all that it entails."

Tears misted her gaze. "I do wish to speak handfast vows with you, to be your wife in truth."

"Then I'll begin." He kissed the tip of her nose, his lips lifting. "I, Tavish William Matheson, of Ivanson Castle, pledge my troth to Julia, of the House of Clan Matheson. With this handfast, I take her as my wife for the next year and a day, and as my soul bound mate for all time." He squeezed her hand. "I long to be your husband, to know none other can ever claim you, except for me. This way you'll be mine, in every single way. None can ever tear us apart. Certainly not a MacKenzie, or their devious demands."

"I cannae believe this is happening." The depth of the vow she wished to speak with him, and the complete rightness of the moment rolled through her. She twined her fingers through his and looked into his eyes. "I, Julia, of the House of Clan Matheson, pledge my troth to Tavish William Matheson. With this handfast, I take him as my husband for the next year and a day, and as my soul bound mate for all time. I will never allow another to tear us apart, and in speaking this vow, I also promise to both trust my mate and his word." Tears slipped down her cheeks, her happiness overwhelming her. "Kiss me."

"Aye, we'll seal the vows with a kiss, then I intend to make love to you, to devour every single inch of you, for you to know you're mine, just as I'm yours." He slid one hand around the back of her head, his fingers sliding through her golden locks. Gently, he drew her forward, captured her mouth with his and kissed her. She swayed forward, grasped his shirtfront and twined her tongue with his in a delicious dance she couldn't help but desire more of. Their kiss grew wilder, more frantic and he tugged the handfast binding off and freed their hands. Rising up over top of her, he toppled her back onto his plaid, gently eased one knee between hers and nudged her legs farther apart. He settled himself fully on top of her, his glorious body a heavenly weight she desired more of.

"My husband." She dug her fingers into his hair, his warm and fresh scent surrounding and embedding itself deeply within her.

"Knowing you can't get away from me right now soothes me beyond reason."

"I dinnae wish to get away." Reveling in his closeness, she glided her hands over his bare back and down his sides. Her fingers itched to touch more of him. "I've always been a curious lass, and there is no one who sparks my curiosity more than you."

"I need to join as one with you, Julia, more than I need my next breath. I long to complete the bond and form the merged link of the mind."

"To have such a merged link, just as Arabel does with Finlay, is something I too desire." Carefully, she caressed over his leather-clad buttocks, wrapped her legs around his legs and rocked underneath him. The sand made a sweetly soft bed, the steam dampening his golden skin and making it gleam in the trace of light filtering through from the vent above. "I want you inside me, all around me, and for us to never be apart again."

"That's exactly what I want as well. You are one very agreeable wife." His lips lifted in a sensual smile and he lowered his head and seized her mouth once more with his. He slipped his tongue between her lips and licked the inside of her mouth, so smoothly and slowly, with such a seductive stroke he left her panting for more.

Raw and primal need swelled within her and she pushed her breasts into his chest and clung to him. Nipping and licking, her mate tasted her with such a soulful and greedy need, need that flared to raging life within her as well. Heat flooded her below and she moaned and scraped her nails down his back.

"I love it when you do that," he whispered against her lips, "and I mean by marking me as yours."

"Aye, you are mine." She dug her fingers into his back once more and he rumbled his pleasure then kissed her deeper, until something brushed against her mind and pushed harder as if trying to find a way into her mind. Cradling his head in her hands, she pulled back a touch and locked gazes with him. The merged link was only possible between mates and his mind clearly battered at hers and demanded entrance. "We truly are mated." Awe laced her words.

"You still doubted it?" His aura expanded and flowed out. "My mind is shoving against yours, trying to gain access. I want the telepathic connection."

"Mayhap just a little part of me still held back on that truth, but not anymore, not when I can sense your need to form the merged link." She gasped as his aura suddenly swarmed around hers, not only tugging but completely surrounding and melding into the rainbow of colors that made up her own. "Oh my."

"What's wrong?" He searched her gaze.

"There is naught wrong. Your aura is saturating mine, fully enveloping me."

"Well, about damn time." He slid one hand around her nape and his warm breath whispered tantalizingly across her lips.

"You are my true mate. Claim me, just as I wish to claim you."

Her grandmother's words reverberated through her mind. *Live as you've never lived afore, my dear. There is warmth and an all-encompassing heat at the end of the tunnel. That is the place you seek. All your heart longs for will soon come to light and from that sacred place, your journey shall begin.*

Aye, her journey had now begun, right here within the all-encompassing heat at the end of the tunnel. She slid her fingers into Tavish's silky black hair and nuzzled his neck. She licked over the mark she'd given him that very morning, right there within the sensitive hollow where his shoulder and neck met. His pulse throbbed under her tongue and dizzy with need, she scraped her teeth back and forth, her only desire to bite him, to mark him fully and completely as hers. "I wish to live, Tavish, to be a part of you, just as you will be a part of me."

"Bite me." He rubbed his body against hers, his aura flaring with more need and flushing hers with the same. Holding her head against his flesh, he sucked on her neck and she clamped down on him and bit him just as he'd asked her to.

He bucked and moaned against her, slid one finger under the shoulder of her shift and eased her sleeve down her arm. A low rumble vibrated in his chest as he freed her breasts and gazed at them, then he dipped his head and licked the hard buds which tightened further under his hot and marauding tongue. "You skin is so flushed. Are you all right?"

"I'm about to lose my mind."

"Then we'll lose our minds together." He curved his palm around her breast, flicked one finger over her nipple and smiled at her. "Say aye."

"Aye."

"Thank you, my love." He covered her mouth with his, captured her lips in a wickedly scorching kiss, his hard body a powerful stamp of heat that embedded itself into each and every inch of her. He licked her tongue and she couldn't help but respond. She sucked it into her mouth and when she did, he delved deeper and growled, his bear rising to the surface and rippling right under his skin.

Mmm, he tasted so good. She melted into a pool of liquid heat, wishing this kiss would never stop. Naught had ever felt so right and a desperate spike of need rushed through her, so strongly, so fiercely. She rubbed her body against his, kissed him wildly in return and reveled in their beautiful bond. Being this close to him was sheer perfection. She seized his biceps and held on as he kissed her over and over, until their breath mingled as one and the heat between them blazed into a fiercely hot fire. "I need skin on skin."

"So do I. Hands up."

She lifted her arms and he swept her shift over her head and tossed it on top of the pile of their discarded clothes.

"Hell, you're so beautiful." With one finger, he traced around her beading nipples then down between the valley of her breasts to her belly button. His aura heated further, as did the molten gold of his shifter eyes. "I can't believe you're all mine."

"As you're all mine."

"Aye, always, from this moment forth and throughout all of time." He clasped her bare bottom, dipped his head and sucked her nipple deep into his mouth.

"There will only ever be you." She arched into him, desperate to rub against the hard length of his erection almost spearing through his black leather trews. She fumbled with the ties at his waist.

"Here, allow me." He eased up, loosened the waistband then shoved the fabric down his heavily muscled legs. His cock bobbed free and brushed his belly, the shaft so thick and the plump head glistening on the very tip. Goodness. How on earth was she meant to fit all of him inside her? Obviously it must be possible since man and woman had been joining together since the beginning of time, only she had no idea quite how.

"What has that worried look flittering across your face?" He kicked his trews away, knelt between her legs, his balls pulling higher and firmer into the nest of dark curls covering the V at his groin.

"Every maid must be worried when first contemplating such a joining."

"I never want to hurt you, only the first time there will be a little pain. I'll do all I can to ensure it's minimal."

"May I touch you there?"

"I'd love nothing more." He gripped her hand and spread her fingers around his long and full length. His cock was so velvety smooth yet also hot and hard.

She caressed his flesh and as a bead of his essence rose and shimmered on the top, she gently smoothed her thumb over it. He groaned, his thigh muscles bunching and his hands clenching. "Does this hurt you? My touching you like this?"

"Your touch feels incredible. This is my first time just as it's your first time. Our mated males wait for our females, never allowing a joining with another. Which means all these new sensations you feel, so do I." He pushed her back until she laid down once more then bent over her and licked her nipple. He drew the tip deep into the glorious heat of his mouth and played the tip to perfection.

She moaned, the sound almost animalistic. Wildly wicked tingles raced through her body, each raspy stroke of his tongue over the sensitive point sending a bolt of pleasure straight to her core. Heat flooded her below and he sniffed and lifted his head.

His hungry gaze swept down her body, from her breasts to her belly then to the golden curls covering her entrance. "Mmm, you smell incredible, like warm, creamy honey and that my mate, is one of my favorite foods. I need to taste you."

"Wait." She squirmed back and he captured her ankles, dragged her back and raised her legs. He hooked them over his shoulders until her bottom lifted off the sand and she lay fully exposed to him. "Tavish, please, you cannae think to taste me there."

"By the end of this day, I'll have tasted every part of you, and most definitely down there. You're so beautiful, so pink and lush and my mouth is watering for more. Don't deny me. Say aye."

She squeezed her eyes shut and somehow whispered her agreement. "Aye."

"Relax, my mate. I intend for you to enjoy this moment, and for me to enjoy it too." He swept his hands along her inner thighs and parted her folds. As he dipped his head, his warm breath feathered across her skin and sent butterflies abounding in her belly. "Look at me, Julia. I want to see your desire when it comes."

She opened her eyes and met his gaze. "I wish to give you all of me. Taste and take whatever you please."

"Good answer." Grinning, he plunged one finger deep inside her and she bucked as pleasure ricocheted outward from her core and hardened her nipples further.

"Oh, that I like."

"If I do anything you don't like, then tell me."

"Keep touching me as you are." She doubted there'd be anything he did which she wouldn't completely adore. "I wish to be loved by you, for us both to live as we've never lived afore."

"All I want is to see to your pleasure." He stroked her harder, faster, then rubbed his thumb across her nub until she arched into his touch. When he added a second finger and lowered his head between her thighs, she sank her hands into his dark hair and gasped as he licked and kissed her flesh in the most intimate of ways. Oh, her mate surely knew how to kiss. Never would she have guessed they could love each other in this way.

Exquisite sensations stormed through her. With each swipe of his tongue and deeply penetrating stroke of his fingers, she couldn't help but lift her bottom higher and rock her hips.

Something sat just beyond her reach, her need for more building higher and higher, until she cried out his name. "Tavish, I dinnae know what to do."

"All you need to do is let go. I've got you, will always have you." He sucked on her nub and sparks sizzled and flared. She hovered on the edge of a precipice she'd soon launch from.

"Cease, please. I cannae take anymore." Except he seemed so determined to stay right where he was. Instinct took over and she reached down and glided over the hard length of his cock. Since he intended to drive her to the point of no return, she would do the same to him. She fondled his hot flesh, his shaft lengthening and heating deliciously in her hand. Stroking him in time with how he stroked her, she tried to hold onto some form of reason.

"Julia, halt." He moaned, long and low. "Or else I'll come before you do."

"I wish to fly. Come with me." She worked him in long pulls, her thumb swiping over the tip now slippery with his essence.

"Hell, you're impossible to say no to." He rose up, pressed every glorious inch of his body down on hers and took her mouth in a hot kiss, his fingers still stroking into her below with such exquisite perfection.

"Please, Tavish. I want to let go, but no' without you." She stroked him harder, everything within her needing his possession. "Come inside me."

"Soon. First I intend to see to your pleasure." He flicked her nub and she gasped and flew, soaring right into the heavens and amongst the brilliance of a million stars. Wave after wave of pure pleasure rippled through her core and a bright array of colors shimmered all around. His aura melded into hers and his gentle purr saturated her. "Are you ready for me, my mate?"

"Aye, beyond ready." She clawed him to her.

His mind battered against hers, demanding entrance, and

she spread her legs wider and wrapped them around his waist. With his hands on her hips, he carefully moved between her legs, slid the head of his cock along her slick folds then nudged at her entrance. "Do you accept me, all of me?"

"You're my mate, my fierce protector. I shall always accept all of you." She grasped his buttocks and looking deep into his eyes, pulled him ever closer. "Join us together and consummate our vows."

With a deep roar, he plunged inside her, tore through her barrier below and as he did, his mind barreled deep inside hers. She welcomed all of him, both body and mind and reveled in their intense joining. There was naught she wanted more than to share all that she was with him, for him to make her his in every way. They were soul bound, each born to be the other's mate, from now until the end of time.

* * * *

Tavish held perfectly still, his body buried deep within Julia's, his mind moving swiftly to forge the merged link that would only ever be theirs. He cemented the link, her thoughts wrapping around his as he whispered into her mind, *"You're my true mate, the one who holds the other half of my soul, just as I hold the other half of yours."*

"Aye, never have I felt so as one with another," she murmured, her grip firm on his butt. *"Or so wholly and perfectly full."*

"I'll take this slow until you to get used to the feel of me." He looked deep into her eyes and she smiled. He could drown in her smile and be a happy man as he did. *"Keep your mind fully open to mine so I'll know if I'm causing more pain than pleasure. I'll stop if I do."*

"I am well, Tavish. There was a moment of pain but now 'tis gone. Look inside my mind and you shall see the truth." She rocked underneath him. *"I cannae halt what my body needs. I wish for you to move, to feel you sliding in and out of me, to feel*

your pleasure in doing so. We were made for each other."

"*You say the most beautiful things.*" He dipped his head, molded his mouth to hers and kissed her. Ever so slowly, he slid his cock back out then as gently as he could, pushed all the way back in. She moaned her pleasure, her eyelids fluttering and every inch of her hot channel hugged him, the exquisite pressure tightening his balls to the point of pain. Hell, he wouldn't be able to hold on for long at this rate, except he had to. He intended to see to her pleasure once more before he came. He wanted her to experience only the sweetest joining with him.

"*I can sense your thoughts. You're thinking of my pleasure first. You wish to come but no' afore I do once more.*" She licked his neck, right over the mark she'd given him.

"*Good. Then you know the plan.*" He nipped her bottom lip then nibbled along her jaw and down her neck until he reached her thumping pulse point. Her soft, creamy skin looked ripe and ready for another mark, an entire series of marks. He intended for everyone to know she was his and no other's.

"*Your thoughts are even more territorial than I thought they would be.*" She rubbed her thumb over the hollow on the other side of his neck and licked her lips, her own desire to mark him in the same way clear to see. "*I wish to bite you again as well, for all to know you are mine and that I've accepted our bond in every way. I belong to you, just as you belong to me.*"

"*I love how you think.*" He moved deeper inside her, and she met each of his thrusts with one of her own.

"*Oh, that feels sooo good. You fill me completely, inside me below and within my mind. There is naught more enchanting than this bond.*" She thrashed underneath him, her teeth scraping back and forth over his neck.

"*Do it, Julia.*" He stretched to give her better access and when she cried out and clamped her teeth down on him, he roared his pleasure and sank his teeth into her neck in return.

Her inner channel tightened wickedly around him and she

lapped the new mark then inched along his neck and bit him again. *"You're my mate, my bear."* Her arousal flew down their link and swamped him. *"Have to—must—"*

Her channel contracted, pulsing over and over and he could no longer hold back. He bit the other side of her neck and bucking into her, came in a hot rush, his essence spurting thick and heavy to her core. No one could ever separate them, not now, not ever. She was his, always his.

"Dinnae leave me." Her lashes fluttered down and she softly sighed. *"Stay right where you are, my handfast husband."*

"I'll never leave you. You're my mate, the one woman I've waited a lifetime for."

"You have my thanks, for bringing me so much pleasure." Smiling, she succumbed to sleep and he carefully pulled out and tucked her safely within his arms.

He tightened his hold on her mind, both him and his bear so content. Through the vent above, the sky darkened and he allowed the pull of the coming night to tug him under. They'd remain here until the morning, then begin the search for her parents once the new day had dawned. He needed this night with her and he intended to take it.

Satisfaction rolled through him as he slipped further toward the dark.

Heavenly sleep took him.

Chapter 7

A bird's pretty trill drifted into the cavern from outside and stirred Tavish awake. Stretching, he opened his eyes while through the vent overhead, the new day's rising sunshine shimmered through and rippled across the chiseled rock walls and basin of water within their sacred underground cavern. Steam plumed from the corner mound of boulders where cold water trickled onto hot rocks. It swirled all about, keeping them both toasty and warm.

Lying on the tartan in front of him, Julia smiled in her sleep, her long blond tresses tangled around them both. He caressed her back and her smile widened. His own smile likely matched hers, the night that had passed all he'd ever hoped for. Speaking vows with her then joining together and creating the merged link of the mind, had soothed his very soul. All he'd ever desired was to find and hold his chosen one and now all his wishes had come true.

Gently, he disentangled himself from her, spread her legs and touched the smear of blood along her inner thigh. His bear stretched and preened under his skin. She'd given him her vow, her body, all of herself, just as he'd given her the same in return.

Needing to take care of her, he leaned over the cool basin of water, scooped a handful of water and gently washed the blood from her thighs before splashing his cock and cleaning himself.

"Mmm, Tavish." She murmured his name in her sleep and he barely restrained himself from taking her all over again. She'd bled and must be hurting. He nabbed her cotton shift, flapped the sand from it then tucked it around her. Keeping her gorgeous body out of his sight would help in ensuring he kept his hands off her too.

"Julia." Leaning over her, he pressed a soft kiss to her lips. "We need to talk. The search for your parents begins today."

"I cannae wait to ride out to the encampment." She stretched and lifted her long sooty lashes. Her blue eyes captured his, the sparks of gold rimming the edge flickering bright as she ran her gaze down his body. "First though, I have a request. You must always wake me with a kiss."

"I already did so."

"I missed it. Kiss me again."

Grinning, he pressed her back into the sand, their bodies fully aligned from head to toe, the only barrier between them her shift. She rubbed against him and a fiery burn invaded his limbs and hardened his cock.

"I would like another kiss, please," she urged him once more.

"When I woke up, I told myself I'd not touch you, that you needed time to heal. You don't fight fair."

"I didnae realize we were fighting."

"I need to take care of you, not to topple you back onto the sand and ravish you all over again."

"Ravishing is good."

"There was blood and you must be sore. Time to heal is what you need, not to be ravished." Cradling her face in his hands, he kissed her, his mouth moving ravenously over hers and she kissed him just as hungrily back. Ragged for breath, he made himself pull away and roll onto his back beside her. Hell, it would take every ounce of his willpower not to succumb to this desperate desire he had for her and take her all over again.

"This need of mine cannae wait, and it appears neither can yours." She sat up, her shift slithering into her lap. Her lush breasts bobbed free, the tips rosy and pink and making his mouth water. Her beautiful creamy skin and luscious pouty lips sent his thoughts into further free-fall.

"Stay right where you are, Julia. I mean it."

"Dinnae turn me away, husband." Smiling seductively, she slung one leg over his hips and straddled him.

How on earth was he supposed to say no to her like this? His greedy bear wasn't helping him right now either. His claws sliced out, his beast riding him hard and his demand clear. He needed to mate. Joining with his chosen one and being as one with her was imperative. His hands moved of their own accord, reached up and cupped her breasts. "Tell me to stop."

"Never." She leaned in and offered him all he desired.

He retracted his claws, eased those delicious mounds together and sucked her nipples deep inside his mouth. He razzed the tips with his teeth and moaned at the delicious taste of her.

"I love it when you touch me like this." She planted her hands on the sand either side of his head and wriggled against his groin, her folds sliding along the length of his erect cock.

Slowly, she moved downward until she grasped his shaft. She eyed his length and smiled, so wickedly, her thoughts extremely clear to see. She wished to take him in her mouth. Hell, the thought of her full and enticing lips sliding around him, of her taking him deep, saturated his senses.

"Hmm, your thoughts are most interesting and in agreement with mine." She eased onto her belly between his legs, licked her lips and touched her tongue to the tip. With one slow swipe, she licked him from root to tip then played her tongue back and forth over the head.

"I'm going to have to learn how to halt certain thoughts from getting through to you." The words barely made it past his dry lips.

"There is naught you can hide from me, not now." She eased her mouth fully down over his shaft. The silken heat of her mouth seared him and sparks shimmered at the base of his spine and rippled around to his groin.

For the life of him, he couldn't stop her, not when her touch was pure temptation and heated torture all rolled into one. Gently, he cradled her head in his hands and urged her on as she bobbed up and down. "You learn fast, my love."

"Your aura also tells me exactly what you wish for, what you will or willnae like. Right now, the sizzling edge of red flares with more need. I believe I shall take you even deeper inside my mouth and see what happens."

"No deeper. I'm not sure if I can handle any more of your aura reading right now, or your very clever mouth."

"You wish to deny me of what I too would like to do?" Sensually soft words as she wrapped her luscious lips around him once more.

His cock pulsed with need and before he lost what remained of his control, he flipped her over onto her back and blood pounding, lavished attention on her. Licking and nibbling, he devoured her breasts before moving in a swirling trail downward. He kissed around her belly button, over her hips and along her inner thighs. Nuzzling her skin, his nose bumped the entrance to her core and he growled long and low as her sweet honey scent drifted around him. He needed to taste her just as badly as he needed his next breath. He slid his hands around her thighs, opened her wider and gave his bear permission to indulge. Lapping at her sweet folds, he rolled around in heaven. This was what he and his beast both wanted, and when her soft cries for more rang in his ears, he dived in and imbibed at the very heart of her.

Sensations stormed through him. His shaft throbbed and he could wait no more. He lifted up and plunged inside her fiery heat, taking her hard and fast, just as her thoughts demanded and just as his did as well. This bond was all-consuming and gave no quarter.

Kissing her, he tasted the delectable recesses of her mouth and claimed every last inch of her. He drank her in, allowing his desperate need for her to take him.

"Tavish!" She screamed his name, clutched his butt and pulled him in even deeper. *"You're my mate, my bear. Make me fly."*

"Always yours, and your wish is my command." He tightened his mind around hers and pounded into her. His thoughts flew as she raked his back, as her inner muscles grasped ahold of him and dragged him in. He roared, his release exploding powerfully from him as she pulsed around him again and again. With his seed coating her womb, he finally eased his pace and rocked gently inside her. As he brought them both slowly back down, he whispered in her mind, *"You're my wife and always will be."*

"Aye, and now I'm a very sleepy wife once more. I need a wee nap after such ravishment." She kissed him and cuddled into him. *"Sleepy."*

"You rest and I'll go fetch us some breakfast. I'll be as quick as I can and wake you when I return." They couldn't leave on any search until they'd eaten. A nap wouldn't hurt her or lose them any great deal of time.

He waited until she'd drifted fully off to sleep, carefully pulled out of her then touched the marks he'd given her either side of her neck and along the top rise of her breasts. She was his mate and such a treasure, one he'd never let go of and always keep safe.

After rising, he tugged on his leather pants, white tunic and stuck his feet into his boots. With his wrist daggers sheathed and his sword belt on, he snuck out of their steamy cavern, slipped through the tightly vented opening and walked along the craggy tunnel into the fresh morning air.

A clear blue sky with only a smattering of white cloud reigned high above and gave the promise of a warm summer's day ahead. White foamy waves sloshed along the sandy curve of the cove while behind him, the cliffs stood tall and strong and the river mouth to the side, sent water streaming smoothly into the sea. He searched along his merged link and touched Julia's mind. She rested, still deep asleep and unlikely to awaken. Certainly if she did, he'd know.

With a determined step, he strode to the beached skiff, removed a snare from a chest under the bench seat and marched toward the river mouth where the forest rose high beyond it. He'd need to head into the woods to set his snare. He followed the river as it weaved inland then veered away and squelched across the wetland. The odd marsh orchid bloomed, a brilliant burst of fuchsia-pink and he couldn't help but stop and pluck a flower for her. The orchid's color matched Julia's sweetly pouty lips to perfection.

Once he reached the edge of the forest, he found a good spot to set the snare then foraged close by for twigs and wood for a fire.

A few minutes later, a soft snap dinged from the direction of his snare and he tramped back to it, removed the rabbit and with his arms full of all he needed, returned to the river and skinned and cleaned his catch.

Down to the beach, he trekked then stole back inside the cavern. Julia still slept peacefully, the sight of her snuggled on his tartan bringing a smile to his lips and warmth to his heart. He dropped a soft kiss on the top of her head, snuck back to the rear of the cave then dug a small pit in the grainy sand. He pulled stringy bark off the wood he'd collected, struck flint with his dirk and coaxed the sparks to life. He built the fire into a crackling blaze with the twigs and wood, the smoke curling upward and floating out the vent above.

The heat of the fire and the steamy recesses of the cavern had the heat rising and dampening his skin. Sweaty, he tossed his shirt aside then set to work fashioning a spit from the thin sturdy sticks that remained. With the skinned rabbit in hand, he threaded the meat into place and set their meal to cook.

The tantalizing scent of roasted meat swirled through the air and near the bath-like basin of water, Julia stretched and opened her eyes.

"You're back." She moved onto her hands and knees and crawled toward him, her full and heavy breasts swaying as she joined him and wriggled onto his lap. "That smells divine."

"What smells divine?" He bent his head and licked one nipple, his naked wife in his arms swiftly stealing his senses.

"The rabbit."

"What rabbit?" He licked her other nipple, the sweet taste of her consuming him.

"I was speaking of the rabbit you're cooking." She looped her arms around his neck and with her body curved into his, offered herself fully up to him. "I'm hungry."

So was he. He seized her lips with his and kissed her until she murmured something about a burning rabbit.

Damn it. The rabbit.

He removed it from the fire and set it to one side to cool. They would definitely need a honeymoon, a month long one at the very least, one he wouldn't mind spending the entirety of within this very cavern. After their mission to find her parents, he was bringing her right back here.

* * * *

Julia giggled as she sat in Tavish's lap while he frowned at the crispy rabbit. "It matters not that our meal is a little burnt. The meat will still provide good sustenance."

"I prefer my meat rare rather than well done."

114

"So does Gilleoin. Do all shifters enjoy their meat rare?" She stroked over his broad shoulders and wide chest, his golden skin gleaming within the heat of the cavern. Oh, and those defined bands across his stomach, they bunched and rippled and completely fascinated her. He was all hard muscles and strong angles compared to her soft curves. She traced one finger down the rigid center of his abs to his waistband and a delicious thrill raced through her. Mother had always said that when one was newly wedded, time was needed between husband and wife to bond. Some couples even spent a month or more away on their own, somewhere close, but also somewhere special. She wished such a time with Tavish, to learn all there was about him, from his intriguing mind to his tantalizing lips and everything in between.

"Aye, all shifters in my clan do. It's a bear thing. The rarer the meat the better."

"What is your favorite meal?"

"It used to be a good steak and roasted vegetables, but now it's the taste of you." He turned her in his lap so she faced the fire, her back to his chest. "How's your head feel this morning?"

"There isnae any pain. I would have told you if that was so."

"I'll check all the same." Gently, he separated her locks and she shrugged her shoulders and indulged him as he wished.

"Is all well?"

"The wound is healing beautifully. I brought you something." He reached over, lifted his shirt off the sand and picked up a bright fuchsia-pink flower that had been lying underneath it. "This is for you. I found orchids growing in the marshland."

"Oh my." She clasped a hand to her chest and touched the orchid. Tears misted her gaze as she reverently stroked its velvety petals.

"Why are you crying? Did I do something wrong?" He

gently wiped a trickling tear away.

"Nay." He would have no idea what such a gift meant to her, but just seeing the orchid sent a flood of warm memories through her. She opened her mind fully to his and shared all she could. "Each time Father walked through the swampland nearby on his way to this cove, he would pick Mother a flower and gift it to her. Mother always tucked it behind her ear or slotted it into her braid. This is a most beautiful and precious gift."

"I had no idea." He slipped it from her fingers and slid it behind her ear. "I'll always pick you one as well, whenever I cross the swampland."

"I will treasure this gift, more than you will ever know." She wriggled her bottom into his groin and dropped a kiss on his lips. "Might I show you just how very much I'll treasure it?"

"I'd like nothing more, but I need to feed you first." He picked up the cooling meat, slid his dirk from his wrist sheath and cut a chunk off. He tore the meat into small slivers then slipped a morsel between her lips and ate a bite himself. He continued to feed her, until her belly was full and she held up her hands.

"No more for me. I need to cool down and wash this steamy heat from my skin." She slipped off his lap, stepped into the basin of cool water and eased back until her head rested against the rim. Taking care not to wet the back of her head, she kept it out of the water. "Come and bathe with me."

"Bathing will likely lead to so much more and I've already taken enough advantage of you." A low rumble sounded deep in his throat, his shifter gaze burning an even richer golden hue. Slowly, he stood and prowled the chamber, from wall to wall before halting in front of her. "You need to hop out."

"Or mayhap you need to hop in." Hands on the basin's smooth base, she pushed up a little and floated on the surface, her breasts bobbing high. "Once we leave to begin our search, there will be little chance for such an intimacy as this. There is also plenty of room here for two."

"I shouldn't." Except he shucked his weapons and trews, his cock springing free and rising thick and high. She quivered with need as he slid into the water in front of her, his legs sliding in underneath her body as he rested his head back on the rim opposite hers.

"Touch me." She stretched toward him, pressed her toes to his chest.

"You are teasing me beyond my endurance." The clear surface rippled as he gripped her legs, ran his warm hands over her calves then slowly skimmed up her legs. Heat raced along the path he touched, his sweet caress moving higher, over her bottom, his hands kneading in firm circles as he traced all the way back down again. "You're a temptation I'll never be able to turn away from. I can't believe you're all mine."

"As you're all mine."

"Aye, always yours." He captured her feet and placed them firm against his chest. She giggled as his crisp chest hair tickled her sensitive soles. "I can already see the urgency of getting a large bath installed in our bathroom at Ivanson. Would you like that?"

"I would love it."

"Whatever is mine is now yours." He lifted one of her feet, massaged her heel, the high arch and around her toes then set her foot back against him and massaged the other. Kneading with delicious strokes, he worked up and over her lower limbs.

She sighed, her long hair swirling around and settling overtop of her breasts.

"Don't dip down any lower. Keep your head out of the water." He flicked her hair away from her breasts and tweaked her nipples. "And no covering yourself up either."

"I didnae mean to." A sizzling tingle radiated from the sensitive tips and rolled through her. "Could you do that again?"

His gaze roamed over her pebbled nipples. "You like it

when I pinch your nipples?"

"Aye, there is naught I willnae like at your hand."

"I intend to offer up far more than just my hands in pleasuring you."

"As I intend to do the same with you." She pushed up, sat astride him and clutched his shoulders, the cool water sluicing down her body as she did. His shaft, so thick and long, saluted her from the water and she fondled the tip then stroked to the root. "Never leave me."

"I won't. You're my true mate."

"Show me." She touched the tip of her nose to his. "I need this."

"You distract me as no other can." He kissed her, hot and hard until he drove every thought from her mind and there was only him and this very moment in time. Gripping her waist, he lifted her up, kissed and licked her neck then drifted lower across the upper swells of her breasts. He rolled one nipple between his lips and as she arched back, he sucked her nipple deep inside his mouth which sent a torrent of tingles racing through her. He bunched his arms around her, his golden eyes twinkling. "I have other places I wish to devour right now."

"Then dinnae let me stop you." The water swished around her as he laid her back down and rested her head gently against the rim once more.

He ran his hands up her legs, lifted them over his shoulders and dragged her closer. Water ran off her and splashed into the pool and with his head bent, he kissed along her inner thighs, his breath puffing hotly against her skin. "If anything hurts, then tell me."

"I promise I shall." She grasped the sides of the pool and softly sighed as he slid his fingers along her folds and rubbed her nub. "More," she whispered. Never had she been so brazen, but he was her mate and she wished to be open and honest with him, to have no secrets. She'd share her greatest desires, just as she shared her body with him.

"I don't consider you brazen. Demand whatever you wish." He spread her legs even wider then licked her flesh with his tongue, his gaze on hers as he built her pleasure to a pinnacle she could barely hold onto.

"You're reading my mind?" Sweet sensations rolled through her and she searched under the water and skimmed the hard length of his cock. She caressed his hot flesh then pumped him in time with how he licked her. "Please, come inside me, Tavish. I dinnae wish to come alone."

"Are you certain you're not too sore?" He released her legs, lifted her against him until his cock brushed her entrance below.

"Never too sore for you." She pushed down on him, melding their bodies in a way she completely adored, until he filled every single inch of her, both body and mind. "Mmm, now this is what I want."

"You are going to be the end of me. I can see it now."

"I certainly hope so." Aching for more, she moved, lifting up and dropping back down. She picked up her pace and he thrust into her, harder and faster, each of his deeply penetrating strokes exactly what she needed. From the inside out, he'd taken her over and she never wanted it any other way.

"Julia, I can't hold on much longer."

"Neither can I."

He flicked her nub and she flew over the edge. Heavenly spasm after spasm rocked through her as he came too, his seed shooting straight to her core. Together, they tumbled right over the edge and into oblivion.

Aye, never would she let him go.

Heart and soul, he was hers, for all time.

* * * *

As Tavish held Julia tight against him, he worked to settle his breathing and slow his pounding heartbeat down. He wished he could keep her here in this magical place forever, only Tor would soon begin to worry if didn't return and so too their mission to find her parents must begin. He kissed her, claimed her mouth once more, just as he'd claimed her body then searching her mind, sought to ensure she'd felt only pleasure and no pain as he'd taken her. Hell, he was insatiable. He and his bear, both.

"I like insatiable." Julia smiled lazily as she gazed into his eyes. "I also enjoy reading your thoughts as you enjoy reading mine. Mostly though, I'm rather glad your bear enjoys devouring me."

"My bear wishes to devour you over and over and never stop but unfortunately we've been gone for far too long and we need to return." He rose from the water with her in his arms and even though he detested releasing her, he set her down on her feet.

"Aye, Arabel too will worry if I'm gone for too much longer." She tugged her linen shift over her damp skin, shimmied into her rich burgundy gown and covered up every delectable inch of her skin. Slippers on, she belted her white crocheted girdle at her waist, the tassels swaying to her knees.

He dragged on his clothes, strapped his sword and wrist daggers in place then cupped her shoulders in his hands. "Ensuring your safety and wellbeing comes first on this trip. It can be no other way and if I feel your safety might be in jeopardy, I'll bring you straight back home. If any harm came to you, I'd never forgive myself. Do you understand?"

"The encampment will be teeming with warriors and although right on our border with the MacKenzie, 'tis still secure and within our Matheson hands. We'll also have the Fae Angel of Love on our side during our search."

Cherub would certainly speed things up with her swift way of travel and he didn't doubt she'd watch over Julia or allow any harm to come to her. He released her with a nod, tossed sand onto the fire, doused it and collected his tartan and war coat. At the tunnel entrance, he held out his hand for her. "Ready to leave?"

"Aye, I cannae wait to begin our search." Brushing her skirts, she joined him with an excited smile.

"Neither can I." He ran his fingers through her long golden locks, tidying her hair then fixed the orchid tucked behind her ear. With his hand in hers, he led her down the darkened passageway, motioned for her to slip through the gap where it forked then walked outside.

She bounded onto the beach and twirled around. The morning sun shone and the rays lit her golden locks and beautiful blue eyes. Such happiness invaded his soul at seeing her so happy and her clear love of this most enchanting place.

"Into the skiff with you." He caught her around the waist and swung her on board while overhead two seagulls squawked and dove into the breakers. Both heaved back up, one with a fish flapping between its beak and the other cackling as it made chase. The wind whispered across his skin, bringing with it the salty scent of the sea and the promise of all he and his clan fought for, this land and their people within it.

"This is such a beautiful place, Tavish, and I love being here with you." She sat at the stern.

"We'll return, however often we can." He uncoiled the rope, stored it under the skiff's bench seat and pushed the boat into the water before hopping aboard. Hell, he'd much rather drag his woman right back into their steamy cavern and send her flying again to the heavens but instead he gripped the oars and rowed until he cleared the bay then raised the sail.

Julia smiled at him, her burgundy velvet skirts fluffed around her and her lips lifted in the most delicious way. "Homeward bound, my fierce protector. We have a great mission ahead of us, the most important I've ever undertaken."

"Aye, homeward bound we go." He'd been gifted with the most precious woman and he'd make certain every hope and dream she harbored was fulfilled. Finding her parents was at the top of that list. To give her what her heart most desired would drive him throughout the coming days. The MacKenzie better well have told them the truth, that he'd never slain Aleck and Adair. He sent a prayer soaring skyward that they lived.

Chapter 8

Through the gates of the House of Clan Matheson, Julia led Tavish after they'd moored their skiff at the sea-gate. Blue skies shimmered overhead and the sun shone and spread its warmth across the land. Her body still ached from her night spent in Tavish's arms, although she adored the change and snuggled her mind deeper into his. Joining as one with him had been so wonderful, then creating the merged link of the mind, such a gift. 'Twas a connection she never wished to give up, couldn't believe was all hers to share with him.

In front of the keep, two lads loaded a cart with supplies for the warriors at the encampment, while across the inner bailey near the far curtain wall, a good fifty shirtless warriors wielded swords in a battle of strength against one another. Finlay, Kirk and Tor were amongst them, the three men training together as a team. They fought with immense skill, the clash of their claymores reverberating through the air, their moves graceful yet holding great strength. "We've arrived in good time. The men still train and the cart isnae yet fully loaded."

"Then I'll join Tor for a bit, warm up my muscles before we leave." Tavish palmed the hilt of his mighty sword. "Stay for as long as you can. I don't care to have you out of my sight just yet.”

“I will.” On her toes, she kissed his chin. “Be careful, because if you suffer even one scratch, I willnae be happy. Certainly whoever harms you will be wishing he never had.”

“I’ll be sure to inform one and all.” He clasped her hips and rubbed his body against hers, his warm and fresh scent wrapping around her. “Right now I’m still feeling a whole lot territorial.”

“I like territorial.” She palmed the mark on her neck then touched the mark she’d given him on his. Gently, she rubbed her thumb back and forth over it and smiled. “Go and train, so that then we might leave.”

“Aye, my wife.” Grinning, he stepped back, slid his sword from its sheath and strode toward his brother and cousins. Swinging his blade in a wide figure eight, he warmed up at the edge of the training men, his moves quick and precise. His shoulders were packed with muscle, his arms so thick and strong and giving evidence of the hours he spent training each day. Everything about him intrigued her, from his gentle healing touch to his fierce fighting stance.

She crossed to the center well draped in ivy where she could watch him with more ease and rested her bottom against the rimmed edge near the swaying pail.

Tor backed away from Finlay and Kirk’s battle and advanced toward Tavish, his weapon held high. “Glad to see you’re back. If you hadn’t returned soon, I would have come in search of you.”

“I needed some time away with Julia.” Tavish thrust his enormous sword against Tor’s as if it were an extension of him and not a massive blade that took such great strength to wield. “We’ve completed the bond and created the merged link of the mind.”

“Congratulations.” Tor beamed as he swung and their two blades crashed hard. “You hear that, Finlay, Kirk? Our clan now has another newly mated pair.”

"That's the best news." Finlay called out as he battled with Kirk. "Iain and Isla too will be thrilled."

"All I can say is I've never felt so at peace. Now, it's time to set out and find Aleck and Adair and if they're alive, to bring them back home." Tavish landed one hard blow after another and Tor met each of his fierce strikes with one of his own. "My mate needs her parents returned to her, and without delay."

"Once the cart is loaded, we'll head out with the traveling party." Tor swung and Tavish caught his high strike and pushed back.

Tavish glanced at her. "Go and pack if you wish."

"Just keep your eyes on the fight." She blew him a kiss.

"The sight of you is far more appealing than the sight of my brother."

"Watch out." Chuckling, Tor swung and Tavish caught his hit. "She might be more appealing but I'm the one with the weapon."

"Then let's battle." The two fought, both moving with such grace and stealth. Sweat glistened on their brows and dampened their tunics while the clash of their blades ricocheted all around the yard.

"Julia!" Arabel dashed out of the keep and hurried toward her, the white ribbons tied around her corseted blue gown rippling in the breeze. Her sister swamped her in a huge hug, her sweet vanilla scent encasing her. "I'm so glad you and Tavish are back. Is all well?"

"Very well." She touched the mark Tavish had given her and smiled. "There's been a development."

"You completed the bond?" Her sister jiggled from foot to foot as she spotted the mark.

"We did, and we now have a merged link of the mind."

"Oh, that's wonderful news. I'm so happy for you."

Cherub shimmered into view near the cart, her skin sparkling in the morning sunshine. She waved out to them and walked across. "I've been out looking for you, Julia, well you and Tavish."

"We spent the night at the underground caverns farther along the loch. We completed the bond and as we did, our auras finally behaved and came into alignment."

"That's the best news." The wind lifted, fluttered Cherub's navy skirts and blew a lock of her blond hair across her cheek. Smiling, Cherub hugged her. "Congratulations. Once you've packed, we'll ride out. Kirk enjoys roaming the countryside on horseback when he can, rather than having me whizzing us through the air all the time."

"I cannae wait to leave." She kissed Arabel's cheek. "I'll keep in touch with you during the mission, however that can be arranged."

"I'll be waiting for news." Arabel tipped her head toward the keep. "Go and pack."

"I shall." With her burgundy skirts in hand, she rushed inside and bumped straight into Matthew. She gripped his shoulders to keep herself from toppling over. "I'm so sorry, Matthew. I wasnae watching where I was running."

"Little has changed since you were a bairn." In his brown tunic and trews, his gray hair thinning at the top, he plucked a red-skinned apple from the woven basket he carried over one arm and offered it to her. "For you, my wee Julia. I'm driving the cart to the encampment and glad I am you've returned in time. Tor told me about your mate, a clever man that Tavish is, a healer of great ability. Tor said they call him a doctor in his time."

"Aye, that is true." She snuck the apple from his hand, rubbed it on her skirts until the red skin gleamed. She took a bite and the sweet apple juice ran down her chin. Wiping it away, she murmured, "Mmm, delicious. Thank you, Matthew."

"You're most welcome. I've heard about the plan to find Aleck and Adair. All within the keep are speaking of it." He tipped his head toward the stairwell. "Be quick now. The sooner we leave, the sooner we can find your parents and bring them back home."

"Save me another apple for later." Munching on the sweet fruit, she dashed up the winding stairwell. Yesterday, she'd stood on the MacKenzie's battlements with Cherub as they'd confronted Jeremiah, and now she was to join their warriors at the encampment and begin searching for her parents. Jeremiah's words echoed through her mind. *They're alive and far from here. When they first arrived, I was the one to personally escort them to their new accommodations, and they've remained there the length of their imprisonment. You can be certain though that when the deadline expires and Julia hasn't been brought to me, then their death will be assured. I'll see to it myself.*

She had to believe her parents lived, that they'd find them in time. No other thought would she consider.

In her chamber, she rolled her shoulders and inserted her never-ending resolve.

"Good morn, my lady." Effie rose from the hearth where she'd cleaned the fireplace. She dusted her hands against her aproned sides and motioned toward the side table where a tray sat with a steaming cup of tea and an earthenware plate holding three of the cook's mouth-watering raspberry and honey tarts. "I was in the kitchens when one of the lads brought the news of your return. I brought you a tray. Do you wish for a bath?"

"I'll forego a bath, but thank you for the tea. Could you lay out my violet riding habit then pack a bag for me? I'm riding to the encampment along with the warriors this morn."

"Aye, my lady. I'll pack all you might need." Effie wandered to her golden curtained ambry and foraged through her clothing. She laid the riding habit, a broad-brimmed hat, and sturdy black boots on the bed, then swept a traveling bag down from the uppermost shelf and carefully folded an assortment of outfits inside.

Apple finished, she crossed to her dressing screen with its length of twine hanging across the inside, slid the orchid Tavish had given her from out behind her ear and strung it up, the bloom facing downward so it would dry. Once it had, she'd store the gift in her keepsake box. This orchid would remind her of the night that had passed, of when they'd completed the bond and joined in all ways.

"Load the cart with additional weapons to send to the men." Finlay's booming voice filtered through her window, ringing with authority from the lower courtyard. Gilleoin couldn't have left their clan in better hands than those of Finlay and Kirk's.

She swished to the window and gripped the stone sill.

Amongst the battling warriors, Tavish wielded his blade with such precision, his biceps rippling and his tunic pulled taut across his wide shoulders. Her fingers tingled with the need to touch him again, to glide over his golden skin and slide through his silky black hair. The hem of his billowy white tunic fluttered free over his leather trews and gave glimpses of his trim waist as he fought. Goodness. She longed to be back in their cavern with him, to have his warm and fresh scent swirling around her, to see his golden shifter eyes spark with desire as he sent her soaring far beyond her body. She'd been gifted with a soul bound mate who'd stolen her heart, a man of many talents, from his dedicated ability to heal to his fierce need to protect. His pure white aura with its sizzling red edge tugged upward and a single stream slipped free and floated on the breeze toward her. She opened her window wider and held out one hand. The tendril swirled in and around her then settled on her palm. Her heart lifted as the tendril kissed her skin with its warmth then soaked into her very being.

"We're almost there, Matthew." Finlay squeezed the elderly cart driver's shoulder then jumped onto the rear of the wooden cart filled with blankets, clothing, armory and other supplies for the warriors camped to the east. Finlay glanced at the cook's son as he stacked a large sack of oats onto the rear. "Alan, bring the loaves of bread the cook set aside this morning, the beans and the fresh fruit the younger lads picked from the grove as well. There's room for it all."

"Aye, sir." He rushed off to do Finlay's bidding.

Tavish and Tor sheathed their swords and strode over to Finlay while Kirk bounded over to Cherub and Arabel as they chatted. Kirk swept Cherub off her feet and her giggles abounded.

At the cart, Tavish tucked the goods into the corner and made more room for the loaves, beans and fruit Alan and another lanky lad returned with. Both lads, brothers with barely a year between them, had brown hair and breeches a good two inches too short on their legs. Their pale blue aura, now tinged with a golden glow, depicted their desire to travel to the camp with the warriors although they were still too young. Mayhap in another year or two they could join the warrior men.

Tavish clapped both the lads on the back and thanked them, a sweet gesture and one that caused their auras to glow brighter with pride. They grinned and ducked their heads under the praise then jogged back toward the side door of the keep.

She smiled too, picked up her tea from the table and sipped the cooling brew then popped a sweet tart in her mouth. So delicious. *"Do you have a sweet tooth, Tavish?"*

He glanced toward her window on the third floor, locked his gaze on hers and grinned. *"I do, and a terribly persistent one at that. How long until you're ready to leave?"*

"I'm about to dress. Do you wish me to have the maid bring your bags downstairs? They're still sitting by my door." She swiped another tart, leaned out the window and whispered, *"Catch,"* as she tossed the sweet pastry to him.

He caught the tart one-handed and popped it into his mouth. *"I'll be up in a moment. I wish to change myself."*

"I'll lay some clothes out for you and have the rest of your

belongings sent down." She scooped his bag stuffed with clothing onto the bed, foraged within and pulled out a blue tunic with the Matheson clan crest embroidered on the front pocket and tan rawhide trews. He could wear his war coat as he rode, should he have a need for the added warmth.

"Is there aught more you need, my lady?"

"Only for you to take these bags downstairs and ensure they're packed with the provisions going to the camp." She snuck the last tart and munched.

"Of course." Effie bundled the bags in her arms and closed the door with a dip of her head as she left.

She shed her gown and shift, flapped out the cream riding shirt Effie had left for her to don and gasped as warm arms wrapped around her from behind. She turned in Tavish's hold and looked into his glittering gaze. "Your clothes are on the bed. Effie took my bags and yours downstairs."

"Thank you, and I believe I need to make a stipulation that whenever you're changing, you only do so while I'm in the room. I'd hate to think I might have missed out on seeing you like this." He pulled her tight against his very hard and very hot body, where every one of those muscles she'd just admired from the window now lay in perfect reach. He'd already shed his tunic and it lay in a puddle of white on the floor, his trews riding low on his hips. She ran her hands over his corded back.

"I wish to make the same request."

"I need to kiss you." He stroked one hand over her bare bottom, swept the other around the back of her head then dipped her backward. "Except kissing will lead to so much more and right now time is ticking away."

"There is always time for a kiss."

"Then I'll need to make that kiss count." He licked her lower lip then sucked it into his mouth. "You taste so sweet."

He kissed her deeper and a fierce heat swept through her, so wicked and wonderful it tightened her nipples and made her weep for him below. She moaned as a storm of need surged through her, as he covered her mouth with his and kissed her with such a soul-searing possession that had her arching into him for more.

Breathing hard, he pulled back, set her back on her feet then whipped her cream shirt over her head. He flapped out her violet riding skirt and knelt at her feet. "Step in."

She did and he wriggled the heavy fabric up her legs and fastened the ties at her waist.

Rising, he brushed his big body against hers then held out her fitted jacket. "Arms in."

"You are dressing me far faster than I ever thought possible." She slid her arms into the sleeves and he fastened the jacket at the front then nabbed her leather boots and after slipping one on each of her feet, laced them up.

"Don't expect me to dress you quite so quickly ever again. I'd love nothing more than to topple you into that bed right now and never let you get back out of it. There is a reason newlyweds always enjoy a long honeymoon, one which we've been denied of."

"I too would like a honeymoon." She pressed one hand to the heated warmth of his chest. "Do you need aid in dressing?"

"I need to wash up and shave first." He strode to the side table and poured water from the jug into the basin. From the pile of cloths, he unfolded the topmost one, dipped it into the water and wiped his arms and chest.

"Here, allow me." She snuck the cloth from his hands, stepped in behind him and stroked down the heavily muscled plane of his back until his golden skin gleamed. "May I shave you too?"

"I'd be a fool to say no and lose the touch of your hands on me." He turned around, perched on the edge of the table and hands on her hips, tucked her in between his spread legs. The black leather molded his strong thighs and she snuggled into the

V as she reached around him and picked up the bar of soap.

"Mother used to shave Father at times." She angled his head to the left and inspected the sharp black stubble that had grown considerably overnight. "Father though preferred to grow a beard and 'twas one as golden in color as his hair, and rather ticklish too."

"What made it ticklish?"

"When I was a child, he would rub his whiskered cheek against mine and make me laugh, Arabel too. Whenever he kissed my poor mother, she'd more often than not end up in a fit of giggles. Her laughter always soothed me. I long to hear it again." Smoothly, she built a lather and smeared his jaw with the foamy bubbles then held out her hand. "Your dagger please."

"Take care with that blade." He slid his dirk free from his wrist sheath and passed it across. "I keep it fastidiously sharp."

"Good. All the better to slice this stubble off with. I prefer you clean shaven so I can see your face and each of my marks on your neck." She turned his cheek with one finger, held the blade nice and close to his skin and ran it in a smooth line down. With care, she drew the dirk along the next portion from his ear to his chin.

"You sound as territorial as I do, and when my stubble gets long enough, it softens." He curled his fingers around her hips to keep her still. "I wouldn't mind tickling you with it." Softly sensual words that had heat flaring through her blood.

"Your words are getting me all hot and bothered." She ran the blade right under his nose. "Dinnae move. I've no wish to cut your beautiful mouth, no' when I'm in constant need of it."

"You think my mouth is beautiful?"

"Aye, as beautiful as your stunning shifter eyes." She tapped his jaw shut and slid the blade along his neck. Done, she dabbed his skin with a cloth, cleared the last of the suds away then leaned in and rubbed her cheek against his. "Mmm, now that is nice and smooth."

"You've done a better job than I ever could have. I'm far more used to shaving with an electric razor." He took the blade from her and sheathed it.

"I have no' seen an electric razor."

"I'll show you mine when we return to the future, whenever that happens to be." He stroked her back, drew her closer and nuzzled her neck. Gently, he licked the mark he'd given her and a deep rumble vibrated in his chest. "My bear would love nothing more right now than to mark you again."

She stretched her neck for him. "Either of you may mark me whenever you—"

He bit down and she gasped.

"—please."

"Time to mount up." Kirk's order rumbled through the open window.

Tavish growled as he released her, nabbed his blue tunic from the bed then donned it and the tan rawhide trews she'd left out for him. He pulled his boots on, eased his war coat over his shoulders and lifted something from the pocket of his pants which beeped when he touched a knob on the side.

"What is that?" She brushed her hair and picked up her jeweled hairpins her parents had gifted her. The sapphire stones sparkled a vibrant blue, just as her mother's eyes had when she'd first pinned them into her hair. With her broad-brimmed hat in hand, she plunked it on and tied the ribbons under her chin.

"This is my cell phone. I must have left it in the pocket of these pants by accident. Cherub would have packed it without knowing. These are interesting devices, but I'll show this one to you later, when there's more time." He pressed the button on the side again, slipped it back inside his pocket, opened the door and motioned her through.

She joined him in the hallway and he set one hand at the small of her back as he steered her downstairs and outside into the courtyard. Next to her mare, he cupped his palms together and gave her a boost into her saddle.

She gripped the reins, a sudden mix of worry and fear rolling through her. The moment of their leaving had arrived, their coming mission the most important one she'd ever embark on. That knowledge both scared and thrilled her. "'Tis time," she whispered to Tavish.

* * * *

"Aye, it's time." Tavish squeezed Julia's thigh as he stood beside her atop her horse, her anxious thoughts pummeling through to him along their merged link. "I'm with you now, and I'll always be right by your side."

"Thank you." She gripped the reins. "You need to mount up."

The last thing he wanted to do was leave her side but he did as she'd bid and walked to his war horse. He nodded his thanks to the stable hand holding the lead and mounted. Reins in hand, he slapped his horse's neck and rode beside Julia as they followed Kirk and Cherub and the rest of their armed party under the arched gate and into the forest. The cart rumbled in behind them, with another two warriors taking the rear.

High overhead, blue sky winked through the thick canopy and birds chirped from their nests. The wind rustled the leaves and scattered the pine-needles covering the well-worn forest path lined with low scrub.

Julia tucked her fluttering hat ribbons underneath the front of her violet riding jacket then lifted higher and snatched an amber leaf as it fluttered down. She slid it into her skirt pocket and softly smiled.

"Do you have a penchant for collecting leaves that I need to hear about?" Everything about her intrigued him.

"When I travel, I like to collect something on each trip to remind me of the moment. Memories stored and kept for a lifetime. The orchid you gave me is drying in my chamber and I'll add it to my keepsake box once it has, right along with this leaf. Do you no' store such keepsakes away?"

"In the future we take photographs to remind us of special moments." He lugged his cell phone from his pocket and focused the camera lens at her. She looked glorious astride her mare, her violet skirts sweeping her horse's sides and the lush green of the forest surrounding her. Her broad-brimmed hat, perched jauntily on the top of her head, dipped forward and backward as she moved with her horse's gait. Golden locks rippled down her back and her beautiful blue gaze with those stunning sparks of gold rimming the edge, locked on him. "Smile for me, Julia, and I'll capture the picture and show you."

"A picture? As in what a painter would paint?" Frowning, she tilted her head to the side. "Of which you have no paints in hand or a canvas to capture such an image."

"Did you see the picture of Tor and me on my oak dresser?"

"Oh, I did." A glimmer of understanding flickered in her gaze. "Does that wee contraption take such an image?"

"It does. Want to see?"

"Aye, very much." She grinned and he snapped the image, took a few more of her then turned around and snapped another of the cart as it bumped along the track behind them, its wooden planked base creaking with each roll of its wheels.

He took one of Tor too sitting astride his war horse then eased his mount closer to Julia's and stretched out one arm to show her the picture of herself first.

"Oh my." She snuck the cell phone from his hand and ogled it. "That is incredible. 'Tis as if I'm on a horse within this very tiny thing." She touched the screen, sliding her thumb reverently over it, which made it flick to the next picture. Gasping, she continued to flick through the shots he'd taken, learning quickly how the mechanism worked. "Could you take a picture of the two of us with this?"

"Of course I can." He'd treasure such a picture of the two of them.

"I would like such an image for my keepsake box, framed too, just like your picture of you and Tor."

"I'll make sure that happens, that we both have one." He snuck his cell phone from her hand and with the two of them riding side by side, he held the camera out as far as he could and at just the right angle to catch them both within the same shot. Perfect. He stroked one finger over the delightful image. Julia's exuberance shone through and his pleasure in the moment did as well. Grinning, he handed the device back to her. "Take a look."

She did and a soft sigh escaped her. Cell phone clutched to her chest, she met his gaze, hers a touch watery and shining bright. "This image is one I shall always treasure. What else can this miraculous wee device do?"

"Not only does it take wonderful pictures, but the primary reason for it is so one can speak to another, anywhere within the country, or even around the other side of the world if needed."

"Impossible." Eyebrows soaring, her look incredulous, she gazed at his surrounding form, as if she was checking his aura.

He searched deep within her mind along their link, found she was. *"Am I telling the truth?"*

"You've yet to speak a mistruth."

"I'll never speak a mistruth to you. You can see my every thought, know exactly what I'm thinking. Do you think you can handle living in my time?"

"As long as you are there, I'm sure it'll be one big, wonderful adventure." Smiling, she handed his phone back to him. "You must look after that device. Dinnae lose it."

"I shall." He powered it off and pocketed it.

Soon, the forest gave way to the rolling moors, the craggy hills of the Highlands rising high on their right, and the inner channel of Loch Alsh just visible beyond the fields to their left.

Julia pointed ahead at the fork in the pathway. "We take the left trail here. The right leads toward the road heading across the Highlands to Invergarry."

Veering left, they rode through the rolling fields of heather awash with wildflowers. His very soul settled at being on this land, his mate so close, and his brother at his back. Trotting on, their traveling party rode alongside a fast-moving river that weaved through the lush green pasture. White-water streamed over wide boulders and flowed toward the inner channel of the loch only a few miles distant. His bear pushed under his skin, his need to shift rolling through him. Splashing through that river then lazing about in the sunshine on the grassy bank to dry off would be heavenly. Another time. Indulging his bear wasn't possible right now.

As they left the grassy trail behind, they picked up their pace and rode along the sandy shore of the loch toward their land border with the MacKenzie. The sun dropped lower along the horizon, its golden rays flaring across the jewel blues of the water.

"There's the encampment. We've made it just afore nightfall." Julia pointed along the curve of the bay where tents dotted the edge of the forest running beside the mountainous border between them and their enemy.

As they passed the warrior on point watch, he sounded an alert, the horn trumpeting and sending word of their arrival to their clansmen up ahead. They rode on, past a large group of heavily armed warriors training right on the water's edge. Shirtless, the men wielded swords in a fierce battle of strength against one another, while another thirty men swam toward a small island in the middle of the bay's waterway, one that held a copse of trees and a wooden shack. As they swam back and reached the waist-depth water, they jogged into shore then swapped out with the battling warriors. They trained hard. Their enemy didn't sit idle, and neither could they.

At the forest's edge, another group of warriors aimed their arrows at a white ribbon tied around a wide trunk a hundred feet distant. Each warrior stepped forward to take his turn with the bow. With impressive accuracy, arrow after arrow thunked into the thin strip of silk.

"I'll go and join the training men before the evening meal. Catch you two later." Tor nudged his destrier past them then galloped toward a makeshift corral of beams hammered between the trees.

Near the central blazing fire pit, two apron-clad women wearing brown woolen kirtles chopped vegetables and meat on a trestle table and tossed the food into two large blackened pots bubbling on the fire. The heavenly scent of seafood stew wafted around him as he pulled his horse to a halt next to Kirk and Cherub who'd dismounted and spoke to one of Gilleoin's captains.

"Mmm, that smells delicious." Julia rubbed her belly. "The dinner hour nears and I'm famished."

"Wait there so I can aid you down." He jumped from his horse, swung Julia from her mount and set her on her feet beside him. Holding her close, he stroked up and down her arms and reveled in being able to touch her so freely once more. "How are your legs?"

"My legs are fine since I ride often, and adore it." She untied her brimmed hat and swished it back and forth with two fingers at her side. "Although I would like to freshen up."

The wind lifted her golden locks and unable to help himself, he threaded his fingers through the long strands and breathed her white rose scent in. "Even though there are so many warriors swarming this area, you're not to wander off on your own."

"I am never alone, not now we have our merged link and you can reach me as you please."

"Julia." Cherub waved out. "Come and join me in the ladies' tent."

"Coming." She reached up on her toes and kissed his cheek, her chest brushing his as she did. "I shall see you soon."

"You will." He grasped her bottom, his hands getting lost

within the mountainous folds of her skirts as he kept her close. "I wish for a proper kiss before any parting."

"That was proper."

"Then I wish for an indecent one." A peck on the cheek would never do.

"I think not." Giggling, she slipped out of his arms and dashed across to Cherub.

"By the way," he called out, "where you sleep, is where I sleep."

"I would never expect aught less." She smiled at him over her shoulder as she cut a path along the grassy forest verge toward the far tent, her beautiful blue eyes drawing him right inside her. Hell, he'd love to be able to take her away from here, to spend days upon days with her, just the two of them and preferably with no interruptions from the outside world. He missed their cavern.

Sighing, he scanned the area. Guardsmen patrolled the entire encampment. His mate would be perfectly safe here, even if not in his direct line of sight. It was time to find her parents—who damn well better be alive—and kick some enemy butt along the way.

Bringing Aleck and Adair home was the one plan he intended to see come to fruition. The sooner, the better.

Chapter 9

Julia heaved the thick tent flap to one side and ducked inside after Cherub. Being separated from Tavish, no matter the short distance between them, sent unease churning through her. She crossed to the center pole, hung her hat on a hook then shrugged off her riding jacket and strung it over the top. "'Tis no' easy being separated."

"Give yourself a few minutes to get used to it. You've just completed the bond too which will make any separation particularly difficult." Cherub wandered toward the corner pile of brown fur pelts, tossed her feathered bonnet onto a wooden crate holding a clay lamp next to it then plopped down on the furs. "Reach out to him along your link as you need to. I can assure you that he too shall be feeling the loss as you are."

"I miss you," she whispered to the man who she couldn't imagine living without.

"I miss you, too. Kirk's counseling me on the intensity of the bond, on how best to deal with the new and strengthened emotions rolling through me."

"What are his recommendations?" More unease speared through her and she frowned. 'Twas as if Tavish were on the move, the distance between them growing farther by the second.

"*Where are you?*"

"*Kirk and I are running a perimeter check. I'm deep in the woods and about to shift with him. Knowing what scents to expect in this area is vitally important to our bears. That way I can better ensure your protection, and that of our warriors in camp.*"

"*I see.*" She sat next to Cherub. "They're running a perimeter check."

"Kirk just informed me too. Shifters are driven by their bears. Their need to ensure our protection rides them hard." Cherub shuffled around and faced her. With her legs crossed under her navy skirts, she rested her hands in her lap. "Let's talk about the days ahead and the best way to move forward in finding your parents. We'll search each and every one of the MacKenzie's holdings by air."

"What is the greatest number of people you can move through the skies?"

"I've transported as many as six afore, but I could push to seven, mayhap even eight. Truly, it comes down to however many can hold onto me. That is the number I can safely transport."

"Does doing so sap your strength?"

"A little, but naught I cannae handle. A short rest in between trips allows me to recuperate sufficiently." Frowning, she squeezed her fingers. "These coming days will be difficult, particularly since we'll be crossing the enemy's land, but we'll return here to the camp each night and ensure we have a safe place to rest. Never forget you'll have all of us by your side and there is naught we wouldnae do for you. I pray that Aleck and Adair live, that we'll find them safe and well."

"It feels as if the hundred yards I can offer in pinpointing them mightn't be enough."

"Yet we shall make the most of it and ensure that hundred yards works in our favor. 'Tis better to have you on hand than to be searching for them with complete blindness. Can you tell the difference between each of their auras?"

"Both are a gentle hum, although my mother's is slightly higher in tune."

"*Julia?*"

"*I'm here.*"

"*Sorry, I just needed to hear your voice again.*"

"*Where are you now?*"

"*Trailing the forest's edge. There are four guards positioned along this line of the border, not enough. Once we return, Kirk will dispatch another four men to double the number.*"

"*Be careful as you track.*"

"*I shall.*"

"Mayhap we too need to stretch our legs as our men are doing." Cherub rose to her feet and tugged her to hers as she did. "There is a glorious loch no' far from here, one I've swam in a number of times. Let's take a walk and enjoy the fresh air afore dinner is served."

"I'd love that." And she couldn't be in more capable hands. No one came up against the Fae Angel of Love and won the battle.

Cherub opened the tent's flap, peered outside then grinned over her shoulder at her. "All is clear."

"Are we supposed to be sneaking out?" The sun lowered further, dancing along the edge of the horizon.

"I sneak everywhere. 'Tis habit, and I dinnae doubt that Kirk has asked a guard to watch over us." Cherub cloaked them both as they stepped out of the tent. "Let's enjoy this moment of freedom while we can."

"You are a terrible influence on me." She couldn't help but smile. "A terribly good influence." Her heart lightened as they left the tent behind. The wind rose and blew all around and the clanging of swords dulled as they moved deeper into the woods.

Overhead, through the odd gap in the dense foliage, a last flare of brilliant red lit the skies as the dark descended. An owl hooted somewhere up ahead and she ducked underneath a low branch and gasped. Surrounded by towering trees, a beautiful loch, small and private and perfectly round, shimmered with the reflection of the rising moon over its smooth, glossy surface. Stars twinkled high above and added to the enchanting scene.

Along the water's edge, they wandered, the odd boulder protruding from the embankment of soft moss. At the far side, a rocky ledge curved around the edge with tall pine and elm trees rising strongly behind it. "This loch is beautiful."

"Even more so than I remember." Cherub lifted her skirts, bounded up onto the ledge and held out a hand.

She accepted the help, hopped up beside Cherub and after toeing her riding boots off, she scrunched her violet skirts to her knees and sat on the stony edge. With her feet dangling in the cool water, she softly sighed. "This is why we fight so fiercely to hold this border, to keep these kinds of lochs and hidden treasures within our hands."

"Aye, the MacKenzie is driven by his greed to have it all, but we'll never hand one inch of our land over to him." Cherub plopped down next to her, her vivid aura beaming a sweetly precious white glow with gold sparks rimming the edge. Cherub's aura tugged toward the east, suddenly and quite strongly, as did her own aura of rainbow colors.

"I believe we're about to have company, bear company."

"Are you sure?" Cherub glanced all about.

"I'm very sure."

"Drat." Cherub frowned then shook her head. "They are very smart bears with a homing beacon that points directly toward us. Although I still cannae believe they found us quite so quickly."

A low growl rumbled then two big bears, their pelts a stunning silky black, lumbered out of the thick tree line and prowled toward them, their noses to the air.

The bear in the front, who had to be Kirk, rose up onto his hind legs, slapped his paws down on the top of the ledge and heaved himself up. He brushed in behind Cherub and she turned, wrapped one arm around his neck and rubbed her cheek against his. "My mate is currently telling me off." Cherub winked at her. "What of yours?"

"*You shouldn't be here, Julia.*" Tavish's bear clomped toward her, his golden gaze targeted on her and no other. He bounded into the water before making the ledge and disappeared under its darkened surface. A flare of bright lights deep within the water shone then her man emerged right in front of her, the water lapping the golden skin at his waist. He shook his wet head and drops flew.

She giggled and wiped her face. "I'm with Cherub, which means I'm perfectly safe, as you well know."

"Thank you, Julia." Cherub stood and hands to her hips, eyed Kirk in his bear form. "See, at least there is someone here who appreciates that I've lived over a thousand years and looked after myself and my kin the entire time."

Kirk prodded Cherub's hand with his muzzle then lapped her palm.

"Dinnae try and sweet talk your way out of this argument, my tempting bear."

Kirk's bear nibbled on her fingertips.

"Or eat me. I am no' your next meal." She dipped her head and kissed the top of his furry head. "Goodness, you are hard to stay angry at for long." Cherub glanced at her. "Mates are beyond impossible at times. I'll speak to you later. Kirk wishes for some alone time afore the evening meal."

"Thank you for bringing me here."

"You are most welcome. On the morrow, we shall head out at first light and begin our search. Be ready, both of you." Cherub nodded at Tavish, cloaked both her and Kirk in his bear form and in a rush of wind, swept out over the loch. Their auras disappeared into the dark, the beautiful streams twirling around and blending together until they whisked away on the wind.

Leaning in, Tavish set his hands down on the ledge either side of her, the water beading on his chest and running in rivulets down. "Some alone time with you is exactly what I need as well."

"Where are your clothes?" She pressed one hand to his warm chest, the heat he emitted washing over her.

"Within the trees." He pointed to the closest and tallest of the massive pine trees. "Just a little way past that one. Care to join me for a dip?"

"I'm under doctor's orders not to get my stitches wet." She nuzzled his cheek where she sat and the sizzling red edge around his white aura exploded with a hungry blaze of starburst gold.

"I'll make sure you don't defy your doctor's orders and get your head wet, the rest of you, not so much." He eased her shirt hem free of the waistband of her riding skirt and lifted her shirt over her head. The cool night air brushed her skin and puckered her nipples. Gently, he eased her breasts together and licked the puckered tips with a hearty swipe and a fierce growl. "Rid yourself of your skirt as well. I'll be able to scent if anyone approaches. We're safe here, well out of sight."

"As you wish." She rose to her feet, tugged the ties of her riding skirt open and shoved her heavy skirts to the ground. She stepped over them and halted as Tavish's golden gaze devoured her, from her head to her toes and everywhere in between.

Heat shimmered through her, a wash of warmth that pooled between her thighs and made him sniff and let out a hearty growl. Claws slicing out and in, he slid his hands around her calves and hauled her forward. She toppled over the edge and fell into his arms. Laughing, she wound her hands around his neck. "It appears you intend on taking advantage of me."

"Absolutely." With her cradled against his chest, he slogged through the water toward the mossy bank, the darkened surface rippling outward and the cool water lapping at her breasts. Carefully, he sat her on the embankment, tipped her shoulders back onto the moss and swept his hands under her bottom then dragged her forward a touch. With a sizzling touch, he caressed her lower cheeks. "I've always been one to make every opportunity count, and right now I've a desperate need to be as one with you."

"As I have with you." She speared her fingers through his wet hair and nipped his lower lip. "This is the second most magical place in the world, the first our cavern. I wish to discover every magical place there is on this land, and only with you."

"Then that's what we'll do." He eased in between her legs, his erection rising out of the water, the plump head deepening to a rich plum color that had her licking her lips.

"You're my fierce protector." She rocked against him, her shoulders resting on the spongy moss as her lower body dipped under the water.

"You're so beautiful, your body a feast I long to indulge in." Head down, he ran his tongue around one nipple then the other. The aureoles beaded further and with one hot stroke across each sensitive tip, he sent a bolt of heat straight to her core and made her whimper with need.

"Again," she pleaded.

"I love it when you get all demanding." He grinned then swirled his tongue around the tip, his heated touch so deliciously divine.

"I never want this moment to end." The sight of his mouth on her, his silky wet hair brushing her skin and the moonlight streaming over them from above, sent her desire for him soaring.

"I can sense what you need along our link. Brace yourself, my love, because I intend to send you catapulting to the stars." He sucked her nipple deep inside his mouth and a torrent of tingles raced through her.

"That feels sooo good. Your touch sends me to another realm all unto itself." She traced the ridged bands of his belly. Hard muscles honed to perfection rippled, layer upon layer, and as she brushed the head of his cock, his shaft, so thick and long, pulsed in her hand. Slowly, she caressed the tip then fondled him all the way to the base and palmed his balls as they tightened and drew upward.

"You own me, every inch of me." His big arms bunched around her. "I wouldn't want it any other way."

"As you own me." She squirmed forward, brought them closer together and rubbed her breasts against his chest. The smattering of dark hair tickled and tightened her nipples and she sighed with delight. "Mmm, this I love. Kiss me, Tavish. I miss having your mouth on mine."

He captured her mouth, his kiss long and dreamy, the stars above them twinkling in and around the moon and adding to the beauty of the moment. Goodness, she needed him, so badly.

She kissed him back, clinging to him as the searing heat inside her intensified. "More," she whispered.

"What my woman wants, she gets." He swept his hands down her sides and along her inner thighs then pushed one finger inside her and when she wriggled closer, he thrust a second finger in.

Her hunger raged, her need pounding down their link. "*I love having your hands on me, having you surround me.*"

"*I'm sure I love it more. Your scent right now is near driving me insane. I need a taste.*" He spread her legs even farther, revealed all of her to his ravenous gaze then with a deep rumble, dipped his head and nuzzled her mound. "*Your body is all mine, a feast I want to devour, inch by incredible inch, starting right here at the heart of you.*"

"*I want that too.*" She rubbed her wet legs against his and as he ducked his head, she tangled her hands in his midnight locks turned a sizzling blue on the ends under the moonlight. His tongue swept across her flesh and a wild storm of sensations rippled out from where he touched. He moved his mouth over her sensitive nub and sucked, hard. She moaned and rocked into his touch, needing more, needing all of him.

Licking her, he sent her soaring even higher, and when she lifted her hips and her legs fell wider, he accepted her offer, seized her bottom and drank from her so deeply, until every part of her belonged only to him and her thoughts raged with the need to join as one.

Panting for a breath, she struggled to hold onto all the intense emotions surging through her. She didn't want to come, not without him, but so too she didn't want him to cease his heart-stopping attention. Oh, she was far too greedy.

"*I adore your greediness.*" He lifted his head as he laved her nub, his desire-filled gaze targeted on hers. "*I want to feel you come on my tongue, and then on my cock when I drive into you. Tell me that's what you want too.*"

"*Oh, I want.*" Rocking her hips, she grasped his broad shoulders, swept over his bulging biceps and down his arms. Her mate was so wickedly strong, each and every roped inch of him. More. She needed more. She stroked over his trim waist, gripped his firm butt and squeezed. Giddy with need, she glided around to his front and smoothed her hand around his velvet-hard shaft and worked him in long pulls.

"*That feels incredible. I love it when you do that.*" He thrust his tongue inside her, curled it into a spot that had her arching her back and crying out. "*Let go, Julia. I've got you.*"

"*Not without you.*" She pumped his cock in time with how he stroked into her and heat pulsed through her. She bucked as he caressed her with his mouth and lips, every flick of his tongue over her inner folds such exquisite torture. Her pleasure rose to the point of pain and she couldn't halt her orgasm from taking her. Her core pulsed as wave after wave of searing pleasure rocked through her. She soared, her aura wrapping tightly around his and his rolling over to swamp hers. Together, they were one, or almost one. "Inside me, now."

She couldn't wait to have him deep within her, for him to be right where he belonged.

"I'm coming." He lifted her up and dropped her down on top of him.

She clutched his broad shoulders, sucked on his neck then bit down.

He growled as he gripped her bottom and surged into her, again and again, his cock buried so deep she'd never felt so completely and wonderfully filled before.

Razzing her teeth back and forth over his skin, she rocked as he thrust and beyond territorial, she bit down and marked him a second time. Her mate, her fierce protector. She'd claimed him and he'd claimed her.

"Aye, I'm your mate, always and forever, no matter that time itself has kept us apart until now." He lapped at the sensitive skin of her neck, his heartbeat thumping against hers then he roared and bit down, his mark all she desired. Her inner muscles tightened and locked him in place and he jerked, his seed exploding from him and shooting inside her.

Blissful spasm after spasm rolled through her, each of his possessive strokes in and out sending her soaring higher than before. He'd taken her over, from the inside out and never had she experienced such heights of pleasure or such a soul-deep peace. *"You feel so good inside me, both body and mind."* She wrapped her legs around his hips to keep him right where he was. *"I love you, Tavish. Always be mine."*

* * * *

"Always, and I love you too." Even though he'd just come, Tavish couldn't halt his rocking or his cock from lengthening all over again. Her beautiful words touched his heart. He wanted his mate, and with a hunger that held a firm hold on him and would

never be appeased. His bear rumbled under his skin, demanding even more and he rubbed his body against hers as he smothered her in his scent.

"I can sense your need for me again in your mind." She scraped her nails down his back and he arched into her possessive touch. "Take me again."

He shouldn't.

"Do it," she demanded.

His mind went dark with lust and he allowed his fierce need its release. He sank his teeth into her neck and thrust. His mate accepted each of his deeply penetrating moves, her body molding to his and her pulse skittering out of time under his roaming tongue. He licked down to the upper swells of her breasts, nipped her flesh then slid one hand down between their bodies and rubbed her nub.

"Oooh, so close."

He flicked her clit and as she gasped and cried out, he took her hard and fast, his essence streaming from him and pumping into her. Sheer bliss took him and saturated his senses until the cool evening air brushed his slick skin and reminded him of exactly where they were.

Slowly, he eased his rocking and brought them both gently back down.

"Oh my." She stretched against him, her beautiful breasts rubbing over his chest and her creamy skin lit a silvery hue under the moonlight. Her slender neck held his mark, and in far more places than one. "That was incredible."

His bear purred his pleasure. Incredible didn't even begin to cover how wonderfully they came together as one.

"I can see and hear that your bear is now finally content." She captured his face between her hands, brought his mouth to hers and kissed him, so sweetly and sensually his cock twitched inside her and she giggled against his lips. "Mayhap I spoke too soon."

"I'll always be hungry for more of you, but right now I need to take care of you." Driven to ensure her well-being, the doctor in him impossible to ignore, the lover even more so, he eased out and hauled himself up onto the mossy bank beside her. "Let me check your back and bottom."

"The moss is soft, and I'm perfectly fine."

"I would still like to check." He lifted her onto her hands and knees before him then he crawled over top of her, his chest to her back as he glided his hands along her spine and over her shoulders. No redness. The moss had definitely cushioned her well.

"See, I told you so." She scooped a handful of fresh water and washed herself, her full breasts swaying against his arms as he remained right where he was with her pert bottom rubbing against his cock as she leaned over the water's edge. He dragged in a long breath, tried to still the desperate need still riding him but to no avail. He went rock hard from one second to the next.

"I want you again." His pushed her down until she lay fully on her front on the moss, his body covering hers. "Tell me to back away."

"Never." She pushed him over onto his back and rolled over top of him, her breasts squished against his chest. "Dinnae move."

"I can't control my bear right now. He's hungry."

"Too bad. I want a taste of you first." She wriggled down his body until she'd settled between his legs. Grasping his length, she slid her lips around him. With one mischievous wink, she sucked him deep inside her mouth and his cock throbbed under the mind-shattering onslaught.

"Julia, halt." Except she didn't. She bobbed up and down over his length and for the life of him, he couldn't stop her, not when her thoughts ricocheted with so much need and love. As his chosen one devoured him, heat shimmered at the base of his spine and radiated out. He gritted his teeth and held on as sheer pleasure coursed through him.

* * * *

Julia intended to love her man every way that she could, and while they were still afforded such privacy. With her hair sweeping Tavish's sides and her mouth on him, she rubbed her breasts either side of his balls and built his pleasure until his thighs shook.

"Julia, please." Groaning, he rocked his hips. "I beg for mercy."

She ignored his plea and kept sucking on him until she found a rhythm that made him buck and groan even harder. Mmm, her mate was very fine fare and she only wished to indulge in him further. She worked him in long pulls with her mouth while he cradled her head in his hands and pushed himself deeper inside her.

"No more, love. I can't take any more." He gripped her waist, flipped her over onto her back and planted his head between her thighs.

"I wasnae done yet."

"You can torture me again later." With the moonlight dancing over their bodies, he spread her flesh below and licked her, again and again before capturing her nub between his lips and rolling his tongue around her.

She shuddered and moaned underneath him, her own thighs now shaking as a whirlwind of pleasure crashed through her. Blindly, she grasped ahold of his arms, dragged him up and gasped as he pushed his cock through her hot heat.

"This is what I need, more of you." He eased back then swiftly pushed all the way back in again. "Open wider for me."

She did then urged him on, meeting each and every one of his powerful thrusts as he took her frantically. Her inner muscles locked tight around him, his balls slapping the insides of her thighs, the full and complete sensation of his possession sending wave after wave of pure pleasure rolling through her. His own pleasure at their joining radiated down their link and she wrapped her arms around him and soared to the stars once more, his seed shooting deep to her core. *"I cannae believe I first denied we were soul bound. You hold my very heart in your hands, Tavish, and I never wish for you to relinquish it."*

"As you hold mine. I will live for you...with every breath I take." He sent a wave of warmth down their link and swamped her in it. *"Always."*

Aye, theirs was a bond to revere.

Overtop of her, Tavish stiffened, the change in him so swift. "What's wrong?"

"Stay very still." He pressed one finger to her lips, pulled free of her and moved into a crouch. He searched through the darkened trees and breathed deep. "Someone comes, the scent not that of the men guarding the border or the warriors back at camp. These men reek of dangerous intent. Clothe yourself, and make it quick."

She scrambled around the edge of the pool, scooped her clothing from the ledge and dressed in her riding habit.

"I'll be back in a moment. I need to dress and arm myself. Go nowhere without me," he whispered in her mind before disappearing into the trees.

All within the forest went eerily quiet. Not even the nighttime creatures made a noise. *"Tavish?"*

"It's certain. MacKenzies come. They've snuck through our border defenses." He returned just as swiftly as he'd left but now clothed in his battle attire, his weapons at his side. With his hands on her waist, he lifted her off the ledge then slung her over his shoulder and raced away with her.

"I can run." Her belly thumped into his rock hard shoulder and she clutched his pumping arms as she searched through the trees for their enemy. *"How close are they?"*

"I spied them, dozens of them, so too close for my comfort. Hold tight, love. I need to get you to safety and warn the others."

The ground blurred at the sheer speed he moved, the trees whizzing by. Everything spun and she squeezed her eyes shut then opened them again as the salty scent of the loch washed over her.

Tavish cleared the forest and halted on the grassy verge of the clearing. A heavy fog had rolled in across the loch and before her the central fire blazed. A serving girl carried flagons of ale and passed out drinks to the men as they sat on the grass and low boulders.

Tavish set her on her feet, released a piercing whistle and shouted, "The MacKenzies come. They've gotten past the sentries along the border."

The men lurched to their feet.

"All to arms," Kirk bellowed as he jumped up from where he and Cherub sat and shoved his sword-arm high into the air. Her kinsmen unsheathed their swords and axes. "Matthew," Kirk yelled to the elderly cart driver, "get the ladies to safety. Everyone else, prepare for a battle. We will not fall, nor allow our enemy to take our land. We fight, as we always have and will, for our freedom and for our very survival."

Tavish gripped her shoulders. "Go with Matthew. I need to know you're well away from here and safe."

"I dinnae wish to leave you." Except she couldn't stay and become a burden in the coming fight. That she knew to the depths of her heart. "Promise me you'll stay safe."

"I will." He dropped a kiss on the top of her head. "We have our connection. You can reach me whenever you need to."

"Julia." Cherub rushed toward her, grabbed her arm. "I need to remain for the battle. Go with the women. I'll check up on you as soon as I can."

"Look after Tavish for me."

"Of course." Cherub nudged her to go. "I willnae allow aught to happen to your mate. Believe that."

"Thank you." Reassured, she stumbled toward the serving

girl and the two cooks. Tears blurred her gaze as she herded the ladies toward the empty cart now unpacked of the supplies they'd brought with them. Matthew hooked up the horses and bounded onto the front bench. She clambered up beside him while the lasses scuttled into the back and huddled together.

The MacKenzies were a thorn in their sides, and the last thing she wished to do was leave Tavish, but right now she no longer had a choice.

Chapter 10

Tavish strapped a baldric across his back and slid a second sword into it as Tor whisked into the supply tent beside him. He wouldn't allow the MacKenzie chief to lay siege to their border and take it. He tossed his brother a black war coat studded with bits of steel. "Arm yourself well. We'll be fighting as never before."

"These MacKenzies are a menace." Tor shoved his arms into the sleeves, slung a bow and satchel of arrows across his shoulders and hauled his sword free. "Kirk's sending a team of warriors to go wide and come in behind our enemy. His intention is to divide their attention and trap them between us."

"They're close, very close." Tavish ducked out of the tent and sniffed, the reek of their enemy now nearing an explosive point.

Cherub stood in the center of the clearing near the blazing fire, her navy skirts swishing about her legs and her white fur cape flapping from her shoulders. She raised her hands to the skies as Kirk stood guard over her. A mass of black cloud whirled and seethed overhead as she churned the air.

"Where does Kirk want us?" he yelled to Tor over the sudden gale.

"We're to remain here and hold the encampment." Tor grasped his shoulder. "We fight together, right at each other's side."

"As we always have." He gripped his brother's shoulder in return.

Shouts boomed all around as warriors took their positions in a strong line along the front of the clearing, their swords, battle axes and pikes in hand.

A fierce battle cry rang out and a good hundred MacKenzies swarmed out of the forest. Cherub sent the wall of wind she'd conjured right at them and half their enemy toppled backward and slammed into the trees. The rest surged forward.

* * * *

A blood-curdling battle cry roared in Julia's ears, coming first from the camp then increasing in crescendo as it boomed throughout the forest. The MacKenzies were everywhere. She clutched the cart's wooden seat under her knees as Matthew slapped the reins across the horses' backs and sent them hurtling through the dark of the night along the trail they'd arrived along only a few hours ago.

As they rattled along the grass and gravel path, the forest caging them in on their left and the loch on their right, a mass of black cloud overhead churned and nearly obliterated the stars and moon. Ahead, one lone MacKenzie warrior burst through the trees and lifted a bow.

An arrow whizzed through the air and thunked into Matthew's side.

She screamed. The reins went slack in Matthew's hands and he toppled from the bench and hit the ground. Nay! She caught the flying reins, hauled the horses to a stop and ran back to Matthew. On her knees, she touched his face. Blood flowed from deep gouges in his cheeks and the arrow wedged deep in his side vibrated with each breath he struggled to draw. This couldn't be happening. Not to Matthew.

"Matthew, please, stay with me." She clasped him to her, the man who'd played sticks with her when she'd been just a child, who'd always picked her an apple or a piece of fruit when walking through the fruit grove. "I'm sorry, so sorry. I willnae leave you."

"Lass, get back to the cart." He gurgled and spat out blood. "You must go. Get to safety."

"I willnae leave you on your own." She lifted his head into her lap and rocked with him in her arms. "Go," she shouted to the two cooks and the serving girl. "Hide yourselves well within the forest."

"MacKenzies, they come," Matthew rasped.

She followed his gaze out over the water. Fog churned and a galley sailed through the mist right toward her. At the center mast a MacKenzie flag flew and at the helm, with a mighty two-handed claymore holstered across his back, Colin MacKenzie stood, his biceps bulging and his legs spread wide. No one could mistake the Chief of MacKenzie, and certainly not her. His aura, a dirty blood-red, spiked with black as his gaze landed on her. 'Twas his true aura, slightly thicker and heavier than his son's, an aura he too had hidden from her until now.

She kissed Matthew's forehead and held onto him tight.

"Take cover, lass. Be away with you." Matthew's breath came harder.

"I'm staying." Tears streamed down her face and splashed Matthew's cheeks and she wiped them away as she held him.

MacKenzie bellowed an order and his men tightened the square sail. The galley cruised toward shore and as the hull scraped the sandy sea floor, Colin MacKenzie bounded out. In the knee-deep water, he surged toward her then stormed onto land. Smirking, he withdrew his sword and pressed it against Matthew's chest as he eyed her. "Get up, lass, or his life will be forfeit."

"I'm no' leaving my kin."

"Aye, you will." He pushed the point of his blade down harder and Matthew groaned as blood bloomed on his tunic under the steel tip. "His final death will be at your hand. If that is what you wish, then so be it."

"Leave him be." She shoved to her feet and slammed her hands into MacKenzie's chest. "What do you want with me?"

"The fae have mingled with Gilleoin's line and his offspring now carry their added abilities. Worse, Gilleoin and his progeny will continue to grow from strength to strength if I dinnae put a halt to it. That is why I want you. No' only are you Gilleoin's niece, but your grandmother is the seer, Nessa. I want the strongest of the village's fae-blooded kind mingling with my direct line, which means you will be marrying my son and giving him sons with your kin's mighty fae skills. I willnae have it any other way." With his fingers pinching into her arm, he hauled her toward his vessel and swung her on board. "Gordon, bind her to the center mast," he snapped at his man.

"Aye, Chief." A hulking warrior stormed toward her down the center aisle.

The wind from the churning storm rammed into them and she toppled into the mast. Her head hit and black dots danced before her eyes. Matthew. She couldn't leave her kin to die alone. And Tavish. She needed to warn him, only she couldn't hold on, couldn't push along their merged link and tell him of what had happened. All went dark and she sank into complete and utter oblivion.

* * * *

In between Tor and Kirk, Tavish swung his claymore at a MacKenzie and blocked the warrior's swift blow. Their blades clashed dead center, steel ringing loud in his ears. "Let's send these MacKenzies back to where they came from," he yelled to his brother and cousin.

"We cover each other's backs while we do." Tor grunted and shoved forward. He met two attackers head on and battled.

"Colin MacKenzie has orchestrated this attack with complete precision," Kirk gritted as he launched himself at the warrior he fought. "Thankfully though he didn't take into account that Cherub would be here. She'll even the odds up as no one else can."

With a fierce shout, another wave of MacKenzies streamed through the trees. High above, Cherub reappeared out of nowhere, twirled her hands and sent a wall of wind at the MacKenzies rushing toward them. Over half of the warriors tumbled head over heels backward then Cherub whisked away and disappeared once more to aid their warriors elsewhere.

"She's keeping the numbers we need to fight against at bay." Tavish swung at his adversary and the warrior slammed his blade into his. With one foot shoved back, Tavish held his position then heaved forward. The warrior lurched back and wobbled. Tavish took advantage of the man's misstep, swept one leg out and toppled him to the ground. Blade in hand, he slammed the hilt down on the warrior's head and knocked him out. Weapons divested, he tossed them onto the blazing fire pit. No weapons, no fight. "Exactly where is the MacKenzie?" he shouted to Kirk. "Does he not lead his men into battle?"

Breathing hard, Cherub breezed in beside them again. "I spotted a galley in the bay and I've just sent a blast of wind at it."

"Just the one galley?" Kirk asked her.

"I'll do a sweep along the loch to make certain there aren't any more. I'll be back shortly. Stay safe." She dissolved into a mist and swept high into the sky.

"They're coming at us from all sides." Kirk bounded forward and fought, matching his next opponent blow for blow. "The constant threat they pose must be eliminated."

"We can't let them get a foothold onto Matheson land." Another warrior swung and Tavish whipped his blade into the man's side.

Grunting, the warrior fell back a step. He grasped his side, eyed the long slice in his steel-studded coat and snarled at Tavish. "You, I will gladly kill."

"You, I will gladly send right back home." He thrust his sword and the MacKenzie blocked his swift blow. They fought, hard and fast.

"Kirk, we have a problem." Cherub reappeared and with one wave of her hand sent the warrior Kirk fought against flying backward. "The cart has overturned. Matthew is hurt and I fear moving him. The ladies are missing and I've no idea where they are."

"*Julia!*" Tavish searched along their link as he ducked his opponent's next blow then twirled around and kicked him in the rear. The warrior went down and knocked his head on a protruding rock. Blood gushed and he moaned and slumped. "*Julia!*"

"Can you reach her, Tavish?" Kirk demanded.

"No, she's not answering me."

"Take command, Gerald." Kirk motioned to one of their garrison's captains. "Cherub, you remain here. I'll call out if I need you."

Tavish sprinted toward the corralled horses. If anything had happened to his mate, he'd never forgive himself. He snagged a destrier from its tethered post, mounted and thrust his knees into the animal's sides and tore along the trail leading around the curve of the bay, Tor and Kirk galloping at his side.

They rode, leaving a plume of dust the rushing wind whipped around in their wake. He urged his mount faster. Massive pine trees swayed on his left and the sea roared on his right. Ahead, Matthew lay on the trail and he hauled his horse to a stop and bounded down. On his knees before the older man, he touched the arrow speared right through his side. "Hold still, Matthew. No moving while I assess your injury."

"You must go. Julia"—Matthew garbled for breath, grasped

his hand and spat blood from his mouth—"MacKenzie. Galley."

"Cherub's already gotten rid of the galley. Did Julia go into the forest to hide? Where are the ladies?" He tried to clear Matthew's airway as best as he could, although there was only one way to save Matthew and that was by taking him back to his time and removing this arrow. He eyed Kirk. "If Matthew's to survive he'll need surgery. Can you spare Cherub from the battle?"

"I can spare her for a few minutes. I'll tell her to come."

Mere moments later the wind rushed all around and Cherub appeared. She clutched a hand to her mouth and sank to her knees next to Matthew. "How bad is it?" she asked Tavish.

"If he's to survive, we need to leave, with all haste." As carefully as he could, he lifted Matthew into his arms.

Cherub nodded at Kirk. "No getting hurt while I'm gone."

"Go, and make it quick." Kirk clasped Tavish's shoulder. "Tor and I will find Julia. I give you my word we will."

"Send word to me when you have." The dark ensued and the three of them fell away into the dark abyss of Cherub's portal. Through the endless streams of time, they moved and mere minutes later they arrived in his medical rooms. Gently, he set Matthew down on the white-sheeted bed, flicked on the lights and hit the red alert switch which would bring his clan's medical team running. The buzzer screeched through the halls and out into the bailey.

"I must go." Cherub kissed Matthew's cheek then eyed Tavish. "I too will aid Kirk and Tor in finding Julia."

"I still can't reach her."

"The link can cut in and out at times, particularly with the wide chasm of time separating you."

The gaping emptiness where his link should be loomed like a black hole. "As soon as you find her, bring her here to me. I won't be able to focus until I know she's safe."

"I shall, the moment I can. Look after my kin." She stepped

back and disappeared within the dark, rushing vortex of time.

The door burst open and Megan and Connor arrived.

He forced his mind back onto the wounded man before him. He had an arrow to remove and a man to keep alive. Julia would be devastated if she lost yet another of her close kin.

* * * *

Julia's head throbbed and her belly rolled as she pitched from side to side within the galley's hull. The boat rocked and dipped. Waves slapped against its sides, the sound pulling her further toward wakefulness.

She opened her eyes and blinked as a new day dawned. Overhead, heavy gray clouds bubbled and brewed, the mass ready to open and spill its load. She touched the back of her aching head and groaned. Nay, she had no time for wallowing. With a wobble, she pushed herself upright and blinked to clear the haze. All around her, MacKenzie warriors rowed from bench seats and her enemy's flag flapped in the breeze from the center mast. Damn. A whole night must have passed since her capture.

"Tavish?" She searched along their link except there was naught but an endless dark. Their connection had been severed, and only two things could cause that, either his moving beyond her reach, or death. Goodness. Death. She wouldn't consider such a thing. Oh dear, Matthew. She'd left him on the trail and his death mere moments away. A tear trailed down her cheek, her heart heaving for the gentle man who'd never raised a weapon in battle yet had perished in a war between their clans all the same.

"About time you woke up, lass." MacKenzie thumped down the center aisle in black boots, his gaze narrowed on her and the jagged scar cutting through his left eyebrow bleeding afresh. Long war braids swayed at each side of his shaggy, brown head. He leaned in and extended his hand to her. "We're about to make landfall and stretch our legs. You may do so too, but only with a guard watching your every step. Allow me to aid you to your feet."

"I'll never accept any aid from you." She slapped his hand away, gripped the closest seat and hauled herself up. On her feet, she swayed, her violet skirts damp from where she'd been lying in the water slopping about the hull. She rubbed her chilled arms, leaned against the mast and surveyed the seas and coastline surrounding them. "Where exactly are we?"

"At Red Point, and we're sailing toward Loch Broom." His dirty aura leeched the blood-red into the fresh sea air and the heavy roar of his aura increased the pounding in her head. She forced her skill to settle until she heard naught but the wind rushing around her and the slap of the oars through the water.

"What's at Loch Broom?" Loch Broom sat a good day's journey to the north of Loch Alsh. She rubbed her brow. Scotland's rugged coastline swept along her right and to her left, the northern-most tip of the Isle of Skye protruded. They'd sailed quite some distance already, any sign of Matheson land well and truly gone.

"Your parents, and by now, Jeremiah as well. After yours and Cherub's surprise visit to my keep, I sent my son to my holding there with the order to slay Aleck and Adair within the fortnight if I didnae arrive with you." MacKenzie bellowed to his man at the rudder. "To land we go. Lower the sail."

Two warriors unraveled the knots securing the great square sail while the warriors rowing, slashed their oars swifter through the water and sent them on a direct course toward Red Point's rocky tip and sandy shore.

As the galley reached the waist-deep waters, two warriors leapt out, seized the bow and hauled it half onto the reddish-gold sands. Colin MacKenzie caught her elbow and steered her toward the bow as he tossed out orders, "Gordon, keep Mistress Matheson under close watch. She is to be my son's wife, so guard her well."

"Aye, Chief." Gordon bounded onto the beach, turned back

and swung her from the galley onto the sand next to him.

She shuddered at the desperately difficult turn of events. *"Tavish, where are you?"*

No answer, and the quiet rang like a death knell in her ears.

Chapter 11

The surgery to remove the arrow from Matthew had taken slightly longer than Tavish had expected, but it had all gone rather well considering the extent of the man's injury. The dawn sun rose as he closed up and left Mathew in recovery under Megan and Connor's expert care.

For the hundredth time, he searched for Julia along their link and came up with nothing. It'd been over an hour since Cherub had last returned with an update, although each and every one she'd given him had ended in the same answer. No sign of Julia.

At least they'd won the battle. Two hours past they'd finally sent the MacKenzies fleeing right back to where they'd come from. Kirk and Tor had even found the two cooks hiding in a cave soon after, although they still searched for the serving girl. Hell, he just needed Cherub to return so he could leave and join them all on their search for his mate.

Exhausted, he shuffled into his bathroom and turned the shower lever on. He shucked his theatre smock and clothes, pressed his palms flat against the tiled wall and ducked his head under the steamy, hot spray. Water sluiced down his body and flowed over tense muscles.

He picked up the metal chair Julia had sat in such a short time ago and tucked it back into the corner against the wall. His thoughts barreled back to that day, to that moment when he'd stood right here with her.

She'd grinned from ear to ear and her words once again resonated deeply through his mind. *That is so fascinating. 'Tis like a waterfall of water, a heated waterfall.*

The water had flattened the thin cloth of her shift to her body, and her laughter and big blue eyes had captivated him. Never had he seen someone so excited by the simple act of watching running water or feeling it cascade over their skin.

He squeezed a glob of shampoo into his palm and scrubbed the bubbles through his hair. The sweet scent of apples wafted with the steam and brought with it another vivid memory. *I feel like I'm in heaven. Thank you for taking such wonderful care of me.* She'd tipped her head back in enjoyment and sighed with delight. His heart had near melted when she had.

He'd take the upmost care of her, for the rest of her life and his. He'd certainly never allow another parting such as this to occur.

With his body soaped clean, he tipped his head back into the spray, rinsed the shampoo out and turned the lever off. From the vanity cupboard, he nabbed a fluffy white towel, dried himself then shaved his jaw, and combed his hair. He had to keep his hands busy until Cherub returned, as well as be ready to leave the moment she did.

In his bedroom, he pulled on a pair of black jeans and a loose-sleeved tan shirt, strapped his sword belt on and sheathed his wrist daggers. From the pocket of his discarded pants, he grabbed his cell phone and turned it on. The last picture he'd taken of him and Julia blazed to life and he stroked one finger over her cheek. His heart scrunched in on itself, his pain intensifying. "Hurry up, Cherub," he muttered as he pocketed his phone and shrugged on his steel-studded gray jacket. His desperate need for Julia beat at him, was carved so deep, right down to the depths of his heart and soul.

At his bedroom window, he gripped the sill and surveyed the inner courtyard below. A good twenty of his clansmen trained. He left his chamber and marched back into the recovery room.

Connor sat in his scrubs next to their patient still in recovery, while Megan, her wavy black bob contained under a white cap, wrote on a chart at the end of the bed then clipped it back in place.

"How's Matthew?" he asked Connor. "Has he stirred at all?"

"Not yet, but his vitals look good."

Carefully, Tavish removed the mask over Matthew's nose and squeezed the elderly man's shoulder. "I need you to wake up, Matthew."

Groggily, he opened his eyes then looked about the white-walled room with its stainless steel countertops and white painted cupboards. "Och, I f-feel…" He blinked and tried to clear his vision, his gaze moving from Connor to Megan then back to him. "W-where am I, Tavish?"

"In my time." He set Matthew's mask aside. "You're alive and all thanks to Cherub who brought us both back through a portal so I could operate on you. Meet Megan." He motioned toward her. "Megan's the chief's wife and a highly skilled healer of this time, also known as a nurse. Connor too aided me in your surgery. He's an anesthesiologist and ensured you stayed asleep during the operation."

"Opera—hell, the arrow." Blue eyes fully clearing, Matthew wriggled one hand out from under the coverings, pushed the white blanket back and stared at his bandaged side. Frowning, he squinted at the IV hooked into the back of his hand then to the IV pole beside him. "The arrow's gone. Well now, you certainly have got some powerfully strong healing skills.

How did you take the arrow out?"

"With great difficultly, but I managed it all the same. You'll also feel more like your old self in no time at all. For now though, I want you to take things nice and slow. You'll be given a chamber across the hallway and you're to allow Megan to care for you. She'll ensure you're up on your feet before the end of the day, just for a few minutes, but tomorrow she'll have you moving around a touch more. There will be some rules during your recovery. No strenuous lifting, and only once I give you the all-clear, can you return to normal duties. I'll be checking up on you regularly, ensuring your wound heals just as it should."

"Wait." Matthew jerked upright then groaned and slumped back down. "The battle. The MacKenzie took Julia. The galley. Did you find her?"

"What?" His world tilted. "Cherub sent the MacKenzie galley whisking back out to sea."

"Aye, but only after it made landfall. The MacKenzie took wee Julia."

"Are you certain?"

"Aye." A tear trailed down his cheek. "Julia wouldnae leave me, but the MacKenzie held a sword to my chest and threatened to take my life if she didnae, said my death would be at her hand. She's such a gentle lass, but with a spark of fire in her soul. The last I saw of her was when the wind hit the sail and sent the galley back out to sea."

Tavish gripped the metal bedrail, his thoughts barreling one over the other. He had to find his mate and get her back.

The air swirled and Cherub, Kirk, and Tor appeared in the midst of the churning breeze.

"Did you find her?" He clasped his brother's arm. "Matthew said he saw the MacKenzie take her."

"We scoured the entire forest and just found the serving girl hiding in a tree. She was the last one missing. She saw everything as the two cooks didn't and recounted exactly what happened. Aye, the MacKenzie has her." Tor blew out a long breath. "Cherub, Kirk and I have already been to the MacKenzie's keep and we've searched it from top to bottom, as well as the entire length of Loch Alsh. There's no sign of either Colin MacKenzie, the galley, or Julia. We can't go any further without you. You need to open your link with her, find out where she is. Are you ready to go?"

"I'm ready." He grasped Cherub's arm and eyed Connor and Megan. "Keep an eye on Matthew."

"Will do." Connor nodded, his gaze filled with compassion. "Find your woman and bring her home. We can't lose a newly mated pair."

"We willnae lose her," Cherub bit out with determination. She opened a portal and the four of them fell away into the dark abyss, all connected as one.

They traveled through time and space and a few minutes later arrived on the top of a mountain in the middle of a long range of mountains sweeping a rugged coastline. A cold wind whipped around and through him. "Where exactly are we?" he yelled to Cherub over the rush of the wind.

"On the mountains near Gairloch, along Scotland's western coastline." Cherub motioned toward the sea only a few miles distant. "We need to search the waterways along this area of the land first. If MacKenzie's still onboard his galley with Julia, then this is the best place to start."

In the valley below, a river wound in and around the hills then snaked outward toward the sea. Across the choppy ocean waves, the northern tip of the Isle of Skye rose, a line of lush green land with a heavy gray cast of cloud swelling overhead. Slowly, he breathed out, closed his eyes and focused on his mate and their merged link.

* * * *

Julia slogged up the sandy length of Red Point beach. The ocean wind slammed into her from behind, plastered her violet riding skirts to her legs then whisked across the moors and over the forest rising high ahead. The cold air wrapped its icy tentacles around her and she shivered, her thin shirt on top not nearly enough protection against the elements.

"Are you all right, my lady?" Gordon offered her his arm and she near rolled her eyes. As if she'd accept any help from the enemy.

"I'm fine." She trudged on, her feet numb within her boots.

"Take my tartan." He held out his MacKenzie plaid.

"Nay, I'd rather freeze than wear your clan's colors."

"Take some water then." Gordon swung a skin from over his shoulder and held it out to her. "Ye must drink."

"*Julia?*"

"*Tavish, I'm here.*" She clutched onto their connection, her pace quickening as she waved off Gordon's offer of a drink and crossed the sand. Following the trail across the moors toward the forest, she sank deeper into his mind and rolled around within his returned thoughts, even as worried as they were. "*Are you all right, Tavish? Where have you been?*"

"*Caring for Matthew, in my time.*"

"*He's alive?*" Dear heaven, please let him be alive.

"*Alive and well, and the arrow gone. Megan and Connor are looking after him, two of our clan's other medical personnel. Tell me exactly where you are.*"

"*At Red Point, on the moors near the beach, along with a good thirty of MacKenzie's men, although I dinnae intend to be here for long. I wish to leave, and with all haste.*"

"*As I intend for you too as well. We're close. I'm with Cherub, Kirk, and Tor on the mountains. I can see Red Point from here.*"

"*I know where my parents are being kept, that's if Colin MacKenzie is telling the truth. They're at his holding at Loch Broom. He sent Jeremiah ahead of him and he should already be there. His desire is to ensure my grandmother's strongly skilled*" *fae line mingles with his own. I'm to wed Jeremiah once we reach his holding.*" She strode past two warriors lighting a fire within the protection of the tree line. With her violet skirts in hand, she hurried deeper into the forest along the scrub-lined path. "*I'm in the forest now, with a pesky guard.*"

"*Wait a moment while I relay everything to the others and we formulate a plan.*"

Snuggling deeper into his mind, she stopped beside a wide trunk and gestured toward a thicket twenty feet to one side through the thick bracken. "Gordon, if you dinnae mind, I wish a few moments of privacy."

He scrubbed his hand over his bristly jaw then nodded. "Go no farther than that thicket. You have two minutes and no more."

"How gracious." This time she did roll her eyes. Although she'd take those two minutes and make them work. She hurried through the brushwood, scrambled onto her knees behind it then skirts bunched up, crawled through the dense undergrowth deeper into the forest. Once she was assured she was out of his sight, she jumped to her feet and weaved through the trees. Up ahead, the sound of gushing water traveled to her. A stream. The thick copse gave way to a river that cut through the forest toward the sea. Rocks lined the bank on both sides and three of MacKenzie's men knelt at the edge filling their skins. Grrr, how annoying. Colin MacKenzie's warriors were everywhere.

She backed up a step, as quietly as she could. "*Tavish, I cannae see a way out of here.*"

"*Cherub has us cloaked and soaring your way. Give me your location, and be as specific as you can. I'll ensure there's a way out.*"

Hope soaring, she clutched her chest. "*There's a river running through the forest, one with three warriors filling their skins. I'm backing away from them now. My guard will be searching for me soon.*"

"*We're over the woods and I can see them. Keep moving*

backward, slowly and carefully. Don't draw any unwanted attention to yourself."

The wind lifted, breezed all around and with it brought an intoxicatingly warm and fresh scent, one holding a sweet tease of apple. It swirled about and saturated her senses. *"I miss you."*

"As I miss you." An arm wrapped around her waist from behind and drew her back against a solid body. Warmth infused her, and her mate's presence calmed and settled her deep inside.

She curled her fingers around his firm forearm and turned around in his tight embrace. Cherub had him cloaked, his form not visible and she dearly wished to see him.

"Cherub's to your left. Grab ahold of her so her cloaking extends over you too. Kirk's behind her and Tor's on her other side." Tavish nipped her ear. *"Hurry, love."*

A bellow sounded. Gordon. She patted the space around her and found Cherub. As soon as she slipped her fingers around Cherub's arm, Cherub covered her with her cloaking and they lifted up.

Gordon stormed along the path and shouted to the warriors at the river, "The Matheson lass has escaped."

"That was close, too close," she whispered in Tavish's mind.

"You should never have been taken from me. I'm sorry I allowed such a thing to occur." He nuzzled her neck. *"Tell me you're all right."*

"I am now."

Cherub took them higher, over the treetops and onward as she breezed toward Gairloch. The forest gave way to the rockier terrain of the Highlands as they swept toward the high mountain peak with its sheer stony sides.

She clung to Tavish as he scraped his teeth back and forth over her sensitive skin. *"Please, bite me."* She stretched her neck. Nothing else would settle her quite like his possessive touch did. *"Now."*

"I shall never let go of you again." Tavish sank his teeth into her flesh and she whimpered for more. *"Where you are, is where I need to be, whether there is a battle raging or not."*

"I agree."

"The moment I get you all to myself, expect a damn sight more than just a bite. I intend to ravish you, right after we rescue your parents."

"Ravishing and a rescue sounds perfect." She swept one hand around Tavish's neck, reached up and sucked on his neck. She licked his pounding pulse point then bit him. His desire surged down their link and flooded her and she went to bite him a second time only they began their descent.

"We're here, everyone." Cherub set them gently down on the mountain peak, the wind churning all around and the gray clouds out at sea swelling toward shore. Rain lashed the ocean then hit Red Point beach.

She released Cherub and Tavish did the same.

He fluttered into her sight, his golden shifter gaze bright as he leaned in and rested his forehead against hers. *"I need to kiss you, except the kiss I wish for is one for behind closed doors."*

"I love having you back in my mind." His passionate words and returned touch sent her thoughts flying. She longed for that kiss, but he was right. This wasn't the place or time. Taking a long breath, she wriggled around in his hold and faced the others. "Thank you all for coming for me."

Cherub hugged her, her soulful aura sparkling, just as her creamy skin did. "I would say anytime, but I'd rather you never fall into the MacKenzie's hands again."

"I second that." Kirk pulled Cherub back to his side, rubbed his chin over the top of her blond head. "It's good to have you back, Julia."

Cherub leaned back against Kirk, her smile wide as she gazed at her mate over her shoulder. "And you, my tempting bear, must cease your mischievousness behavior when we are in flight. Distractions can cause me to drop people."

"What mischievous behavior?" In tan rawhide pants and a white tunic under his loose fur vest, Kirk twirled Cherub around and grinning, kissed the tip of her nose. His claymore sheathed snugly at his side, gleamed as it swayed. "I have no idea what you're talking about."

"You are the worst liar." She giggled and kissed the tip of his nose in return.

Tor clapped Tavish on the back then hugged her, his black war coat flapping in the breeze. "Julia, I'm so glad to see you've suffered no serious injuries at the MacKenzie's hand, although no more high-tailing it off with them. We've been searching for you all night."

"What of the battle?" She stretched back against Tavish, soaking in even more of his delicious scent.

"We won the war." Tor rubbed his hands together. "And sent those damn MacKenzies fleeing."

"That's wonderful news."

"Aye, and now we need to find and rescue your parents." Cherub swatted one of Kirk's roving hands then offered her arms to them all. "We need to travel to Loch Broom, with all speed."

"Hold on." Frowning, Tavish touched the back of her head and blood spotted his fingers. He spun her around. "You hurt yourself again? When did this happen?"

"A small injury. I knocked my head on the mast when the galley flew out of the bay."

"I'll need to take a closer look at it." He shrugged out of his steel-studded gray coat and slipped it over her shoulders. "Arms in. You look cold."

She pushed her hands down the sleeves, his heat trapped within the cloth warming her through. "Thank you."

"Chin down." His tone brooked no argument.

She did as he bid while he parted her hair and assessed her injury.

"It's a new wound, an inch lower than the last one and thankfully not deep or long enough to require stitches. Did you lose any awareness at all?"

"I may have."

"For how long?" He turned her again, the worry in his aura spiking out in sharp waves.

"Not too long."

"How long? And be exact."

Clearly she wasn't getting out of answering this question. "The entire night, although I would like to point out that one usually rests during the night once one is asleep. That was all I was doing. Resting and sleeping." She reached up on her toes and brushed her thumbs along the darkened shadows under his eyes. "Which it appears you didnae do at all."

"This conversation isn't about me but you. Keep your eyes open." With one hand, he tipped her chin up and peered directly into her eyes, his golden gaze so intent and those luscious lips of his so close. "Do you feel faint at all?"

"Aye, very faint." She swayed toward him, her heartbeat racing. Goodness. She needed to regain her focus. Tor, Kirk, and Cherub stood waiting, and she needed to find and rescue her parents. No more could she delay. Swiftly, she ducked under Tavish's arm and grasped ahold of Cherub's hand. "I'm ready to leave."

"Julia Matheson." Tavish caught her around the waist. "You should be in bed, resting. Losing consciousness is dangerous, particularly for a solid night."

"Yet I just woke up. I dinnae need any more rest. What I need is to find my parents, and then I shall rest once that is done. You may oversee that rest if you like."

"I'm sorry, Tavish." Cherub arched a sympathetic brow at him. "You really can't argue with a woman when she's in this kind of a determined mood. The sooner we leave, the sooner we can return, then you can tend to your mate to your heart's desire."

"Thank you, Cherub." Julia squeezed her hand. "I need to get my parents back and now we have a destination, to Loch Broom we go."

"Aye, to Loch Broom. I'll open a portal and take us directly there rather than fly us through the skies. There's an inn I've visited afore, one close to the loch's entrance and at a good guess, I'd say his keep will be close to that point." She glanced over her shoulder at Kirk. "Ready to leave?"

"Always, my elusive imp." He banded his arms tight around her waist. "How are you holding up?"

"My energy is depleting. I'll soon need a rest, but for now I can manage one more jump through time." Cherub swirled one hand through the air and the wind rose and tunneled around them. The dark ensued and they all fell away into the churning abyss.

Moments later they reappeared on the rise overlooking Loch Broom. Dark and ominous clouds gusted in from the sea. Loch Broom weaved inland for several miles with the odd longhouse nestled along its rocky shoreline. Cattle grazed within the lower pastures and sheep dotted the craggy hills rising high either side of the waterway. This ruggedly wild land was so difficult to reach when one traveled the dangerous mountain pass directly across the mainland.

Cherub swayed and Kirk turned her in his arms and eyed her. "You need to rest now, before we go any further."

"Aye, an hour or so to replenish my strength would be appreciated, a meal as well if possible. Transporting so many so far can be draining."

"You also haven't rested since well before the battle. We've got time on our hands right now. Not only will Colin MacKenzie be searching for Julia but Red Point is still a half day's sail away from here." Kirk motioned toward the winding downward trail where at the base, nestled amongst a stand of towering elm trees, a quaint stone building with smoke puffing from its chimney, beckoned travelers. "We'll head to the inn for a meal. None of us are wearing our Matheson plaid. We'll appear as no more than any other warrior or traveler would."

"We also need to keep a low profile," Tavish added. "Ensure no one discovers who we are or where we've come from."

'Twas a sound idea and Julia nodded her agreement. She too longed for a hot meal. At the side of the inn, a wooden beamed enclosure housed horses and a lad with a woolen cap, his tunic's sleeves rolled to his elbows, brushed a horse tethered within. Two other horses dug their snouts into a wooden pail holding feed and gobbled it down.

"Look, right there." Cherub pointed toward the loch's entrance. On the jutting, rocky tip overlooking the ocean, a castle stood, its stone curtain wall rising high. The MacKenzie's banner flapped from the uppermost corner of the gatehouse. "That must be our enemy's holding."

"That's it all right." Tor's gaze narrowed on the very strategic location the MacKenzie held. "From that point, the MacKenzie will be able to keep an eye on one and all sailing these seas."

"Let's go. I'll rest, restore my strength then we'll be underway once more." Cherub tugged on Kirk's hand and started down the trail, her white fur cloak resting over her shoulders and her navy skirts flapping. Tor followed them and so did she.

"Julia, slow down for a moment." Tavish tilted his head in that angle she was fast learning meant business. "If you feel unwell at any time, then you must tell me."

"I promise you I shall. Now cease worrying." Before he could issue yet another demand, she picked up her pace and skipped ahead down the trail to prove she was mightily well. This mission was far too important to allow a little head wound to get in her way, one that bothered her not at all. So too Arabel was counting on her and she wouldn't let her sister down. Not again. Bringing her parents back home was all that mattered, however it had to be done. Surely they lived. The MacKenzie had been so adamant that they did, and she wouldn't allow herself to think otherwise.

Tavish grumbled as he caught up to her. "I will worry as much as I like."

"You are one very stubborn mate." Thunder rumbled overhead and a drop splashed her nose. "We're about to get wet."

Cherub glanced skyward. "'Tis best I allow those clouds to remain where they are. No' only do I need to conserve what strength I have but sweeping them away will alert the MacKenzies to my arrival. Our enemy's warriors have seen me in action, and far more than once." The heavens opened and Cherub tugged her cloak's hood over her head and dashed toward the inn's front door with its low hung eaves and stony facade.

Kirk chased her and Tor loped after them.

Two lively children squealed from under an apple tree at the side of the inn and with baskets in hand, tore barefoot into the stables where the lad tending the horses too had sought shelter from the rain.

Julia grasped her skirts and darted around a lanky brown-haired dog in the center of the yard and ducked in through the front door, Tavish one step behind her. She brushed the rain from his gray jacket and handed it back to him. "I'll warm up quickly now I'm inside. This search is becoming quite the adventure."

"Adventure or not, just don't forget whose land we're on." His golden gaze blazed as he leaned in and nipped her ear. "I won't lose you again."

"How can I help ye fine folks?" The innkeeper, a crinkly-eyed man wearing breeches and a loose plaid tossed over one shoulder, ambled over from the bar toward them. "The wife has beef stew cooking and fresh bread warm from the oven. There are travelers aplenty here today."

"Beef stew and fresh bread would be most appreciated." Kirk tucked Cherub under his shoulder, her head tipped down within her hood and her cloak fully protecting her identity. Cherub always took great care with whom she allowed to see her. Her glimmering skin was a physical attribute held only by the eldest child born within the ancient royal line of the fae and since Cherub was the king's firstborn and she'd yet to conceive a child, she was also the last to hold the unique skin trait. It certainly made her easily identifiable.

"Then find yourselves somewhere to sit. I'll have the barmaid see to ye all." The innkeeper plodded off through the side door into the kitchens.

"I'd love a moment to freshen up." Cherub peeked at her from under her hood. "What of you, Julia?"

"Aye, I've a great need to freshen up." Her windblown hair must look a fright and she wouldn't mind washing the blood from her hair. With the blood out of Tavish's sight, mayhap her new injury would also be out of his mind. A side stairwell led upward to the top floor of the inn and a young maid of perhaps ten and four swept the floors near the bottom step. She squeezed Tavish's hand. "Cherub and I will be back soon."

"Keep your mind open to mine."

"I shall." She crossed to the lass with Cherub at her side. "Excuse me, we've a need to freshen up. Is there a chamber available where we could?"

"Aye, my ladies, right here on the lower floor. Come with me." She set her broom in the corner, tucked one errant brown lock under her white frilly cap and led the way along the lower corridor. At the end of the hallway, the lass opened the paneled door and motioned them inside. "This is Mama and Papa's best chamber and has a view right across the loch as well as a side door and a private garden. 'Tis all yours for as long as ye need it."

"You have our most heartfelt thanks." She smiled at the lass and walked inside. A large bed covered in a patchwork quilt of bright blues and greens stood against one wall and a posy of wildflowers sat in fluted holder on the bedside table next to it. The window faced the loch, offering a perfect view of the sea entrance and the MacKenzie's stronghold sitting on the jutting point only a short distance away. She opened the door to the outside garden and gasped. Lavender bushes and scattered wildflowers surrounded a pathway leading down to the loch. "I would dearly love to stay here for a day or two, to enjoy the countryside, that's if this inn were no' on MacKenzie land."

"This is a lovely spot, although a sure shame to be located right here." Cherub joined her underneath the covered doorway and motioned toward the castle where guardsmen patrolled the barbican. "Do you sense any hum?" Cherub kept her tone low so as not to be overheard by the maid as she lit the fire across the other side of the chamber.

Eyes closed, she focused on the castle and her parents possibly imprisoned within. Once she heard the gentle hum of their aura then she'd know for certain that they lived. She touched her chest, right over her rapidly beating heart, but not a trace of a hum resonated toward her. "There's naught." She opened her eyes and blinked the hot burn of tears away. "I need to get closer, Cherub. I'm still too far away."

"I'll take you straight into the castle myself, the moment I've restored my strength." Cherub had expended such a great deal. "Soon, very soon."

Julia faced the castle once more. Several warriors heaved slabs of stone from the rear of a cart and handed them to a stonemason and his team who disappeared around the other side of the keep. Another cart rumbled past the inn and down the bumpy trail toward the castle, the rear stacked with the same stone blocks. "They are at work on constructing the outbuildings."

"Aye, I'd say 'tis a relatively new keep."

"Is there aught more you need, my ladies?" The maid rose from the blazing fire and dusted her hands against her aproned skirts.

"Nay, thank you for your aid. We'll be fine now." Julia smiled at the lass.

The girl dipped her head and closed the door behind her as she left.

Cherub pushed her hood back and picked up a drying cloth from the side table and dabbed her wet cheeks.

Julia pulled the garden door shut, slid her sapphire jeweled hairpins from her tangled hair and set them on the side table.

"Here, let me aid you with your hair." Cherub patted the chair before the looking glass. "We'll need to get rid of the spots of blood at the back if you wish to keep Tavish calm."

"I cannae believe I hit my head again. 'Tis just as well I didnae hurt myself too badly." She sat and Cherub carefully cleaned the blood away. Sighing, she sank even deeper into Tavish's mind and rolled around within the exquisite space. *"The chamber is lovely and looks right out over the loch toward the castle. There's a door leading to a private garden."*

"I'd rather you be right here with me in this main room. Hurry it up, love."

Cherub set the washcloth aside then gently worked the comb through her hair and detangled the knots.

"I'm not quite sure what I did afore this merged link took form." She smiled at Cherub over her shoulder. "Although now I'm mated to Tavish, I hate to think of only living in the future and completely leaving my kin here behind."

"You'll never have to leave them behind. I'll gladly bring you and Tavish back and forth through time as needed. My duty is to my people and I will never forsake any of you, no matter what time or place you reside in." Cherub finished tidying her hair then brushed her own and set the comb down. "All done."

"Thank you." She hugged Cherub, squeezed her extra tight. "Never have our people been so lucky as to have you as our princess."

"'Tis my pleasure to aid my people, however and wherever I can." Cherub squeezed her back. "You are my sister, just as Arabel is."

"*Julia, how much longer will you be? I can't stand this separation.*"

"*I'm coming.*" She walked to the door with a grin. "Tavish is getting anxious."

"So is Kirk. Mated men are quite the handful at times." Grinning and with her hood back in place, Cherub swished past her and led the way along the corridor to the main room.

Julia followed, weaved past a score of patrons seated at small tables then alongside a fire roaring within the wide hearth. Each table was separated from the other by wooden screens, and farmers and travelers all partook of the stew and tankards of ale while they chatted. In the far darkened corner, the men sat with a clear view of everyone within the room and the front door. She joined Tavish as he stood, his gaze sweeping over her.

"Do you feel better?"

"I do." She sat down and Tavish slid in next to her, securing her safely between him and Tor. Leaning against him, she pressed her cheek to his shoulder and allowed the peace of the moment to roll through her. Being this close to him soothed her very soul. "My mate," she whispered in his ear. "Always mine."

"Aye, always yours." He slid one arm around her back, and stroked his thumb in a slow circle over her hip.

Mmm, she wriggled even closer, almost purring under his delicious touch. She'd missed him terribly while they'd been parted. Thankfully she'd been out of it for most of that time, would never have wanted to experience the endless hours of fear as he unfortunately had. "Thank you for saving Matthew's life. I cannae wait to see him."

"He'll make a full recovery, and I don't doubt he can't wait to see you either. As soon as he woke up from surgery, he told me what had happened to you. Until then, I'd had no idea."

"I never want to lose our link again."

"Agreed."

"Here we go, my lovelies." A barmaid flounced in, a tray of tankards in hand and her bountiful breasts almost spilling from her blue kirtle's low neckline. "My apologies for the wait."

"Thank you." Tor accepted a tankard from her.

"One of the lasses will be out shortly with your meals." Raising an appreciative eyebrow at Tor, she leaned in and gave him a rather stunning eyeful of her wares. "Be sure to holler out if ye need aught more. I have a willing hand, no matter what ye might need it for."

"Cheeky, lass. Go on with you." Tor swatted her bottom, which sent the lass giggling as she sashayed away.

The serving lass who'd shown them to their chamber hurried through the kitchen door and across to them with a platter of breads and cheeses. She set it on the scratched wooden tabletop while another lass with an apron tied around her waist brought out a tray holding bowls of stew. She passed one to each of them, laid out spoons then whisked back to the kitchens.

Kirk slid his dirk from its sheath, sliced the bread and handed them each a piece.

Julia dunked hers in her stew and bit into the end. Delicious. The richly flavored beef juices danced on her tongue and the hot meal warmed her belly.

"Where are your hairpins?" Tavish tucked an errant lock of her hair behind her ear. "You had them in before you left for the chamber."

"Oh dear." She patted her head. "I left them on the table when Cherub combed my hair. They were a gift from my parents and I cannae lose them." She slipped off the bench. "I'll be back in a moment."

"I can retrieve them for you if you wish." He rose.

"Nay, I'll be quick." With one hand on his shoulder, she pushed him back down then snuck around the room and down the darkened corridor. In the chamber assigned to them, she picked up her hairpins and pinned them back in place. These had been the very last gift Mother and Father had given her. *These sapphires match your eyes*, her mother had said then slid a matching set into Arabel's hair as well. Mother had hugged them both, held them tight. That moment was embedded in her mind, her precious hairpins a most treasured keepsake. Soon, she'd hold Mother again. She had to. For if they truly were dead, then her grief would rise as sharply and as painfully as it had the first time. Mourning them all over again, would break her heart.

Outside the window, the rain eased and the clouds broke apart. A glimpse of blue sky dotted through. She thrust open the garden door. At the castle, a guard shouted and the portcullis rose from within the arched front gate, its clunky sound reverberating along the shore and across the grassy field toward her.

Horses' hooves pounded and a dozen armed warriors rode out of the bailey. In single file, the warriors galloped along the trail leading farther around the craggy tip then disappeared.

Another warrior rode out of the keep in leather pants and a thick fur vest over a dark shirt. He galloped along the grassy verge of the inner channel of the loch and on a direct path toward her. His fiery red hair brushed his shoulders and his dirty blood-red aura swirled all about.

'Twas Jeremiah.

Her heart leapt within her chest.

Chapter 12

"*Tavish, Jeremiah rides this way.*" A gentle hum whispered through Julia's mind and her heart lost one very necessary beat.

"*Are you certain?*"

"*Very.*" Clutching Jeremiah from behind sat a cloaked woman. "*Mother's with him. I hear the gentle hum of her aura.*"

"*Stay right where you are. I'm coming.*"

"Mother!" She screamed her name as she stumbled outside. Rushing along the path with her mother's gentle hum increasing in tempo, she yelled frantically and waved her hands.

Jeremiah hauled his horse to a stop next to her and sneered, a look of victory sparking bright in his eyes. "Well, well. If it isnae Julia, my wife-to-be. About time you arrived."

"I will never be your wife. I am here to rescue my kin and naught more."

"Julia?" Mother pushed her hood back, heaved free of Jeremiah and jumped to the ground. Mother grasped her, held her tight. "What are you—I cannae believe you're—how did you—oh goodness, I've missed you."

"You're alive. You're really alive." Tears pooled in her eyes and flowed down their mashed cheeks. "Where's Father?"

"At the castle. He's gravely ill and Jeremiah agreed to bring me to the healer for the herbs I need. I must bring his fever down if he's to survive."

"I agreed on one account." Jeremiah bounded to the ground, his holstered claymore bobbing at his back. "You were to keep your hood in place and no' expose yourself, even to the healer."

"But my daughter—"

"Julia!" Tavish roared her name as he raced across the field toward her, Tor, Cherub, and Kirk one step behind him.

"Damn it," Jeremiah spat. "And now we have even more Mathesons here on our land." He grabbed Julia around the waist, tossed her up onto his destrier and bounded in behind her. Arms pinned tight either side of her, he slammed his knees into his horse's sides and they flew back along the trail toward the castle.

"Mother! Tavish!" She shoved against Jeremiah's punishing hold. Behind them on the trail, Tor nabbed her mother and whisked her back through their chamber's open garden door. The others had gone, had disappeared in the blink of an eye.

A breeze churned the grass and whipped the long stalks about then a blast of wind hit her. Jeremiah's horse reared onto its hind legs and whinnied. Its hooves crashed down and she went flying.

"Got you." Tavish scooped her out of thin air and plastered her against his rock hard chest. Cherub and Kirk stood right behind him. "Let's just get one thing straight, for once and for all. Where you are, is where I need to be."

"Aye, I agree."

"Julia, come." Cherub nabbed her hand and tugged her backward.

Jeremiah bounded from his horse, landed on the ground and stormed toward Tavish. He swung his claymore from its holster and Tavish thrust his sword high and blocked Jeremiah's fierce blow. "Who are you?" Jeremiah scowled at him.

"Tavish Matheson, Julia's mate and her handfast husband."

"If you're her husband, then you stand in my way."

Jeremiah came at Tavish, slashing again and again in a clear attempt to take him down as quickly as he could. "Be prepared to die. Julia will be my wife afore the end of the day."

* * * *

Tavish sprang forward and fought. It was time for Jeremiah MacKenzie to learn that no one would ever take his wife from him, a message he intended to make certain got through. He certainly had no greater incentive than to fight for his woman. He slashed and Jeremiah met each of his deadly strikes.

"Whistle out if you need me, Tavish." Eagerly rocking from foot to foot, Kirk palmed his sword from the sidelines, his gaze narrowed on Jeremiah. "I want in on this fight."

"This is my battle, one I intend to win." He was a Matheson, and no one ever tangled with the 'Son of the Bear.'

"Those are strong words, Matheson, but you're on MacKenzie land and we dinnae spill our own blood here, only that of our enemy's." Jeremiah's gaze glinted with determination and he slammed his blade hard into Tavish's, one hard strike after another.

Tavish grunted and fell back a step then bounded back. He struck, his blows strategic as he came at Jeremiah first on one side and then the other, all wielded in order to weaken his enemy. He blocked Jeremiah's next high swipe then dropped low, rolled clear and came up on his adversary's flank and struck again, swiftly and surely.

"Nice move, Tavish." Kirk gritted his teeth. "Now bring him down so we can find Julia's father and be done with this lot."

"I'll be right with you." He met each of Jeremiah's blows with the same intensity as the aggressive warrior heaped on him.

"Tavish!" Julia pulled free of Cherub and rushed toward him, her golden locks streaming behind her. "Dinnae get hurt, no' one scratch. Do you hear me?"

"Get back." He glared at Kirk. "Keep her behind you and

safe."

Kirk hustled Julia out of the way.

Jeremiah struck his ribs, the blow ricocheting and rattling his teeth. Damn it. He should have been keeping his focus on the warrior he fought and not on his mate. Julia screamed as MacKenzie swung again.

He caught the next blow and arms shaking, shoved his two-handed sword hard against Jeremiah's. He heaved forward and battled. Whisking his blade through the air, he caught MacKenzie off guard and sliced into his arm.

Jeremiah grasped his bicep and growled as blood poured through his white-knuckled fingers. Not a death blow, but a damaging one all the same for a warrior who would need his sword arm if he wished to fight.

"This battle isnae over." Snarling, Jeremiah nabbed his horse, bounded onto the beast and rode toward the castle, his injured arm swinging loose at his side.

He should have expected the man to run once injured, wanted to chase him and put an end to the fight only Julia ran toward him and he caught her in his arms and gripped her tight.

"We have to reach my father afore Jeremiah does." She clasped his face and kissed him. "Thank you for coming to my rescue."

"You're to go straight to your mother. Tor will watch over you while Cherub, Kirk, and I see to your father's rescue. We'll find him, that I promise you." He dug his fingers into her hair and kissed her with all the fierce need contained within his soul. Seeing her in MacKenzie's hands had nearly halted his heart from beating. "We'll meet you on the hill where we first arrived. Tell Tor. He'll get you and your mother there without any issue."

"My father is ill, sick with a fever. Mother never had the chance to explain more than that. Be careful." She kissed him again. "Stay safe and come back to me."

"Always."

Julia raced back to the inn and he wiped his blade on the grass, sheathed it then grasped ahold of Cherub. He had a mission ahead of him, one he couldn't falter in. "Let's be away."

"Hold tight. We are running out of time and I'm going to make this flight quick." Cherub cloaked the three of them and took them high. They flew over the curtain wall and descended down into the bailey before the tower house.

Jeremiah galloped through the main gate. "Secure the keep. Our enemy has arrived," he bellowed and all hell broke loose.

* * * *

Fear and worry coiled deep in Julia's gut as she left Tavish and ran back to the inn. Leaving her mate to fight this battle without her at his side had been the most difficult thing she'd ever done. With her heartbeat a raging mess, she stumbled through the garden door and inside the chamber. She drank in the returned sight of her mother. Even though she looked pale, dirt smeared across her cheeks and her skirts ragged, she was still alive and that was all that matter.

"Mother." She grasped her close, ran her hand over her fair hair pulled back into a long plait and let the tears flow. "I love you."

"I love you too." Mother rocked her in her arms, the gentle hum of her aura a sweetly soothing sound she'd known since the day of her birth and that had only ever brought her comfort. "Tor just explained everything to me, that you're mated to his brother, Tavish, and that you're here to rescue your father and me."

"Did Tor explain that they're from the future?"

"Aye, that your sister is mated to a man named Finlay, who's from Tor and Tavish's clan. The 'power of three' has been unveiled and Nessa's prophecy set in motion." She shook her head as if dazed. "I cannae believe all that has happened while we've been gone."

"What of Father?"

"He's so sick. A week past, he suffered a nick to his arm

from one of the warrior's blades and the wound festered and a fever rose. It rages strong and willnae abate. I convinced Jeremiah to take me to the healer. He didnae care to lose his prisoner afore the fortnight of time had expired. Jeremiah told us of the MacKenzie's demand sent to Gilleoin."

"Tavish is a gifted healer, one they call a doctor in his time. Father couldnae be in better hands once Tavish finds him." She glanced at Tor. "Tavish said to take us to the hills where we first arrived. He'll meet us there with Father, the moment they've rescued him."

"Then let's be away, before the enemy storms this inn." Tor opened the outside door and gestured them through. "To the stables. We'll ride."

She gripped Mother's hand and tugged her out the door and around the side of the inn to the stables.

Tor halted next to two horses tethered to a post, cupped his palms and tipped his head toward her. "You first, Julia. Speed is of the essence."

She set her foot in his hold and he hefted her up then aided Mother as she mounted in behind her.

"Hold tight." With the reins in hand, she slapped her horse's neck and bolted from the inn, her mother's arms wrapped firm around her waist. Tor galloped in beside her and they rode up the hilly trail to the crest. "Where's Father exactly?" she shouted over her shoulder. "I can inform Tavish. We have a merged link of the mind."

"Your father's on the upper floor of the main tower."

"Tavish."

"Tell me you're safely away."

"I am. Father's being kept on the upper floor of the main tower."

"We've already searched within the dungeons below and we're heading that way now."

"Then hurry." She urged her mount onward and upward,

made the top rise and sat high on her stead. MacKenzie's stronghold sat on the jutting rock at the tip and guardsmen swarmed the battlements. *"They know you're there."*

* * * *

With Julia's warning ricocheting through his mind, Tavish negotiated the cramped inner stairwell of the main tower in the near dark, Kirk and Cherub right behind him. The space was tight, designed that way to ensure a man couldn't swing his sword should the tower be under siege. He made the second landing where a trace of light trickled through the slatted boards covering a narrow window and he nodded at Kirk and Cherub. "Two more floors to go. We're almost there."

He scaled the next two flights then halted at the very top, his senses on full alert. The gloomy corridor, this one lit by one single candle in an iron wall sconce, held three cells with wooden doors and a mail-clad warrior standing on guard outside the last one.

As the warrior straightened and glanced their way, Cherub nabbed him and Kirk and swiftly cloaked them.

"Tavish, I've got this one," Kirk whispered.

They crept closer.

A clunk sounded and the guard grabbed his steel helm which now held a dent in the top that matched the length of a blade, Kirk's blade. The guard's eyes rolled to the back of his head and he slithered to the floor, his keys jangling at his side.

"Nice hit," he slapped Kirk on the back as Cherub released and uncloaked them.

"They drop fast when they don't see you coming." Kirk grinned as he tapped the downed man's steel helm once more with his sword. "The next one's yours."

"Thank you." The urge to fight still flared strongly through him.

"Hopefully there won't be a 'next one.'" Cherub lowered to the guard's side, hauled his keys from his belt and tossed them to

Tavish. "Unlock the door and let's pray there's a window. I need fresh air in order to work with my element."

Tavish turned the key and shoved the door open.

A candle flickered on the floor next to a single pallet wedged in the corner. A ratty gray blanket covered the legs of a man who could only be Julia's father. Aleck Matheson's arms were outstretched and each of his wrists restrained with cuffs and pulled back against hooks.

"Who goes there?" Aleck rasped, his voice weak and his gaze cloudy. He rattled the chains, his hands fisted as if he were fully prepared to fight even though immobilized. "I demand you bring my wife back to me."

"Aleck, 'tis Cherub." She rushed to Aleck's side and pressed one hand to his forehead. "You're hot, very hot."

"Cherub?" He blinked, his body burning with a fever and the heat easily reaching Tavish. They'd arrived just in time. He waited one step back as Aleck got his bearings and understood they were here to help him, not hurt him. "Is it really you, Cherub?"

"Aye, 'tis me, and Adair is safe and waiting for you on the hills beyond this castle. I've brought my mate, Kirk, and his cousin, Tavish. They're Mathesons, from Gilleoin's future clan and Tavish is mated to Julia, your Julia."

"Nessa's prophecy has been unveiled?"

"Aye. You and Adair have missed a great deal during your imprisonment. Are you ready to leave?"

"Aye, and quite some time ago." His pale hair, dirty and long and shaggy, swayed about his sunken cheeks as he shoved his wrists out.

"Here, I've got the key." Tavish knelt before Aleck, rustled through the keys and slotted one that appeared the right fit into the lock. With one swift turn, he released the lock and the cuffs clanked open and fell away. Aleck tried to hold himself up, but he swayed. Weak he might be, but strong of heart he was. "I've got you." Tavish heaved Aleck up and slid his arm under the man's shoulder. "Brace yourself against me as needed."

"I'll un-board this window." Kirk slid his blade between the wooden slats over the window and cranked one of them off then tore the rest free with his hands and flung the window open.

Tavish whistled at the sheer drop that would see any man who tried to escape this way end up a mangled mess on the jagged rocks below. The sea crashed in and sprayed high. "There isn't a chance we can all fit through this window, Cherub."

Footsteps thumped up the stairs.

"I dinnae need the window, Tavish, just the fresh air." Cherub stepped through the door into the darkened passageway, twirled her fingers and sent the wind streaming through the open window whooshing past her and slamming into the warriors pounding their way. Grunts and bellows sounded. Hands dusted, she closed the heavy wooden door and shoved the bolt home. "My apologies, there is a need to lock us in since I dinnae wish for any of our enemy to jump into the portal I open. This will be a trip for four and no more."

"A sound idea, my imp." Kirk clasped Cherub around the waist. "Grab ahold, Tavish."

Supporting Aleck at his side, he nabbed Cherub's other arm and motioned for Aleck to do the same.

Once they were all connected to her, the Fae Angel of Love grinned then did as she was born to do, her duty, that of protecting and guarding her kin. A more dedicated protector of their people, Tavish had never known. With a flick of her fingers, she swirled the fresh air tunneling around them and sent them falling away through the most blessed portal ever.

A few moments later, they reemerged in the clear light of day on top of the rise overlooking the inn, the wind churning all about and his mate sitting astride a horse with her mother behind her and Tor atop a second horse. Relief poured through him.

"*I love you,*" he whispered then sent that love swarming

down their link.

* * * *

"I love you too." Fresh tears streaked down Julia's cheeks as Tavish's love saturated her along their link. She tossed one leg over her horse, jumped to the ground and bounded into his arms. She ran her hands over him, checking him for any sign of an injury. No nicks or even one scrape. She grasped her father, his body gaunt and hot but oh, he was alive and that's all that mattered. "I cannae believe I have you and Mother back," she cried as she hugged him. "I've missed you, Father, more than my heart could bear at times. I see you've met Tavish. He's my mate and handfast husband. We've no' long spoken vows."

"I've missed you too, cannae believe you're here." Father held out his hand for Mother and she dashed across and joined them, snuck under Father's other arm and helped to hold him up as Tavish did too.

Jiggling about, she hugged both her parents and allowed her sheer joy and happiness its release. "Father, Tavish is a healer in his time, and you must allow him to look after you. He'll rid you of your festered wound and fever."

"All I desire is to have my family close and to be together once more." Father glanced at Tavish. "Thank you for coming to my rescue. Glad I am to see my daughter has such a courageous and loyal husband."

"I would do anything for you, for both your daughters or your kin." Tavish glanced at Cherub. "Have you enough strength to transport us back to the future? The sooner I tend to Aleck, the better."

"Of course. I have rested up enough, and seeing my kin safe and well has given me an added boost of energy." Cherub swished into the center of their group and twirled her hands through the air. "Everyone hold onto me. We're heading to Kirk, Tavish, and Tor's time."

They all did as she bid and the air churned.

Tavish caught Julia close as they fell away into the dark and breezed through the endless streams of time. Gently, he stroked the back of her head, each soft and loving caress warming her through from the inside out.

She snuggled deeper into his embrace, her parents either side of her. Wonder and love filled her heart. She had her parents back and she'd never let them go again, or the man she'd been gifted with as a mate. She opened her mind more fully to his and shared every one of her thoughts. *"Thank you for returning my family to me. You've given me the greatest gift."*

"They're safe and I'll ensure your father is soon well." He kissed her forehead. *"The day you arrived with Cherub to be tended, is the day I received my heart's desire. I now live for you."*

"I need to kiss you."

"I need to bite you." He chuckled as they bumped down inside his medical rooms. *"Soon,"* he promised as he aided Father across the room and onto the white-sheeted medical bed. Mother whipped to Father's other side as he lay down and rested his head on the pillow.

Cherub, still standing beside Kirk, swirled the air once more. "We'll be back soon. Arabel and Finlay need to be here."

"Travel safely." Excitement bubbled inside her. Soon her sister would be here and their family would once again be complete.

Tavish tossed his jacket onto the side chair, washed his hands in the metal sink, dried them then pulled a tray of utensils forward. He returned to Father's side, removed the bandaging around his wounded arm and eyed the pussy mess. "Let's get you all cleaned up. I'll have you back on your feet as soon as I can." He struck a look at Tor. "Could you bring the IV pole over here?"

"Sure." Tor did so and her mate took charge, cleaning the wound then stitching it closed.

"Well, this is rather handy." Blue eyes twinkling, Father's mouth lifted in a smile. "Glad I am to now have a healer for a son."

"My profession certainly comes in useful at times." Tavish inserted what he called an IV into Father's wrist then fiddled with a bag he hooked up onto a pole.

"I've always had such a love of the healing craft." Mother watched him, her interest piqued, just as Julia's was. "What does this bag of liquid do?"

"This bag holds fluid which contains some wonderful nutrients, including pain relief as well as the necessary medication to heal your husband's festered wound. With all of that medication combined, and with it traveling straight into his blood, his fever should begin to recede fairly quickly."

"And the stitches?" Mother quizzed.

"They're dissolving ones. Aleck may bathe if he wishes, although afterward I want you to ensure he keeps his wound dry and out of the water until the stitches have gone, which will be in about a week's time."

"Did your mate say dissolving?" Mother asked Julia as they both aided Father into a seated position on the bed.

"He did. This time is so very different to our own and great medical advances have been made." A time she couldn't wait to embrace.

"You should tell your mother how we met." Tavish winked at her then said to Mother, "The wound was shallow and even though infected, only three stitches were needed, although if you feel your husband's wound looks worse and isn't healing as it should, then call out. My chamber is just one door farther down the hallway from this medical room. I'll make sure you're given rooms on the same floor."

"Thank you." Mother hugged him, her smile bright. "I shall adore having a doctor for a son as well."

Megan breezed into the room in a red woolen skirt and

white blouse with a ruffled neckline, her dark wavy hair bobbing on her shoulders. Surprise lit her eyes. "Well, hello one and all. Tavish, you're back. I wasn't aware you'd arrived."

"Meet Julia and Arabel's parents, Aleck and Adair."

"Oh my." Megan clapped and beamed then rushed across and hugged them. "This is such an incredible surprise. I'm Iain, Finlay, and Kirk's mother, which means we're all now very close kin."

"There's an awful loud ruckus coming from in here." Barefoot, Matthew clomped in, his IV pole in hand as he wheeled it alongside him. His great plaid was belted at his waist and a peek of the bandage wrapped around his upper body showed through the thin white linen of his loose-sleeved tunic.

"Matthew." Julia raced across the room and gathered him in a hug. "You're walking about and oh, you look so very well. The arrow is gone. 'Tis incredible what Tavish has done."

"Aye, your mate removed the pesky thing, and all while I slept. Just dinnae ask me how he did that. Make sure you keep your mate close, lass. He's a keeper." He shuffled toward Aleck and Adair with a grin on his face. "'Tis about time you two returned. Your daughters have been quite the handful to watch over of late, both of them whisking here and there and without nary a word of where they're going."

"'Tis so good to see you, Matthew." Father gripped Matthew's forearm and Mother embraced Matthew, as gently as she could with his wound.

A rush of wind swirled and Cherub and Kirk arrived with Arabel and Finlay.

"I cannae believe what I'm seeing." Tears flowed down Arabel's cheeks as she dashed toward their parents and clutched them to her. "You're both back and alive. You're alive, truly alive."

"We have our parents back." Julia wrapped her arms around Arabel and their parents. A fresh wave of tears fell, soul-cleansing tears. From the day Gilleoin had told her and her sister the devastating news of their parents' death, a piece of her heart had died, but now her heart was once again alive and bursting with so much happiness and joy. This moment was one she'd cherish forever.

A click sounded from behind her and she glanced over her shoulder.

Tavish blew her a kiss, his clever device in hand. "Smile, love."

She beamed as he circled their group and snapped pictures of them.

Chatter abounded, each of them talking over the other in their rush to share all their news.

An hour or more passed before Megan declared the evening meal would soon be served, and for those who wished to join the rest of their clan downstairs in the great hall, could do so after they'd had time to bathe and change. Megan grasped Mother's hand. "I'll bring all you might need to your chamber, clothes and such for you and Aleck. The one a few doors down shall be all yours, and for as long as you need it."

"You have my most grateful thanks." Mother squeezed Megan's fingers in return. "I cannae wait to see more of this time since my daughters will soon be living in it."

"Then I hope you and Aleck will consider Ivanson Castle your home just as your daughters soon will. You are both welcome here whenever Cherub brings you for a visit."

"Aye, I will gladly bring one and all." Cherub twirled around with a giggle. "This is a most wondrous day."

"It surely is." Julia nabbed Arabel's hand, caught Cherub's hand too, and the three of them all danced around in a circle together.

Dizzy, Arabel stopped and grabbed a breath. "All right, time to show Mother and Father to their chamber." She kissed Julia's cheek then Cherub's. "I've never been so happy."

Neither had Julia. She opened the door for everyone and Matthew padded out then her sister led their parents down the hallway to their room.

Kirk swiped a blue pen from Tavish's countertop and tossed it to Finlay with a grin. "Here's your pen, as promised."

Finlay chuckled and pocketed it, one hand on the doorway. "Thanks ever so much, but now I'm leaving you in charge of Gilleoin's accounts and ensuring the rents are received, as well as watching over his lands and clan. I'm going to stay here for a few days with Arabel and get to know her parents while they heal. Are you up to holding the fort while I do?"

"Absolutely." Kirk glanced at Tor. "Want to give me a hand back on the other home front?"

"Of course. That's where my mate resides and where I'll need to be to find her come the next full moon." Tor clapped Tavish on the back. "Will you remain here for a bit too?"

"Aye, until Aleck and Matthew are all clear to return. We may even take some time out to show Julia's parents and Matthew the sights." Tavish pulled his brother into a hug. "I'll see you when we return to the past. I don't want to miss your journey in finding your mate."

"Aye, I long for the next full moon when I can begin the chase. I'll stop at nothing to find her."

"Then let's be away." Cherub held out her arms for Kirk and Tor and the two men joined her. The wind swirled and the three of them disappeared through time.

Finlay closed the door behind him as he headed after the others, leaving her and Tavish completely alone.

"Goodness, it's so quiet now." She leaned against the wall and smiling, crooked a finger at her fierce protector. "Whatever could we do now we're all alone?"

"I know exactly what we're about to do." He pulled out another set of instruments from a drawer, set it on the bed then steered her across the room and settled her on top of mattress and moved in behind her. He directed the light on the overhead metal arm over her head until the light shone on the back of her head. Carefully he separated her hair at the back.

"Tavish, this isnae quite the kind of 'whatever' I was referring to. You also said my new wound wouldnae need stitches and Cherub has already cleaned my hair and the wound site for me."

"I'll give it all another clean with my sterilized water. I need to ensure no bugs are introduced to the open area. Definitely no stitches needed though. That I promise you." He nipped her ear from behind. "And I also haven't forgotten you lost awareness for several hours, which means I'm going to have to wake you throughout the night to make certain all is well."

"Wake me as often as you please, just ensure you make it interesting when you do." She giggled and clamped a hand over her mouth. "Goodness, I cannae believe what now comes out of my mouth. You have completely corrupted me, Tavish Matheson."

"I hope so." He gestured toward the window overlooking the inner courtyard. A fiery red sunset beamed, its brilliant rays searing the forest's treetops beyond the curtain wall. The dark descended and stars twinkled in the night sky. "Since it's so late, would you care to take a shower with me before bed?"

"Most definitely. Now, hurry it along."

He chuckled, finished tending to her then swept her off the mattress and carried her into his chamber and knocked the door shut with his hip. A mischievous glint lit his golden shifter eyes as he strode past their big bed and into his bathroom.

"'Tis hard to believe I now live in two times."

"A new world has opened up for both of us." He crossed the sandy colored floor tiles, slid her down his body and onto her feet. He unbelted his weapons, laid them on the countertop then shucked his tan tunic and black trews until he stood unclothed before her. With one finger, he teased along her lower lip. "May

I undress you?"

"I'm no' quite sure why you haven't already." She pushed her fingers into his silky black hair, cupped the back of his head and tugged his mouth down to hers. His warm lips caressed hers, so softly, so deliciously, then he rubbed the entire length of his body against hers, all hard and hot heat that had her panting for more. She pulled back an inch and grinned. His pure white aura with its sizzling red shifter edge swarmed around and completely covered hers. "You're my one and all."

"As you're my one and all. I wish to wrap myself around you, inside and out." He unfastened the ties of her violet riding skirt, allowed the fabric to slither to the ground then lifted her cream shirt over her head and whisked her to the shower and sat her on the metal chair. He flicked the shower lever on and stuck his hand under the water. "I'll wash your hair for you."

"I'm allowed to get my hair wet?"

"You are. The wound is healing nicely, and the stitches fairly close to dissolving." He slid the shower head from the slider and passed it to her. "I also want to watch you bathe, as you did the last time we showered together."

"Mmm, this I will enjoy." She ran the warm water over her locks, down her back and over her breasts before relaxing back into the chair and into Tavish's hands.

He worked the creamy shampoo into a foam and ran the bubbles through her hair. The sweet scent of apples swirled within the steam, a fragrance that saturated her senses, just as her mate's warm and fresh scent did.

A soft sigh escaped her, the water soothing her tired muscles as she rinsed the shampoo out.

"Would you like a massage?" Tavish knelt at her feet, a bar of vanilla soap in hand.

"Aye, very much." She craved his touch, however he offered it.

He massaged her feet and calves, stroked upward, over her

knees and along her inner thighs. Leaning in, he bumped his nose against the entrance to her core and with a low growl, breathed her scent in deep. His claws sliced out and in. "My bear is clawing for a taste of you. You smell like the sweetest, warmest honey and he wants to devour you."

"Devouring sounds good." She hooked one leg around Tavish's back and drew him ever closer. "I intend to request daily showers with you, from this moment forth."

"That request I'll gladly grant." Gently, he stroked over her hips, around her breasts and back down her sides. Rubbing his body against hers, he whispered, "You're clean, from top to toe. Rinse off so I can actually begin the devouring."

She rinsed them both, rose from her chair and slid the shower head back onto the slider.

Tavish crowded her from behind, one hand sweeping her wet hair over her shoulder and the other sliding around her waist. Water pummeled into her, his erect cock brushing over her lower cheeks as he rubbed against her. Nuzzling her neck, he razzed his teeth back and forth over her most sensitive spot and growled under his breath. "Look at me."

She turned around in his embrace, looked deep into his eyes as she traced the tip of his impressive erection with one finger then palmed his balls with the other.

"You have an exquisite touch." He bent his head, suckled one nipple then moved to the other.

"So do you." Heat rippled through her and she captured his mouth with hers and kissed him, until every wonderfully muscled inch of his body was wrapped fully around her. This was what she needed, to join as one with him.

"I need to join as one with you too." His mind moved swiftly through hers as he read her thoughts. "I also want to know your every dream and desire. Tell me them, so I might fulfill each and every one."

"I want you to make love to me, right here in this shower, in our bed and wherever else you might fancy. Once we return to the past, I want to spend time with you in our sacred cavern, all alone."

"You have a deal." He gripped her fingers, flattened the backs of her hands to the slick tiled wall behind her and licked his lips. "Anything else?"

"I wish for your babe, to start a family with you, a child all of our own."

"Then be prepared for a loving like no other. I'm about to make you mine, in every single way." He eased her breasts together, swiped his thumbs over her stiff nipples then licked around her aureoles. Greedily, he kissed each nipple, sucked them deep inside his mouth until every inch of her sizzled and burned for more. She needed this, needed him. She always would.

Delicious heat radiated through her and she arched her back, thrust her breasts ever deeper into his exquisite touch and whimpered. Her legs shook. "Tavish, I'm no' sure I can stand on my own two feet for long."

"One second." He nabbed a fluffy white towel from the handrail, spread it over the tiled floor under the water's spray and laid her down on top of it. "This better?"

"Infinitely."

"I aim to please." Between her legs, he knelt then grasped his cock and rubbed the head over her nub. White-hot pleasure radiated through her. "Are you about to come, my love?"

"I believe so. Mayhap you can love me hard and fast right now, then slow and easy in our bed later."

"Aye, my love, as you wish." He clasped her hips and before she could draw her next breath, he plunged inside her. Pounding into her, he gave her everything she'd asked for and more, his mind barreling into hers and locking around tight.

Her inner muscles clamped around him, the sensation of both his body inside her and his mouth on her neck, sending her senses soaring. He bit down and pleasure stormed through her. She'd been gifted with a mate she'd never expected, with a soul bond as deep as time itself. Grasping his shoulders, she held on for the ride of her life. *"Thank you for saving me from the enemy, for rescuing my parents, for being mine and for offering me all of your love. Your kisses are what I'll always crave, always desire, and always demand you give me more of."*

"I love you, Julia, and demand away. I'll give you everything you ask for and more. This I promise you." He thrust and she met each of his deeply penetrating moves then urged him even deeper. He plunged balls-deep inside her, his seed shooting to her core and sending them both flying over the edge and streaking toward the heavens.

Her next mission had begun, one she intended to spend a lifetime pursuing, that of tying her mate to her in every possible way, heart, body and soul. They would always be one, from this moment forward and throughout all of time.

* * * *

Tavish soaked in the beauty of his mate lying underneath him, her tight channel squeezing his cock and dragging him ever deeper inside her. Such a wildly desperate need to mate with her still consumed him. She was the only woman he'd ever hold deep in his heart, ever kiss, ever crave, and ever desire. She was his true mate, his heart and his home, his everything and all.

With such a ravenous hunger rolling through him, he scooped her off the damp towel on the floor and wrapped her in a fresh clean one before carrying her to their bed. "I want your scent on my tongue, to have you so deeply entrenched within me that you're as much a part of me as I'm a part of you."

He laid her down on the large mattress covered in his thick black fur.

"Get ready for round number two, my mate." He tugged the towel off her, slid onto his belly between her knees and raised her legs. Over his shoulders, he hooked her feet until her bottom lifted off the bed and she lay fully exposed to him. Time to give both him and his bear exactly what they both desired, more of her. Out the window, the night sky twinkled with a myriad of stars. Moonlight beamed in and played over her lush body. He stroked along the pinkness of her lower folds. So beautiful. So enticing. She was all his and with her inner thighs spread, he plunged one finger inside her.

"Oh, aye, that I love." She bucked and moaned, her beaded nipples hardening even further and his cock lengthening and filling as if he hadn't just come. "Come here, my fierce protector."

"You'll have to wait until I've finished devouring you. Are you ready for more?"

"Aye, always." She fisted the fur bedcover either side of her, a delicious grin on her face. "Devour away."

He stroked into her harder and faster, rubbing his thumb across her nub until she arched into his touch and panted. Then he added a second finger, dipped his head and licked her flesh as he desired and as his bear demanded. The other half of him, contained so deep within, rumbled his appreciation. Aye, this was just the beginning. He removed his fingers and thrust his tongue inside her, stroked the inside of her channel then retreated only long enough to begin doing the same all over again. Building her next orgasm to a peak, he lapped and pleasured her with his mouth and tongue alone.

"Tavish." She tunneled her mind deep inside his, her passion rising to such a height the desire she shared with him had his cock throbbing, so heavy and full as he drank at the very heart of her. "I cannae take any more."

"Wait there, my sweet love. I'm coming." He took one last lick of her below, lifted up and covered her mouth with his. He kissed her, twining his tongue around hers and gorging himself on her full lips. She was his, an intoxicating and heady blend he would never be able to get enough of.

"Inside me." She gripped his shoulders, her nails digging into his flesh and making his bear roll around with pleasure at her very clear marking. He kissed her and she swished her hands down his front, brushed the head of his cock with the soft pad of her thumb then with her sweet fingers firm around his erection, worked him in long pulls.

His spine tingled and the pressure in his shaft built, with such a swiftness he could barely contain himself. Kissing her, he savored the luscious recesses of her mouth then gave into the need to join them both together. Blood pounding, he pushed his cock deep inside her hot sheath, her mouth-watering scent bathing him below.

"More," she moaned against his lips. She clutched his butt, pulled him in even deeper and rocked underneath him. *"You're my fierce protector, the other half of my soul."*

"Just as you're the other half of mine. From this moment forth, we'll always be together. No one will ever separate us again, not the enemy and certainly not time itself." He thrust deep, every inch of her welcoming heat pulling him in further. *"Bite me, my love, the same time as I bite you. I want your full possession."*

"That I will never deny you of." With her mind open to his, her body wrapped around him, she sucked the skin of his neck between her lips.

He slid his hand around the back of her head and held her against him as he razzed his teeth over her fiercely beating pulse. *"Now,"* he demanded.

She sank her teeth into him and he bit her in return. Bucking into her, his pace wild and feverish and driven by the very heart of his bear, he marked her and made her his, forever and for all time.

Meeting each of his pounding thrusts, she bit him again on the other side of his neck and he roared his pleasure, bit her again in the same way and sent them both spiraling over the edge and flying straight to the stars.

Never had he experienced such a perfect union, his shifter soul connecting and locking tight with hers. Forever, they'd keep each other safe and close, a forever he desired with all of his heart and soul.

Chapter 13

Inside their sacred cavern two weeks later, Julia slumped on top of Tavish, the sand underneath them a heavenly bed and the bath-like pool of water next to them offering a cool reprieve from the steamy heat. Happiness and peace invaded her soul as she played her fingers through her mate's silky black locks.

The day before, Cherub had brought them, her parents and Matthew—all now fully healed—back to the past and that very day their clan had celebrated their safe return with a hearty feast, a celebration that had lasted all day and night until the two of them had finally been able to sneak away.

"You certainly do keep your word," she whispered in his ear. "Do you recall all of my requests?"

"Let's see." Smiling, he caressed down her back and over her bare bottom. "We've made love in my shower and our bed, many times over, and now we're back in the past, we've also done so here within our sacred cavern." Slowly, he rolled her over on their tartan blanket and came up over top of her. A delicious spark lit his beautiful golden shifter eyes. "But you also requested I give you my babe, for us to start a family all of our own."

"That I did." Her courses were late, only by two days, but

still two all-important days.

He breathed deep, scented the air then released a low growl, one that rumbled in his throat and vibrated against her chest. "You smell incredible. Like vanilla and hot honey all rolled into one, but there's something else, a heady new aroma I've never caught the scent of before."

"What do you think that might be?"

"Have I ever told you our shifter males can scent when our mates are at their most fertile, as well as the change within our chosen one's body when they conceive?"

"Nay." How intriguing.

"It's been that way since the very beginning. Your scent calls to the very heart of both me and my bear." Wriggling down, he dragged in another deep breath and on his knees between her legs, spread her thighs wider. Gently, he smoothed one hand over her hip then bent and nuzzled her flat belly. "You're carrying my cub."

"Aye, a babe all of our own. I may even have conceived right here in this cavern, the very first time we came together."

"The timing would be just about right." A sensual grin lifted his lips. "I need to make love to you again."

"I need that too."

"I love you, Julia. You're all I could ever desire in a mate, all I could ever hope for as a wife and the mother of our children." He rose up and kissed her, so deeply and passionately her core pulsed, and when he slid so perfectly inside her, his aura fully enveloping hers, joy overwhelmed her.

Her mate held her very soul in his hands, just as she held his in hers.

Love. Theirs had transcended the endless streams of time, and forever would.

Coming in Highlander's Heart, Book Five is Tor's story.

Author's Note

Clan Matheson descends from a twelfth century man called Gilleoin, a man who was believed to have been from the ancient Royal House of Lorne. The name Matheson has been attributed to the Gaelic words Mic Mhathghamhuim which means "Son of the Bear," and the clan chief's arms carry two bears as supporters. In the twelfth century, clan Matheson settled around the area of Loch Alsh, Loch Carron, and Kintail, and gave their allegiance to clan MacDonald whose chiefs were the Lords of the Isles. Clan Matheson became a large and powerful clan with a force of around two-thousand men, although by the middle of the sixteenth century they'd diminished greatly in size and influence due to the blood feuds raging across the isles at that time. This warring left them to possess less than a third of the original Matheson property on Loch Alsh.

It's time for the whispers to reignite. Clan Matheson are the "Son of the Bear."

This story is woven with as much accuracy to the period and locations as possible, although any mistakes made are mine alone.

Please feel free to search for any of my other works. I simply adore strong heroines, and have a ton of fun matching them with their honorable alpha heroes.

**Also available in paperback
Scottish Historical Romance**

Traveling through time…for a Highlander.

Highlander Heat Series

Highlander's Castle, Book One

Highlander's Magic, Book Two

Highlander's Charm, Book Three

Highlander's Guardian, Book Four

Highlander's Faerie, Book Five

Highlander's Champion, Book Six

by Joanne Wadsworth

Looking for more sexy Scottish adventure?

Catch a teaser excerpt of the next book in
The Matheson Brothers series.

Highlander's Heart

The Matheson Brothers, Book Five

by Joanne Wadsworth

Highlander's Heart

The Matheson Brothers, Book Five

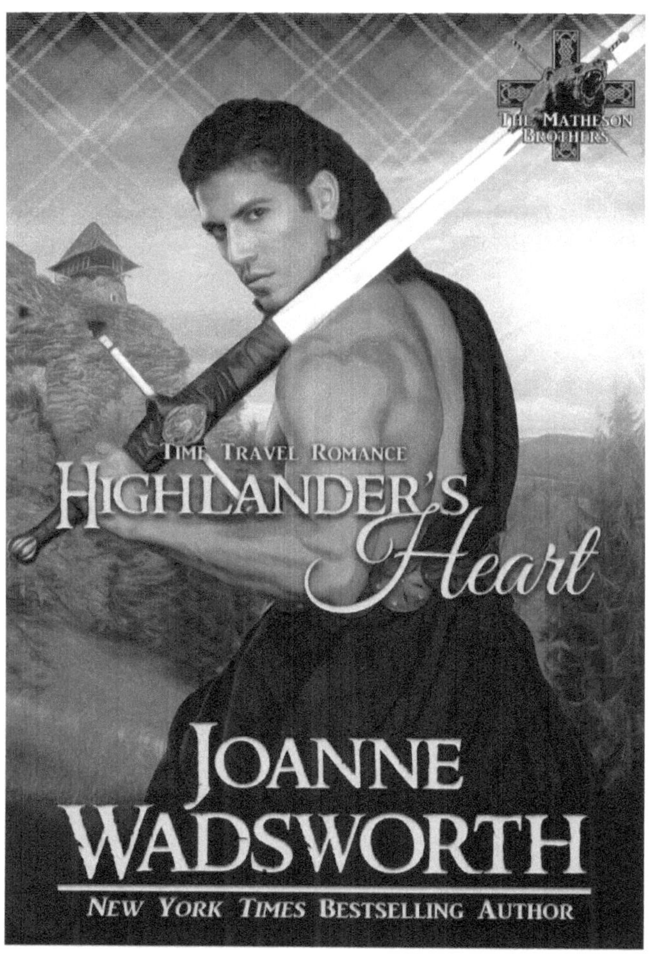

Teaser Excerpt

Layla should never have allowed Tor to take her from the meadow. Now, she was trapped here in this remote cavern in an underground pool with a determined man and his resolute bear so very close to the surface. She couldn't be his mate, no matter his desire for her was clear to see and apparently continuing to deepen. "Wait right there, Tor."

She needed to keep some space between them.

"My bear will want your touch."

"I mean it." She did, only as the moon blazed brighter through the vent overhead in the craggy ceiling, her very soul ached at the thought of keeping him at bay.

"There will be no marriage between you and Donnan MacDonald." Tor surged forward through the pool's water, grasped her dangling legs as she sat on the overhanging ledge. "This is our night, and the sooner you acknowledge it, the better." Challenge lit his gaze and his luscious lips lifted, not that she should have noticed his lips. Except she always had, wished only to lean forward and lick them.

"What are you doing to me?" He had her thoughts in total disarray.

"It's our bond taking form, your soul calling to mine and

mine to yours." He rubbed upward, over her knees, his thumbs swirling in a slow circle along the inside of each leg and his golden eyes heating to a smoldering hue. "When one shifts, it causes quite a lightning bright display. Close your eyes or turn away if you need to, but be warned, my other half might get a little possessive over you. He knows you're ours and that you're fighting to keep your distance from us. He's also far more insistent and forceful than I am."

"I can handle your bear. I'm rather insistent and forceful myself. Shift. Show me your other half."

"Of course, and by the way"—he winked at her—"demanding I show you my other half is a very mate thing to demand." He stepped back and shifted, bright lights bursting a myriad of sparks before one very large bear with silky black fur reared up onto its hind legs in the water and roared. He came back down, his paws slapping against the stone ledge either side of her, his teeth sharp and snapping together.

"Calm down." She wriggled back, her back coming up hard against the slick stone wall and her heartbeat racing. Nowhere else could she move to get away from him.

JOANNE WADSWORTH

The Matheson Brothers

Highlander's Desire, Book One
Highlander's Passion, Book Two
Highlander's Seduction, Book Three

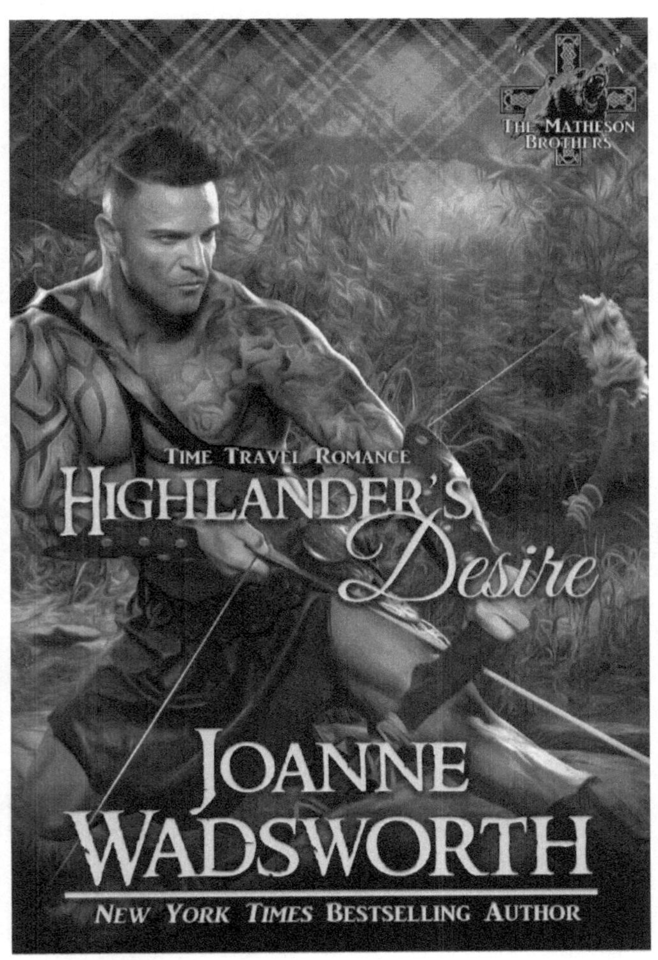

The Matheson Brothers Continued

Highlander's Kiss, Book Four
Highlander's Heart, Book Five
Highlander's Sword, Book Six

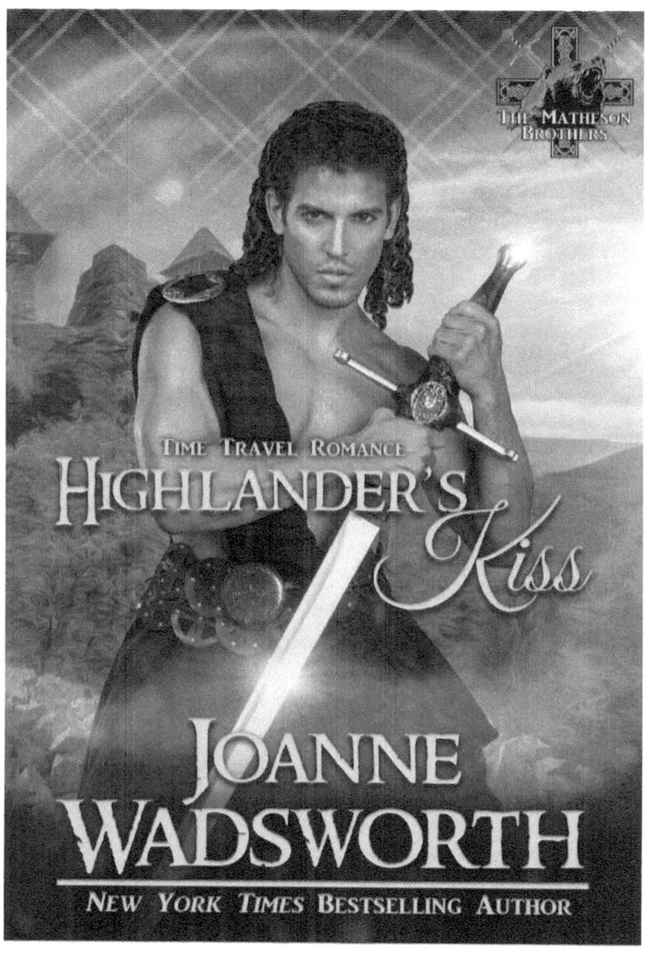

The Matheson Brothers Continued

Highlander's Bride, Book Seven
Highlander's Caress, Book Eight
Highlander's Touch, Book Nine

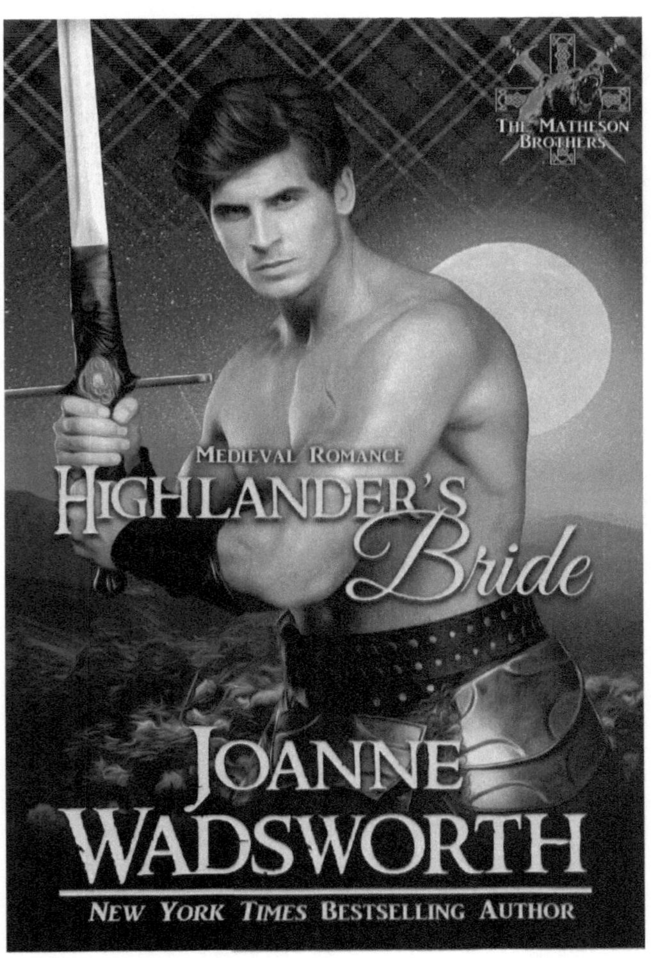

The Matheson Brothers Continued

Highlander's Shifter, Book Ten
Highlander's Claim, Book Eleven
Highlander's Courage, Book Twelve
Highlander's Mermaid, Book Thirteen

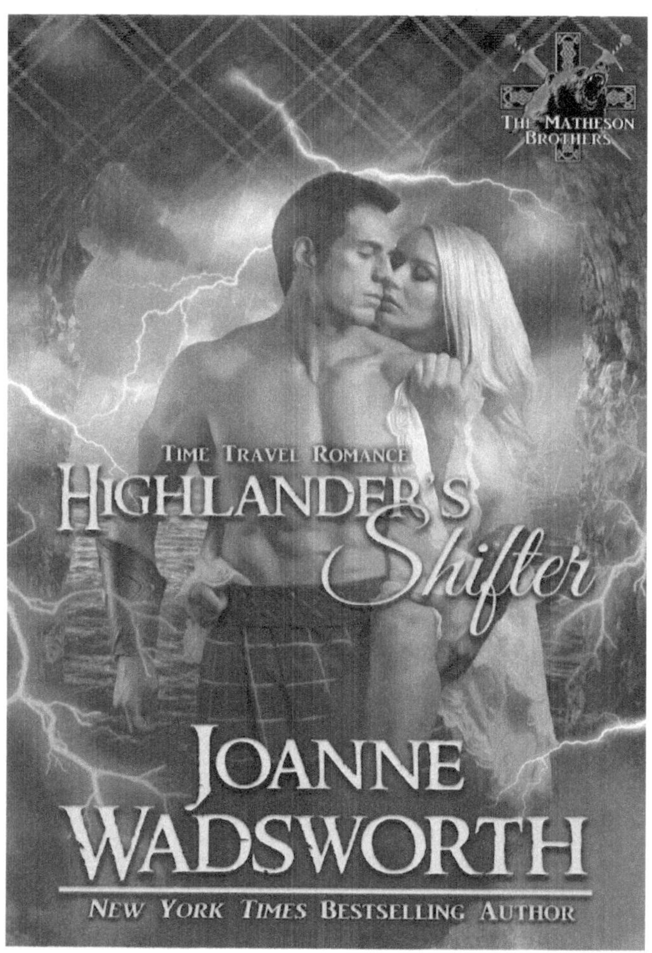

Highlander Heat

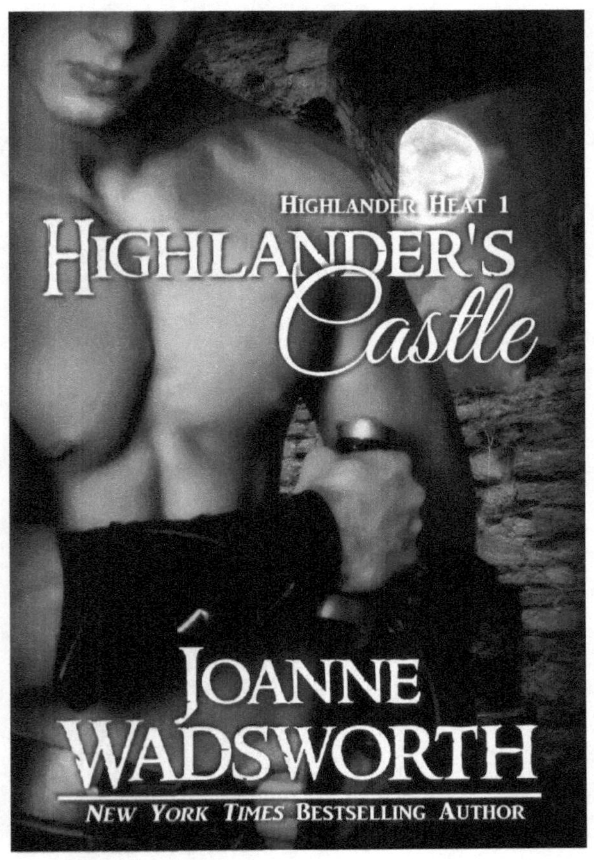

Regency Brides

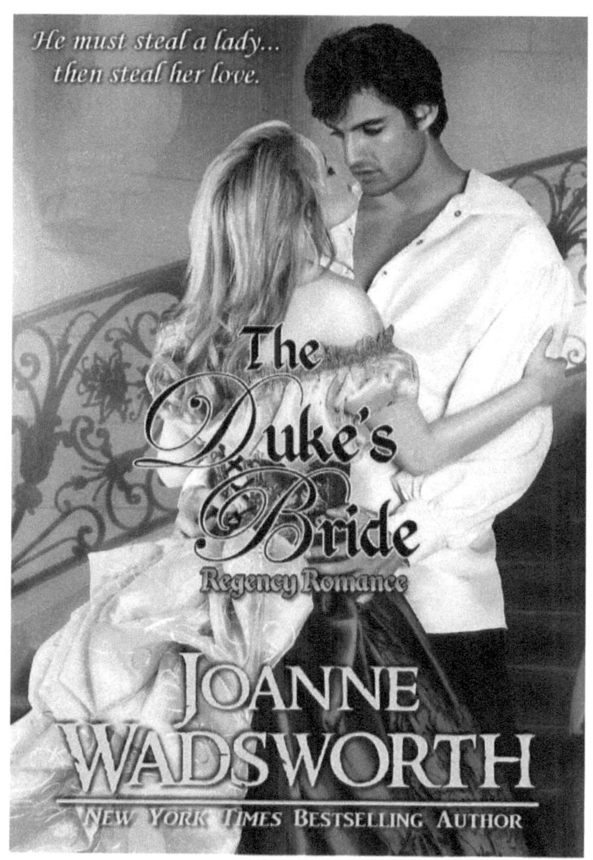

JOANNE WADSWORTH

Princesses of Myth

Protector, Book One
Warrior, Book Two
Hunter (Short Story - Included in Warrior, Book Two)
Enchanter, Book Three
Healer, Book Four
Chaser, Book Five

Billionaire Bodyguards

Billionaire Bodyguard Attraction, Book One
Billionaire Bodyguard Boss, Book Two
Billionaire Bodyguard Fling, Book Three

JOANNE WADSWORTH

Joanne Wadsworth is a *New York Times* and *USA Today* Bestselling Author who adores getting lost in the world of romance, no matter what era in time that might be. Hot alpha Highlanders hound her, demanding their stories are told and she's devoted to ensuring they meet their match, whether that be with a feisty lass from the present or far in the past.

Living on a tiny island at the bottom of the world, she calls New Zealand home. Big-dreamer, hoarder of chocolate, and addicted to juicy watermelons since the age of five, she chases after her four energetic children and has her own hunky hubby on the side.

So come and join in all the fun, because this kiwi girl promises to give you her "Hot-Highlander" oath, to bring you a heart-pounding, sexy adventure from the moment you turn the first page. This is where romance meets fantasy and adventure…

To learn more about Joanne and her works, visit
http://www.joannewadsworth.com

www.ingramcontent.com/pod-product-compliance
Lightning Source LLC
Chambersburg PA
CBHW030822210726

48290CB00002B/712